CARLA NEGGERS

ABANDON

**Doubleday Large Print
Home Library Edition**

MIRA

This Large Print Edition, prepared especially for Double-day Large Print Home Library, contains the complete, unabridged text of the original Publisher's Edition.

MIRA

ISBN-13: 978-0-7394-8235-3

ABANDON

**This Large Print Book carries the
Seal of Approval of N.A.V.H.**

CARLA NEGGERS

ABANDON

To Bettye-Kate Hall

One

Andrew Rook focused on a seed that had broken loose from a thin slice of lemon in his ice water, because if he didn't distract himself, he was going to jump across the polished, black lacquered table and throttle J. Harris Mayer, the would-be informant who had set up this meeting.

If they switched drinks, Rook thought, maybe Harris would choke on the lemon seed.

They were sitting along the back wall of a quiet bar in an upscale hotel four blocks from the White House. In his day, Harris had served two presidents. But it wasn't his day anymore.

He was an outcast, caught five years ago in a gambling scandal that had cost him his job and his reputation, if not his trust fund or his freedom. Many people—including Rook—believed criminal charges should have been filed against him, but Harris, once a federal judge, had managed to skate.

"We've been here a half hour," Rook said. "Get to the point."

Harris ran a pinkish fingertip along the rim of his beer glass. He was sixty-nine but looked older. His hands were trembling and heavily veined, a wet cough sporadically rattling his thin frame. Brown spots and moles dotted his fair, finely wrinkled skin and showed through his thin white hair. He wore a starched shirt and a sport coat with one of his ubiquitous bow ties, and his wingtip shoes were polished but had just enough sign of wear to suggest he was a man, nonetheless, who still got around Washington—who still mattered.

Lifting his beer, Harris gave a paternalistic tut-tut. "You have a short fuse, Special Agent Rook."

"You might want to keep that in mind."

"I chose you because you're a rising star with the Bureau. You're familiar with fraud and corruption investigations." Harris spoke with a nasal, affected patrician voice. "You need to learn patience."

Rook grabbed his glass and took a long drink. He didn't care if he swallowed the damn lemon seed. *Patience.* He'd been patient. For three weeks, he'd played Harris's game, treating seriously his vague tale of Washington intrigue, blackmail and extortion. Financial shenanigans. Sordid secrets. Fraud. Possible conspiracy. Harris Mayer knew all the buttons to push to get and keep Rook's attention.

Now it was time for results. So far, Harris had produced nothing of substance, and Rook couldn't waste any more time indulging an old man's fantasies of regaining lost prestige, being a player again.

He set down his glass, hard. Harris didn't seem to notice. Rook wore a dark gray suit, not a cheap one, but not as expensive as most of the suits the other men in the bar had on, including his wannabe informant. Rook hadn't worn a bow tie since first grade.

"Are we waiting for someone to show up?" he asked.

"Ah. There we are. The federal agent at work, applying his deductive reasoning to the situation at hand." Harris licked his thin lips. "Of *course* we're waiting for someone to show up."

Rook considering shoving the lemon seed up Harris's nose. "When?"

"Anytime now."

"Here?"

Harris shook his head. "Observe the guests walking up the hall to the ballroom. Beautifully dressed, aren't they? I still have my tuxedo. I haven't worn it in a long time."

Rook ignored the small play for sympathy. The table Harris had chosen provided a strategic view of everyone in the bar, as well as everyone who passed by in the gleaming, glittering hall. About two hundred guests were gathering in the ballroom for a cocktail reception to benefit a local literacy organization. Rook had recognized a number of high-powered guests, but no one involved—at least as far as he knew—in criminal activity.

Harris could call the shots tonight. He was the informant. It was his show.

"There's Judge Peacham." The old judge almost chortled as he gestured toward the hall, smiling as if he were in possession of a secret that confirmed his natural superiority. "I knew she'd be here."

"Why do I care if Judge Peacham is at a charity function?"

"Just wait."

"Mr. Mayer—"

"Judge," he corrected with a sniff. "It's still appropriate to refer to me as Judge Mayer."

"Seeing Judge Peacham again doesn't help me."

"Shh. Patience. We might have to go into the hall. I hope not—I'd prefer Bernadette not see me."

Bernadette Peacham paused in the hall just outside the bar, her attention focused on something—or someone—behind her. For the past ten years, she'd served as a judge on the U.S. District Court for the District of Columbia. Before that, she'd been a federal prosecutor and a partner in a prestigious Washington law firm. But her roots were in New Hampshire, where she owned a lake house that had been in her family for more than a hundred years. She often told people she planned to die there, as her parents and her grandfather had.

Rook had done research on Judge Peacham, and he'd testified in her courtroom a half-dozen times in the three years since he'd worked out of the Washington Field Office. He didn't know if she'd recognize him if she walked into the bar, but she'd sure as hell recognize J. Harris Mayer, the old friend who had lured her to Washington thirty years ago.

She'd never win any awards for best-dressed judge, Rook thought with amusement. Tonight's outfit looked as if she'd pulled it out of a paper bag stuffed under her desk in her chambers. Apart from the obvious wrinkles, the black floor-length dress and brightly colored sequined shawl somehow didn't go together. Not that Rook had an eye for clothes, but Bernadette Peacham was a train wreck when it came to style. No Botox and face-lifts for her. No hair dye, for that matter. Damn little makeup, either. People tended to notice her because of her presence and her obvious intelligence and grace. At fifty-seven, she was regarded as a firm, fair, articulate trial judge and, despite her generous nature, no one's fool.

She was perhaps Harris Mayer's last friend in the world, not that he would let friendship or anything else stop him from feeding her to the wolves.

Or, if it came to it, the FBI.

Harris would calculate the benefit to himself and act accordingly.

Rook drank more of his water, although he was only a notch less impatient than he'd been five minutes ago. "It looks like she might be expecting someone to join her. A date?"

"Oh, no." Harris shook his head as if Rook couldn't have come up with a dumber idea. "She hasn't started dating again since her divorce was finalized earlier this month. Cal still lives with her, you know. Don't you think that's odd?"

"Maybe it was an amicable divorce."

"No such thing."

Her marriage to Cal Benton, a prominent Washington attorney, had surprised people far more than their divorce two years later. It was her second marriage; her first, to another lawyer, had lasted three years. No children.

"Supposedly he's not getting a dime from her," Harris continued, his voice more shrill now, as if he was growing impatient himself. "That can't make him happy, but it doesn't matter—Cal will never be satisfied. He'll always want more of everything. Money, recognition, women. Whatever. For some people, there's never enough. Cal is one of them. *I'm* one of them."

"I can't launch an investigation because you think Bernadette Peacham deserved better than Cal Benton—"

"I'm well aware of what you require to proceed." Harris regarded the woman in the hall with a sudden, almost palpable sadness. She'd been a protégée, and she'd left him in the dust in terms of her career, her reputation, her ever-widening circle of friends. His expression softened and he said quietly, "We're not here because of Bernadette's love life or lack thereof."

Rook didn't respond. Harris had lived in social and professional exile for a long time, but, as prickly as he was, he was observant, experienced and very smart. He had a long career behind him, and even now, people owed him favors and came to him, quietly, for advice.

He gave Rook a supercilious smile. "Thinking you'd be smart not to underestimate me, aren't you?"

"I'm thinking you need to get to the point."

Harris leaned over the small table and said in a dramatic whisper, "Don't forget. I know where a lot of the bodies in this town are buried." He sat back abruptly and grinned, his teeth yellowed from age, cigarettes, drink and neglect. "Figuratively speaking, of course."

Rook sucked in his impatience. "If you're looking for action at my expense, Judge, you're looking in the wrong place."

"Understood." Harris nodded wistfully at the middle-aged woman in the hall. "Bernadette used to stop by my office just to say hello, grab a cup of coffee. We don't see each other that often nowadays."

"It's to her credit she didn't drop you altogether."

"I suppose it is. Ah. Here we are." Harris seemed relieved. "Finally."

Another woman came into their line of sight.

Rook took in her dark red hair, her big smile as she greeted Bernadette Peacham.

Hell.

Harris's eyes lit up. "Mackenzie Stewart," he said with relish.

She was barely thirty and slim, wearing a slip of a deep blue and carrying an evening purse just big enough for a .38 caliber pistol. Rook didn't know women's purses. But he knew guns.

"She's a deputy U.S. marshal," Harris added. "A fugitive hunter, a protector of the federal judiciary. A fellow federal agent. Doesn't look like Wyatt Earp, does she?"

Rook kept his reaction under tight wraps. He wasn't there to entertain Harris. "All right. You've had your fun. What's going on?"

The old man's eyes lost some of their spark "Deputy Stewart isn't here in a professional capacity. She's not protecting Bernadette. In fact, she's known Bernadette all her life."

Well, hell, Rook thought. A half-dozen dates, and more or less all he'd learned about Mackenzie was that she was new in Washington, new to the Marshals Service and a native New Englander blessed with great legs, a kissable mouth and an unstoppable sense of humor.

They hadn't gotten around to discussing which state she was from and what friends she might have in Washington.

The two women continued on down the hall toward the ballroom.

"Bernadette saved her," Harris said.

"Saved her how?"

"When she was eleven, her father was maimed in a terrible accident while building a shed for Bernadette at her lake house. He was laid up for months, and Mackenzie was left on her own for much of the time. She got into trouble. Stole things. She blamed herself for what happened."

"Why? She was eleven."

"You know kids."

Actually, Rook thought, he didn't. He tried to picture Mackenzie at eleven. Freckles, he guessed. He bet she'd had a million freckles. She still did.

Harris lifted his glass, almost in a toast, and took a long drink, his eyes darker, more focused, ending any doubt in Rook's mind whether the outcast judge should have faced charges for his gambling shenanigans five years ago. The man thrived on risk, playing it close to the edge. "You didn't know your marshal grew up across the lake from Bernadette, did you, Special Agent Rook?"

"No, I didn't."

"They call Bernadette Beanie. Everyone in her hometown. Not here in Washington. Beanie Peacham. I never have." Without waiting for a response, Harris belched and got to his feet, gesturing to his near empty glass. "Government will pay?"

"I'll pay. Hang on, and I'll walk out with you."

The old man laughed, clapping a bony hand on Rook's shoulder. "You've taken this news well, I have to say." The affected lockjaw accent was back. He dropped his arm to his side and winked with amusement, a sense of drama. "Don't worry. We'll talk again."

Rook lot Harris go. Management of confidential informants was a tricky business under the best of circumstances. As a prosecutor, a judge and an advisor to two presidents, J. Harris Mayer had seen all kinds who'd come forward with tips, information, theories, evidence, although he'd probably never imagined himself in that role. But he would know how to play it.

Even now, after almost a month, Rook couldn't say for certain if he was dealing with a man in the know, with secrets that troubled him, or a rambling, self-important has-been desperate to be part of something important again.

Or both, Rook thought, watching Harris turn briskly down the hall toward the hotel's main entrance. Whether he was on the level or a phony, he clearly hadn't made up the friendship between Mackenzie Stewart and Judge Peacham.

"Just your luck, pal."

Rook had met Mackenzie three weeks ago, on the night Harris had sent him to a Georgetown restaurant to witness Bernadette Peacham having dinner with her ex-husband, the significance of which remained a mystery to Rook. As he'd left the restaurant, the oppressive heat had given way to a steamy, torrential downpour. He'd found himself ducking into a coffee shop to wait out the rain, at the same time as a slim, blue-eyed redhead.

Not entirely a coincidence, apparently.

They'd exchanged phone numbers and met for a movie a couple of nights later.

So much for his relationship with Mackenzie Stewart, Rook thought. He couldn't date someone who was even peripherally involved in his investigation. He left a few bills to cover his and Harris's tab. He and Mackenzie had a date for dinner at his place tomorrow night. His nineteen-year-old nephew, who was living with him, would be off to the beach with friends for the weekend. Perfect timing.

Not anymore. After Harris's little bombshell, Rook had no choice. He couldn't mix business with pleasure. He had to cancel dinner with Mackenzie. He had a job to do.

Two

Mackenzie Stewart shoved a flannel shirt into her backpack with more force than was necessary. She had the air-conditioning turned up, but she was hot—hot and agitated and in no mood to have Nate Winter, perhaps the most observant man on the planet, in her kitchen with her.

Although it wasn't technically *her* kitchen.

She was a temporary resident in a corner of a historic 1850s house in Arlington. Nate's archaeologist wife, Sarah, was in charge of getting it open to the public, a task apparently fraught with twists, turns and setbacks. Just when she thought everything was under control, the place sprang unexpected, unexplained massive leaks. Some people were convinced the leaks were the work of the ghosts of Abraham Lincoln and Robert E. Lee, long-rumored to haunt the house. Mackenzie didn't believe in ghosts. She blamed worn-out plumbing.

Nate and Sarah, pregnant with their first child, had moved into a house of their own in the spring. Sarah had offered the caretaker's quarters to Mackenzie when she arrived in Washington six weeks ago. While she looked for a place of her own, Mackenzie could be a presence at the historic house, discouraging ghosts and potential vandals, and staying alert for new leaks.

She zipped up her backpack. She was in shorts, but was still hot. "Nate, did you and Sarah ever encounter Abe and Bobby E. while you were living here?"

Sitting at the small kitchen table, Nate watched her with a level of scrutiny that got to most people. He was a feet-flat-on-the-floor senior deputy marshal, tall, lean and notoriously impatient. He, too, was from Cold Ridge, New Hampshire, and Mackenzie had known him all her life. He was like the big brother she'd never had, and he didn't scare her.

"I never did," he said.

"Meaning Sarah did?"

He shrugged. "You'd have to talk to her."

Mackenzie suspected that if Nate had his way, her first assignment as a federal agent would have been in Alaska or Hawaii, not his backyard. He worked at the U.S. Marshals headquarters in Arlington, and she was assigned to the Washington district office—still too close for his comfort. If she flamed out on her first assignment, better she wasn't right under his nose.

If he'd *really* had his way, she'd be writing her dissertation and teaching political science back in New Hampshire, uninterested in dipping a toe into his world.

Since he didn't have his way, he was doing what he could to help her get acclimated to her new profession. Which, on most days, she appreciated.

"You're taking a long weekend," Nate said.

"That's right. I worked it out with my chief."

"You've only been in D.C. for six weeks."

His tone was mild, without any detectable criticism, but Mackenzie knew he didn't approve. She still had boxes stacked against a wall in the kitchen, and bags of paper cups and plates were on the counter, signs she hadn't fully moved in yet—physically or emotionally. She could feel Nate wondering if she'd changed her mind about staying, about remaining in law enforcement at all.

He'd never believed she'd get through the weeks of rigorous training at the federal academy. He wasn't alone. No one had believed it. Not one solitary person, including her own mother. They didn't lack faith in her or want her to fail—they just didn't believe she was meant to be a cop of any kind.

To be fair, Mackenzie wasn't sure she'd believed it herself, but when she finally secured her spot at the academy, she went all-out. She didn't let doubts—her own or anyone else's—deter her. She refused to let anything derail her, not her size, her level of fitness, her temperament, her sense of humor. She figured she'd either discover she hated law enforcement and quit, or she'd shoot off her mouth and get the boot.

"Why take a personal day now?" Nate asked.

Because she needed to get her head screwed back on straight after making the classic new-in-town mistake of dating a guy she'd met in the rain. At first she thought Rook was a good-looking Washington bureaucrat. Instead, he turned out to be an FBI agent, violating one of the rules she'd established for herself at the academy—no getting involved with other law enforcement officers.

But she told Nate, "I'm still getting acclimated to the heat."

"You didn't have trouble with the heat in Georgia."

The Federal Law Enforcement Training Center was located in Glynco, Georgia, a hot climate, but Mackenzie refused to let Nate throw her off. She wasn't telling him about Rook. Period. "I didn't say I was having trouble."

"You were in town last night for a literacy fund-raiser."

She glanced at him. "How do you know?"

He shrugged. "Someone mentioned it."

"Who? Beanie?"

"No. I don't see a lot of her."

"She invited me. She wanted to introduce me to people. I only stayed a half hour. I think she's just trying to be a friend now that I'm in Washington, but she's not quite sure what to do with me."

Nate stretched out his long legs. "Next time, tell her to invite you for pie and coffee."

He paused, watching as Mackenzie used her foot to push her backpack against the wall next to the door. "Who did you see at the party?"

She hadn't expected that question. "What do you mean? I saw Beanie. She introduced me to a few people, but that's about it."

"Did you see Cal?"

"For about ten seconds. He showed up late and left early."

Nate got to his feet. He seemed more settled since his move to USMS Headquarters and his marriage to Sarah Dunnemore, but he was hard-bitten, impatient, unrelenting. When he was seven—before Mackenzie was born—his parents had been caught up in the mountains, on notorious Cold Ridge, in unexpected, frigid, difficult conditions. They'd died of hypothermia and exposure before help could reach them, leaving behind Nate and his two younger sisters, Antonia, five, and Carine, just three. Their father's twenty-year-old brother, Gus, just back from Vietnam, had stepped in to raise his orphaned nephew and nieces.

"I think it'd be smart for you to make new friends," Nate said now.

"Cal's not a friend. I've never had much

use for him." Mackenzie let out a breath, aware that she'd let Nate throw her off balance. "I don't know if I'd call Beanie a friend in the sense you mean. I've known her all my life. She's a good neighbor."

"A neighbor in New Hampshire. Not here. Here, Mackenzie, she's a member of the federal judiciary. You're a deputy U.S. marshal. There's a difference."

"Thanks, Nate, I couldn't have figured that out myself—"

"I'm trying to look out for you."

She knew it was true, but her usual good nature had taken a thrashing when she got back last night and listened to the voice mail from Rook. He hadn't even had the decency to ax her in person.

"Sorry, Mac, can't do dinner. I'll see you around. Maybe we'll run into each other on the job. Good luck."

Low. Very low.

The "good luck" had really ticked her off.

"Mackenzie?"

She jerked herself back to the present. Thinking about Rook wasn't smart. If she even pictured him in her mind, she swore Nate would know. Somehow, he'd figure it out. She made herself smile at him. "Sorry. I let the heat get to me."

"It's about forty-seven in here with the way you have the air-conditioning cranked up."

"It's seventy-two. You're just used to the Washington weather. If you had to go back to New Hampshire—"

"I'd get good gloves for the winter."

She grinned at him. "Are you saying I can't take the heat?"

He didn't smile back. "Mackenzie, I know you're new in town, but you have to trust me."

Obviously, he knew something was up with her. He started to go on, but she raised a hand. "I appreciate your help and support, Nate. Don't think I don't. I just . . . Give me this weekend, okay?"

Even that didn't satisfy him. "Your parents are house swapping with an Irish couple. You're staying at Beanie's place on the lake?"

"Do you know *everything,* Deputy Winter? Beanie offered—"

"When?"

"I stopped by her office after work."

Mackenzie didn't explain further. She hadn't mentioned Rook's voice mail, but

Bernadette had obviously sensed something was wrong and immediately invited Mackenzie to stay at her place at the lake. *"I'll think of you while I'm sweating here in Washington and falling asleep at my desk."*

Sweating, Mackenzie believed. Washington was in the middle of a heat wave that was brutal even by its standards. But Bernadette Peacham's work ethic—her ex-husband would say workaholism—would never permit her to fall asleep at her desk.

Nate ran the toe of his running shoe along the bottom edge of Mackenzie's backpack, as if it might yield some of her secrets. "I'm not going to lecture you," he said.

"I appreciate that."

"You've been here only six weeks. Any sense that you're distracted—"

"I'm not. I'll be back at my desk first thing Monday morning, hunting fugitives."

Her stab at humor didn't seem to register with him. "Sarah wants to have you over to dinner." He gave a half smile. "She has a new casserole recipe she wants to try."

His wife, a native Tennessean, was famous for her southern casseroles. Mackenzie smiled in turn. "So long as she makes fried apricot pies for dessert, I'm game."

Nate started to say something else, but broke off. "All right. I'll keep my powder dry for now and see you back here next week."

Mackenzie took a breath, debating whether to press him on what he wasn't saying. Did he know about her involvement with Rook? Possible, but unlikely. She hadn't told Nate she was seeing someone. Not that she was hiding it—the subject just hadn't come up.

Still, Rook was a hotshot FBI agent, and Nate had been around a long time and knew everyone.

"Nate—" She stopped herself, deciding there was no point in dredging up a few dates with a guy who'd just dumped her. "Thanks for stopping by."

"Anytime, Deputy."

After he'd left, Mackenzie checked the air-conditioning. It *was* cool in the house. She turned the temperature up slightly, then listened for ghosts. "Abe? Bobby E.?" She whistled as if calling them. "I sure could use your advice right now."

Yeah, she thought. *About why I'm talking to ghosts.*

Because it kept her from thinking about Rook.

At least she didn't have to worry about him blabbing to a senior federal agent who treated her like a third sister. Rook was ambitious, as well as humorless, and a snake, and he'd keep mum about having given her the boot.

She'd be more careful next time some good-looking man got out of the rain with her, but she couldn't bring herself to regret the movies and dinners with him—and the kisses, she thought. The brush of his fingertips on her breasts, her back . . .

What had prompted him to cancel—correction—to dump her altogether? Had he learned something about her that he thought would hurt his career? She hadn't been on the job that long. She was closely supervised. She hadn't had a chance to screw up or develop a bad reputation.

Bernadette? Did Rook not approve of her friendship with a federal judge? But that made no sense. Bernadette was a solid, fair judge with an excellent reputation.

A knock on the back porch door startled Mackenzie out of her obsessing.

Cal Benton, looking awkward, gave a curt wave through the glass panel.

She opened the door. "Hey, Cal. I'm glad

you're not a ghost. You had me worried there for a second."

"A ghost?" He seemed to have no idea what she was talking about. "Mackenzie, are you all right?"

"Never mind. Please, come in."

She stepped aside, and he strode past her into the small kitchen. He was in his late fifties, tanned, healthy, aging well—and not a man anyone who knew Bernadette would ever have expected her to marry. Before their relationship had soured, they'd said they admired each other's intellect and experience. They could laugh together, and they enjoyed each other's company. Apparently, something was missing, or something had gone wrong.

"I won't keep you." Cal was dressed in a pale gray suit, crisp-looking in spite of the heat. "Bernadette said you were going home for the weekend."

"I'm flying into Manchester at the crack of dawn."

"She said—" His cheeks reddened, and he sniffed awkwardly, then continued, "I understand you're staying at her house on the lake."

Mackenzie yanked a chair from the table

and sat down, stretching out her legs and suddenly feeling tired, even more out of sorts. "I haven't told her, if that's what you're wondering."

He glared at her as if she hadn't done him any favors. "Bernadette and I are divorced. Who I see is no longer any concern of hers." He paused, obviously for effect. "Or yours."

In the three years since Bernadette had met and married Calvin Benton, Mackenzie had tried to like him. Now, she didn't bother. "Unless you and one of your ladies of the hour sneak onto Beanie's property for a little skinnydipping on the sly—"

"We didn't skinny-dip."

"Close enough."

Earlier in the summer, before she'd left for Washington, she'd accidentally caught Cal and a woman at least thirty years his junior at Bernadette's lake house. They weren't officially divorced at the time, but it didn't matter. Divorced or almost divorced, he still had betrayed Bernadette by using her home for an illicit romantic weekend.

"I've never liked the lake." He spoke through half-clenched teeth, his tone acidic. "The water's always cold. The house is run-down. Bernadette would never listen to me about improvements. It was a bad idea to take a friend there."

"You don't want her to find out, but you like knowing how hurt and angry she'd be if she did."

"Maybe so, but don't be too quick to judge me. You don't have a clue what it's like to be her husband. The sainted, brilliant Judge Peacham."

"If you're here to convince me to continue to keep my mouth shut, you don't have to worry. I have no intention of telling her about your little liaisons at the lake. But they have to stop, Cal. No more."

"They've stopped." He inhaled through his nose, and for the first time, Mackenzie sensed he was embarrassed. "And that's not why I'm here." He seemed suddenly to notice the heat, still oppressive despite nightfall, and rubbed the back of his neck. "Have you seen Harris Mayer?"

Mackenzie tried to conceal her surprise. J. Harris Mayer was one of Bernadette's longtime friends, but not someone Mackenzie knew well. "Recently?"

"Since last night."

"I didn't see him last night. Was he at the party?"

"No, but he was—" Cal stopped himself, straightening his spine, showing no hint now of his earlier discomfort. "Never mind. My mistake."

"It's okay, but what do you want with Harris?"

"We were supposed to get together tonight for dinner. I'm sure he just forgot. It's not like I've never been stood up before."

But he'd never knocked on Mackenzie's door looking for his missing dinner mate. She'd met Harris Mayer when he and his wife would visit Bernadette at the lake, long before the gambling scandal that had forced him into early retirement and disgrace. He'd lost money he couldn't afford to lose, he'd lied to his family and friends, he'd used everyone he could think of to get any kind of advantage—and while he hadn't gone to jail, he'd paid for his compulsions. His wife had left him. Their two grown children had little to do with him. His friends had deserted him.

Except, of course, for Bernadette, who was loyal and forgiving to a fault.

"Why would you get together with Harris Mayer?" Mackenzie asked.

Cal looked uncomfortable. "Because he

asked. I'm sure he just decided to get out of this heat for a few days and forgot about our dinner. The years haven't been kind to him. Sorry to disturb you."

"Did you try to call him?"

"Of course—and I stopped by his house. It was just a stab in the dark to stop by here and check if he'd said anything to you last night. But I gather I was mistaken, and you didn't see him."

Mackenzie frowned. "Cal, what's wrong?"

"Nothing."

"If you're worried about Harris, you should talk to the police—"

"I'm not worried. I also wanted to talk with you about the other matter. What you saw at the lake. I'm sorry, Mackenzie. I shouldn't have put you in the position of keeping a secret from Bernadette." He seemed surprised by his own words, but added quietly, "You've been a good friend to her."

"And she to me. But, Cal—"

He glanced at his watch. "I have to go."

Short of siccing her ghosts on him or finding a reason to arrest him, Mackenzie had no way to make him stay and tell her what was on his mind. But his car wasn't out of her driveway before she dialed Nate Winter's cell phone. "J. Harris Mayer?" she asked after he clicked on.

She was met by silence.

"Nate?"

"What about Mayer?"

Mackenzie related her encounter with Cal Benton, leaving out, as she'd promised, any mention of his liaisons at the lake.

When she finished, Nate said, "Strange that those two have hooked up at all. Mayer could want to retain Benton as his lawyer for some reason. It doesn't matter. If I were you, I'd just forget about it."

"If you heard I was at the literacy fundraiser last night, did you hear Harris Mayer was?"

Nate was done with the conversation. "Have a good weekend," he said, and hung up.

Mackenzie didn't throw her phone at the wall, but was tempted. She debated calling Bernadette. If she did, Bernadette would ask questions, and Mackenzie knew she was too agitated, too irritated, to answer them without giving herself away. Then there'd be more questions, and just to keep from telling Bernadette about Cal and his cute brunette, she'd no doubt mention Rook, their three weeks together, how he'd dumped her.

It'd be a mess. Bernadette could always see through her. She would be able to tell—no matter how Mackenzie tried to hide it—that the one-time-hellion kid she'd saved had fallen fast and hard for an FBI agent.

Mackenzie locked the porch door and turned up the air-conditioning another notch. She hadn't let firearms training and defense tactics and learning to drive a car like a bat out of hell derail her. She wouldn't let Andrew Rook. She would get control of her emotions, just as she had during training when she'd faced fresh challenges, new fears.

She went into her little sitting room with its worn wood floors and simple, tasteful furnishings. Sarah Dunnemore Winter's touch.

Aware of the silence of the historic house, Mackenzie sat on a cozy love seat and studied a pair of old prints hung side by side on the wall opposite her. One depicted Abraham Lincoln giving the Gettysburg Address months after that bloody battle. The other was of Robert E. Lee on his horse—she didn't recognize when or where. She didn't know the story of how the two well-known nineteenth-century Americans supposedly had ended up haunting the house. It was in the brochures Sarah had so meticulously researched and written for prospective tourists.

Mackenzie promised herself she'd read one.

"In the meantime," she said aloud, sighing at the two adversaries, "if you boys are around, now would be the time to show yourselves."

But there was no answer, only the creak of old floorboards, and she gave a mock shudder of relief at the silence. *Thank heaven,* she thought, jumping to her feet. Bad enough if she ever had to explain Rook to her marshal colleagues. If ghosts started talking to her, she'd be kicked back to her campus ivory tower in New Hampshire, and be writing her dissertation in no time flat.

Three

Harris staggered out of the hole-in-the-wall Georgetown bar, an old favorite where he could place a gentleman's bet and not have to worry about anyone sniffing in disapproval. He was tired and he'd had too much to drink. After twenty-four hours, he could no longer drum up any energy for steering clear of friends or enemies. He had no attention span for going into hiding.

It was late on a dark, hot summer night. Who the hell would bother hunting him down now?

When he reached M Street, he recognized a *Washington Post* columnist and a prominent U.S. senator getting into a private car, and gave them a surreptitious middle finger, hating them for the life he'd squandered. Once, he'd had his own driver. Now he was reduced to cabs, buses and an ancient Honda that was a bother to keep on the road. It wasn't a question of finance as much as of prestige.

People who had nowhere to go didn't need drivers or fancy cars.

He smelled of stale cigarette smoke, sweat and alcohol. He walked past nice bars, nice restaurants, heard music and laughter and saw people who looked good, *were* good. He'd been like them once, filled with hope, ambition—and hubris. He'd known he was smarter than most people. He could not fail.

Now he had the FBI hunting him.

And worse.

The heat and stifling humidity started him sweating again. His shirt stuck to his back. His eyes stung. He wanted to vomit, but not on M Street. Not in front of people who used to respect him.

Then again, why the hell not? Who did *they* think they were? They had their own secrets and compulsions. Everyone did.

"Harris, for God's sake."

For a moment, Harris didn't realize who was speaking to him, but he looked up and saw Cal Benton, as if he'd materialized out of nowhere. "Cal?"

Cal hooked a hand around Harris's forearm just beneath the elbow. "You're drunk."

"Tipsy. I have higher standards for drunk."

Cal smelled of antiperspirant, as if he'd given himself a fresh swipe before getting out of his car. He was sweating, too, but he'd have to be inhuman not to sweat on such a night. "In here," he said, tugging Harris toward a nearly empty coffee shop.

"If we're seen—"

"We won't be." Cal opened the glass door, pausing to glare at Harris. "Unless your new friend Special Agent Rook is on his way."

Harris licked his lips. Even after three beers, he felt dehydrated, parched. "Who?"

"You slimy, corrupt son of a bitch, Harris."

Cal's reaction was a sign of panic. Incipient fear. "Here's the pot calling the kettle black, isn't it?"

"Damn you to hell."

Harris didn't respond. What was the point? Over the past five years, he'd grown accustomed to people damning him to hell.

Cal shoved him onto a rickety chair and briskly went to the counter, soon returning with two coffees.

"Those paper cups burn my fingers," Harris said, hearing the whininess in his own voice. He'd always hated whiners. "Don't they have any of those little cardboard holders?"

"No. Start drinking. You need to sober up."

"I am sober." Harris leaned over slightly, so that he could inhale the steam from his coffee. "Too sober."

"Damn it, Harris," Cal said with a hiss. "I've been looking for you since last night. I saw you at the hotel with your FBI agent. What the hell were you doing? *Anyone* could have seen you."

"Special Agent Rook and I were just having a quiet drink. I know a lot of FBI agents."

"I checked him out. Rook's a tough customer. He's not talking to you out of the goodness of his heart." Cal placed his elbows on the small table and clenched and unclenched his fists, staring at them. Finally, he regarded Harris not so much with hostility as disdain. "He'll throw you under the bus, you stupid bastard."

"I haven't told him anything about you, Cal. I wouldn't. You're not the one—"

"Rook doesn't care about you." Cal didn't raise his voice. "He cares about what information you can give him to help him advance his career. That's it."

"He's ambitious, but he's not dishonorable."

"Dishonorable?" Cal snorted in disbelief. "Only you, Harris. People don't care about honor anymore. They care about results."

Harris wished he could think clearly, but thoughts floated by him, just out of his grasp. Nothing felt nailed down. It was as if he was on a current of air that was taking him wherever it wanted, and he had no control.

He leaned over his coffee, the steam rising into his eyes. "Rook can save Bernadette."

"From *what?*"

"From you, Cal." Harris raised his gaze to the man across from him. "And from Jesse."

There. He'd said the name. *Jesse Lambert.* The devil.

Harris had known Cal even before he'd started seeing Bernadette, but only in the past three months had their fates become intertwined. Cal was hard-driving and ambitious, a womanizer who had seemed, at least in the early days of his marriage to Bernadette, ready to settle down.

Bottom-feeder that he was, Jesse Lambert had sensed Cal was ripe for the picking. With impeccable timing, he'd pounced at Cal's weakest moment.

And Harris had helped.

"You should give him the money," he said. "Trust me, Cal. I know of what I speak. Give him the damn money *now.* Then get out."

Cal averted his eyes. "If I give Jesse the money, there'll be no getting out. Ever." He returned his gaze to Harris. "I'll turn into you."

"If you don't pay him, he'll kill us both."

"He's a dealmaker, Harris, not a killer. We're offering him a deal. Don't weaken now."

Harris could hear the disdain for him in Cal's voice. After all, Harris was the one who'd brought Jesse Lambert into Cal's life.

Into *Bernadette's* life.

That was what ate at his soul. In using Cal, Harris knew he was also using the one friend he had left in the world.

"Jesse is the devil, Cal," Harris said quietly. "And we made a deal with him."

Cal didn't respond right away. He drank his coffee, eyeing Harris, his expression unreadable. Jesse Lambert had walked into Harris's life five years ago, preying on his insecurities and compulsions—and Harris had let himself be victimized. The gambling scandal that had ended his career was the least of his transgressions. Because of Jesse, he had betrayed his friends and the public's trust for financial gain.

You let the devil have his way with you.

Three months ago, Jesse had returned to Washington, wanting fresh meat in return for his silence about Harris's wrongs.

Harris had thrown him Cal Benton.

Cal's work and his marriage to Bernadette Peacham provided him with the kind of access and information that Jesse could use. He stayed in the background, maneuvering, manipulating. But when Jesse came to collect, Cal had refused to pay up.

"It's time to give the devil his due, Cal."

"We will, but on our terms. We're not stealing his money. We're delaying payment in return for Jesse getting out of our lives."

"We?"

Cal leaned forward. "Don't think Jesse doesn't know you helped me."

Harris could feel the blood drain from his face. A few weeks ago, he'd dropped one tidbit about Jesse Lambert to Cal, and Cal had run with it, uncovering Jesse's true identity. Cal had a complete dossier on their devil. Names, addresses, bank accounts. His insurance policy, he called it. His game was straightforward but dangerous. Using information Cal provided, Jesse blackmailed people—among them a popular U.S. Congressman, a powerful Senate aide and a well-to-do, well-connected Washington widow. Jesse remained in the background, anonymous. Cal and Harris were the ones who arranged payments. In three months, they'd amassed $1.5 million. In cash. They were to split five hundred thousand, and Jesse was to get a million.

Only Cal was withholding the million until Jesse exited from their lives.

He'd keep the dossier. If Jesse ever breathed Washington air again, it would end up in the hands of federal investigators. They wouldn't need to know a thing about Cal or Harris's involvement with Jesse to nail him.

"Going to the FBI won't save you," Cal said.

"I haven't given them anything. I just thought if they were looking . . ." Harris trailed off and blew on his coffee, wishing he could understand his own motives, his own thinking. When he'd first gotten in touch with Andrew Rook three weeks ago, his plan had seemed so logical and sensible. Now, he didn't know. Finally, he shrugged at Cal. "I guess I hoped Jesse would think twice about killing us if I'd talked to the FBI."

"Does he know?"

Harris shook his head. "I don't think so."

"You're a sniveling weakling, Harris. You're trying to save your own skin. That's all."

"If only you'd been faithful to Bernadette . . ." Harris pushed aside his coffee and sank into the cheap wooden chair. He felt crumpled, saggy and old. He'd broken so many promises over the years— to his ex-wife, his children, his friends. To himself. "I don't want her to get caught in the cross fire."

Cal's jaw tightened visibly, and he spoke through half-clenched teeth. "She won't." There was no hesitation in his tone, no regret, no guilt.

Harris stared at his coffee, a film forming on it as he tried to get his head around his thought. "But it's not fear of humiliation that sucked you into Jesse's orbit, is it, Cal?" He looked up, giving Cal a knowing, bitter smile. "You wanted the action. The risk. The same impulses that prompted you to take your little tootsie to Bernadette's house for the weekend got you into the pickle you're in now."

"Would you have preferred I'd capitulated

and let Jesse put out the pictures for the world to see? How would *that* have helped your good friend Bernadette?"

They were graphic pictures. Harris had seen them. Cal Benton copulating with a very young, inexperienced, beautiful Congressional aide in the bedroom he and his wife had once shared. They were the kind of scenes that would not only ruin him, but the aide and Bernadette. Her authority in the courtroom would be diminished with those images in people's heads.

But Cal hadn't cooperated with Jesse Lambert for noble reasons—or even just to protect himself. He liked living on the edge. Jesse had seen that quality in him and used it to his advantage, luring Cal into his world of blackmail, extortion and fraud.

"I played Jesse's game," Cal said. "Now I'm pushing back, hard, because that's all he'll understand. You don't fool me, Harris. You don't give a damn about my sainted ex-wife."

"What do you want from me?"

"I want you to stop talking to the FBI."

"I haven't told them anything of substance—"

"Good. Don't." Cal gave him a long look.

"You can't weaken. You can't waver. Stick with me, Harris. I know what I'm doing."

"No, you don't." Harris couldn't remember when he'd felt so tired. "You don't have a clue."

Cal sniffed with impatience. "Go into hiding, then. Leave Jesse to me."

"I already have gone into hiding. I just— tonight . . ." He broke off, not knowing how to explain his actions. "No one knows where I'm staying."

"Rook?"

Harris shook his head. "No one."

Cal slumped in his chair in relief. "That's good, Harris. Excellent."

"My advice, still, is to give Jesse his money and the dossier you have on him."

"He won't know if I've made copies of the information—if I have it all stored in my head. No, we've done what we've done, Harris. I have his money, and I have enough to put him away for decades. He'll cooperate."

Harris didn't think so.

But Cal was on his feet. "Go, Harris. Leave Jesse to me." He smiled, his arrogance and confidence back. "Hide."

Harris didn't respond, and Cal left, not so

much as glancing into the coffee shop as he passed by the window on the street outside. Harris remembered himself in court, holding the attention and respect of everyone present. He'd squandered his reputation—that life— because of weakness, greed and the constant search for excitement. But he'd learned a few things during those years. He could recognize a violent man when he saw one.

And Jesse Lambert, he thought, was a violent man.

Twenty minutes later, Harris stepped out of a cab in front of the shabby rooming house on a bad street in southeast Washington. He'd fled here last night after his meeting with Andrew Rook, terrified of the consequences of his own actions. Harris had fought a sense of impending doom all day. It was what had driven him to the Georgetown bar. His fear had made him careless.

The odor of fresh dog excrement permeated the hot, humid night air. What the hell was wrong with people, not cleaning up after their pets? With a hiss of disapproval, Harris unlocked the separate entrance to his small studio apartment, in an ell off the run-down main building. He could hear someone vomiting down the street. Thanks to the smart management of a family trust by a financial advisor who loathed him, Harris remained in possession of a beautiful home on a prestigious street in Georgetown. But he couldn't go back there, at least not for now.

He pushed open the door, then shut it tight behind him, blocking out the vomiting, the cars, the heat, the smell. He caught his breath, letting the cool air and his isolation soothe his taut nerves. He could ignore the seedy furnishings.

"Feeling sorry for yourself, Harris?"

Harris swung around as if he had heard a ghost. Or had he imagined the voice?

The devil's voice.

"I'd feel sorry for myself if I were you," the hidden intruder went on, his voice deadly calm and familiar.

Jesse Lambert.

Harris recognized the arrogance, the flat, bland accent.

At his worst, he would never match this man for pure evil.

"What are you doing here?" Even to his own ear, Harris's voice sounded pinched and frightened. "Come out where I can see you."

"By all means." Jesse moved into the

doorway of the tiny entry. Behind him, the studio apartment—rented by the day and sometimes by the hour—was dark, casting his face into shadows. "Don't think the FBI will come save you. They're not out there, Harris. They haven't found you. You're not important enough for them to have you under surveillance."

"That's because I haven't told them anything. What do you want?"

Jesse was dressed entirely in black. His hair was black, with random flecks of gray. He'd let his beard grow. He was in his early forties and looked wild, as if he'd just come out of the mountains or off a pirate ship.

But his eyes, Harris noted, were virtually colorless, utterly soulless.

Jesse held a knife in one hand. Casually, as if it should cause no concern.

Harris was no expert on weapons, but he knew it wasn't a kitchen knife. One side of the blade was serrated, the other side smooth. Both would cut. An assault knife of some kind, he thought.

"You don't need that," he said.

"I'm afraid I do." Jesse ran a thumb along the smooth edge of the blade, as if he wanted to test its sharpness, see his own

blood. "A knife is fast, quiet. In many situations, it's more useful than a gun. You agree,
don't you, Harris?"

Harris tried to ignore the thudding of his
heart, and summoned the last shreds of his
dignity, his honor. He'd let himself be lured
and manipulated by this man and by Cal
Benton, by his own greed and compulsions,
his own need for drama.

Stonily, he said, "It's Judge Mayer."

Jesse laughed, a hollow sound that con-
veyed neither pleasure nor fellow-feeling. "I
like that. You'd go to the gallows with a stiff
upper lip, wouldn't you?"

"I would hope not to go to the gallows at all."

"A little late, Judge Mayer."

"I suppose so," he said without flinching. "I
made my deal with the devil."

"Oh, yes." The colorless, soulless eyes
flashed, and the light seemed to dance on
the knife blade. Jesse lowered his voice. "So
you did."

In the cheap entry mirror, Mayer recognized his own stark look of fear.

No, he thought. *Not fear.*

Dread.

He took in a shallow breath. "I don't have
your money, Jesse. I don't know where it is.

That's the truth. Double-crossing you wasn't my idea."

Outside, car tires screeched, but it was silent in the small, rented room. Harris had stayed here before. It was his refuge—his hiding place. He'd been so sure no one would think to look for him here.

"How did you find me?" he asked.

"You're a creature of habits."

"The bar . . . you followed me. Did you see me having coffee with Cal? Why didn't you follow *him?*"

"He's not the one who went to the FBI. Don't try to pretend you're the innocent here. Cal couldn't have betrayed me without your help."

Harris thought of his foyer at home, with its antique mirror and half-moon table. Once it had been filled with the sounds of running children and his wife's welcome when he came home. He'd lost them all.

One beat, two beats passed. Harris absorbed the reality of just how much trouble he was in.

Finally, Jesse went on. "How much do you and Cal know about me?"

Harris didn't hesitate. "Everything."

He should have laid it all out for the FBI

from the start and let the chips fall where they may. Instead, he had tried to play Andrew Rook the same way he'd played everyone else in his life who'd wanted to help him, to trust and believe in him. Subterfuge and betrayal were his art. His entertainment. He'd thought, why not practice what he was good at on the FBI? Rook was investigating, but he had little to go on. Harris had seen to that. He'd kept his revelations vague, promising specifics in future visits—keeping Rook's interest without giving him anything concrete. Rook was in fish-or-cut-bait mode now. At their next meeting, he'd want details.

But Cal was right, Harris thought. He didn't care about helping the FBI. He cared about saving his own skin.

The devil had come for his due, indeed.

"If you knew everything about me, Harris, you and Cal wouldn't dare try to double-cross me."

As if to further drive home his point, Jesse pressed his thumb onto the tip of his knife, drawing a pearl of his own blood.

"You're a violent man, Jesse." Harris felt some of his former presence on the bench come back to him. He'd never flinched in the face of what he had to hear and see in the courtroom. "You don't use violence as a tool to get what you want. Violence *is* what you want."

"That's my secret, is it?"

"It's your secret and it's your weakness. Your obsession."

Jesse smirked as he licked the pea of blood off his thumb. "You Princeton types. You've read too many Greek tragedies. I want my money. I want everything you and Cal have on me. I want to know what you know."

"I'd never use what I know against you, and Cal won't, either. It's his insurance policy—to keep you out of his life. Jesse . . ." Harris gulped in air. Did he dare hope he could negotiate a deal with this man? "Jesse, you can trust me not to talk."

"Seeing how you've been meeting with an FBI agent, no, you lying son of a bitch, I can't trust you not to talk." Jesse sprang forward and placed the knife blade at the side of Mayer's throat. "I want my money."

"I can't—"

"You *can,* Harris. You can get my money." He lowered his knife and stepped back, the split second of explosive anger dissipated. "We'll find a way. Together."

Through violence, Harris thought.

Through death.

"In the meantime," Jesse said calmly, with a smile so cold it could only be the devil's, "tell me something. Just between us."

"What?"

"Who was the redhead with Judge Peacham last night?"

Four

On Friday morning, Rook awoke early to catch a flight to New Hampshire. His head pounded, and he was in a foul mood. He'd anticipated a very different weekend for himself. He'd expected to show Mackenzie the small Cape Cod house he'd inherited when his grandmother died a year ago. After seven years working in south Florida, he'd been offered an assignment in Washington, his home turf. Leaving him the house was his grandmother's way of getting him to stay.

It was on a quiet, tree-lined street in Arlington. His two older brothers lived within walking distance. His younger brother was a short drive away. Andrew was surrounded by Rooks, every one of them in law enforcement. He'd been infected by the Rook sense of responsibility, the hardworking, straightforward Rook values, the Rook propensity for home and hearth. He was thirty-five. The pressure was on. It was time for him to settle down. Time to start a family. All he had to do was look at the work to be done on his house, see the remnants of his boyhood tree house up in the big oak in the backyard, and he could feel it.

With a soft curse, he headed for the downstairs bathroom. It still had the Cupid wallpaper his grandmother had hung herself, with help from her grandsons. The house sorely needed renovating. A lot of de-old-lady-ing. He'd worked as a carpenter in high school and through college and could do most of the jobs himself. He'd gotten a good start, but he hadn't had a chance to tackle the Cupid wallpaper.

He took a quick shower, threw on a suit and headed for the kitchen.

T. J. Kowalski was at the front door, right on time to take Rook to the airport. Also a special agent with the FBI, T.J. wasn't impressed with Rook's rationale for heading to New Hampshire. "Packed and ready to go?"

"Just about."

T.J. wandered into the kitchen. Except for the two-inch scar under his eye, he was the classic G-man stereotype with his dark, close-cropped hair, square jaw and neat suits. "Your J. Harris Mayer is a dead end."

"Maybe." Rook grabbed a notepad and jotted instructions for his nephew. "I have to know. You drop me off at the airport. I fly to New Hampshire. I look for my missing informant. I fly back tomorrow night. Easy."

"Nothing's easy with you, man. Not these days."

Without responding, Rook folded the note, wrote "Brian" in big letters on the outside and propped it up against the pepper mill. His nephew would see it.

"Mackenzie Stewart's from New Hampshire," T.J. said.

"That's how she knows Judge Peacham."

"And Harris?"

"Presumably. He used to visit Judge Peacham there. He and his wife rented a cottage on the same lake a few times. He's taken off—he left me a message yesterday saying he was off to cooler climes. What does that tell you?"

"It doesn't tell me he's in New Hampshire."

Rook knew T.J. had a point, but he was restless and didn't believe Harris had just suddenly decided to get out of the heat. "Checking out Judge Peacham's lake house makes sense."

"Can't hurt, I guess," T.J. said, still skeptical.

"It's worth two days of my time." Rook picked up his soft leather bag and nodded to the note. "Think my nephew will see it? He gets back later today from the beach."

"Can't miss it." T. J. Kowalski wasn't even pretending to be interested. "Brian's a good kid. He's not going to burn down the house. You're only going to be gone overnight."

Brian had surprised and pissed off his parents when he'd abruptly dropped out of college in the spring, then asked his uncle Andrew if he could move in with him for a few months. He'd work, put some cash together, figure out what was next in his life. Scott, his father, a federal prosecutor, had agreed. His mother had gone along with the decision, but she obviously didn't like it. According to Scott, the eldest of the Brothers Rook, she tended to baby their two boys.

So far, Brian hadn't lived up to his end of the deal.

That was a problem for later.

When Rook and T.J. headed out, the morning was already a scorcher, the heat wave locked in for another few days, at least. If he was nineteen and unemployed, Rook thought, he'd stay at the damn beach, too.

A black SUV pulled into the driveway behind T.J.'s car, and Rook recognized the grim-faced driver, Nate Winter. Winter was damn near a legend in the USMS. T.J. had run into him during an investigation in the spring, confirming Winter's reputation as a serious-minded, impatient hard-ass—and ultraprofessional.

He got out of the car. "Good morning, gentlemen."

"Nate," T.J. said by way of greeting. "I'll be in my car. You want Rook here, right?"

Winter gave a curt nod, and T.J. slid into the car, immediately starting up the engine, the windows shut tight for the air-conditioning. Rook didn't blame him. Winter was from the same New Hampshire town as Bernadette Peacham and Mackenzie Stewart. In the past thirty-six hours, since learning Mackenzie was friends with Judge Peacham, Rook had done a little research on her. Never too late, he thought.

"Heading somewhere?" Winter asked casually.

"Airport." Rook had no intention of playing games with this man. "I'm flying up to New Hampshire."

"I'm from New Hampshire." It wasn't an idle statement. "My sister Carine lives there. She has an eight-month-old baby boy." He kept his focus on Rook. "She and Mackenzie Stewart are friends. They're planning a 'girls' night out' at Judge Peacham's lake house tonight— toasting marshmallows, catching up."

Rook said nothing. He glanced back toward his house. He could bag his trip and wait for his nephew, work on his motorcycle, deal with the gold faucets and the Cupid wallpaper in the downstairs bathroom. He'd considered how to explain them to Mackenzie when she came for dinner.

He turned back to Winter. "I'm not seeing Mackenzie while I'm in New Hampshire."

"Did you know she's headed there?"

"I've heard." But he hadn't mentioned the fact to T.J., although he'd planned to get to it on the ride to the airport. "She's not my reason for going."

"You want to find Harris Mayer," Winter said.

There was no reason for him to know the details of the preliminary investigation into J. Harris Mayer's ramblings and whether they meant anything, but it wouldn't surprise Rook if Winter did. He was one of the most trusted and capable federal agents in the country, and Rook had no real desire to go up against him. But he supposed he already had, given his behavior toward Mackenzie. The way he'd backed out of their relationship. Dating her in the first place.

"That's the main reason," he said. "I'm also trying to figure out if he's on the level with me."

"And going to New Hampshire will help?"

"I hope so."

"Cal Benton stopped by to see Mackenzie last night. He asked her if she'd seen Mayer lately."

Rook kept any reaction under wraps. "Had she?"

"No. Cal saw you and Harris at the hotel on Wednesday."

"Is that what he told Mackenzie?"

"Not in as many words. She doesn't know, but she'll figure it out soon enough." Winter paused a moment before going on. "My uncle is taking Carine's baby overnight. Should I figure out a way to get Carine and Mackenzie to cancel their plans at Judge Peacham's?"

"There's no need for that. I don't know what Harris is up to, but I can't see how he'd be a threat to an evening on a New Hampshire lake." Rook glanced at his watch. "If I make my flight, I can get out to the lake and be gone before Mackenzie and your sister arrive. They don't need to know I'm even in town. I don't expect to find anything. I'm just covering all my bases."

"Where are you staying tonight?"

"I don't know yet."

"See my uncle if you get in a jam. Gus Winter. He'll be discreet."

"Thanks," Rook said, then added in a more conciliatory tone, "I'll be in touch."

Winter didn't soften. "If not, I'll be in touch with you."

He climbed back into his car without another word.

When Rook settled into T.J.'s car, his partner and friend shook his head. "Winter will bury you in his uncle's backyard if you cross him."

"Nah. Too much granite up there. He'll toss me in the Potomac instead."

"In pieces, Rook. Lots of little pieces."

Five

Mackenzie set a new flashlight and a package of batteries on the old wooden counter at Smitty's, a well-known outfitter in her hometown of Cold Ridge. Its owner, Gus Winter, had never had much patience with her, but she smiled at him. "I'm not taking any chances if we lose power up at the lake."

Gus looked at the price tag on the flashlight. He was a tall, lean man in his late fifties, widely respected for his knowledge of the White Mountains, and for the duty and courage he'd shown first as a soldier in Vietnam, then as the young uncle who'd raised his nephew and two nieces after they were orphaned on Cold Ridge, which loomed over their town and gave it its name.

He pulled a gnarled ballpoint from a mug. "Doesn't Beanie have flashlights?"

"From 1952."

"She's always been tight with a dollar." He grabbed a pad of generic sales slips—no scanners and computers at Smitty's—and jotted down the prices of her purchases. "You and Carine will have good weather for the weekend. Beanie'll be up here at the end of the week and stay through Labor Day, like always." He grunted. "At least this year she won't have that greedy jackass husband of hers with her."

Mackenzie smiled. "I guess you're not neutral about Cal."

"Doesn't matter what I think. Matters what Beanie thinks." He looked up from his sales pad. "Is this all you need? Anything else? You can pay me later."

His gruffness was more pointed than usual, and Mackenzie stood back and frowned at him. "Gus, is something wrong?"

"Didn't mean to bite your head off." He tore off his copy of the sales slip and set it aside, then tucked hers into a bag with her batteries and flashlight. "We've got a missing hiker up in the hills above the lake."

"Are search teams—"

"I'm meeting my team as soon as I finish ringing you up." An expert in mountain rescue, Gus knew the peaks around Cold Ridge better than most. "With any luck, this woman will be back by the time we get our gear together. She's in her midtwenties, in good condition. Her friends say they spent the night in a shelter, but she took off on her own early this morning. They can't raise her on her cell phone or pick up her trail."

"Anything I can do?"

He shook his head. "Not right now. Carine's gone up to Beanie's already. Maybe this woman worked her way down to the lake, who knows. Let me grab my stuff and I'll give you a ride up there."

The original plan was for Mackenzie to meet Carine, a nature photographer, at her studio, and hang out there until Gus finished work and could take the baby. They would then head up to the lake. But Mackenzie didn't mind going early. She waited for Gus outside, where the bright afternoon sun was baking the quiet village street of Cold Ridge, which was tucked in a bowl-shaped valley among the White Mountains.

Compared to Washington, the weather was warm and pleasant, but by northern New England standards, it was a hot afternoon. Mackenzie felt strange not having a car, but she'd flown into Manchester and caught a ride to Cold Ridge with another deputy marshal out of the New Hampshire district office. Driving from Washington would have eaten up too much of her weekend, and renting a car when she was saving up for a place of her own was out of the question. But not having her own transportation underscored her new role as a nonresident—an outsider.

Gus joined her, and they climbed into his truck and headed out of town, turning off onto a dirt road and finally pulling into the sloping driveway that led to Bernadette Peacham's classic New Hampshire lake house. It was built close to the water, amid tall pines, oaks and sugar maples. Across the small, isolated lake, Mackenzie could see her parents' house. She checked in with them once a week at their Irish cottage and had met the couple they'd swapped with a few times. She had no idea if Bernadette had met them, or if they'd seen Cal with his young brunette girlfriend. There were few houses on the lake. Bernadette owned much of the wooded shoreline, with no plans to develop any of it.

"Need a hand with anything?" Gus asked, coming to a stop behind Carine's truck.

"No, thanks. I packed light."

"You're missed around here." He gave her a grudging smile and added, "Deputy."

She grinned at him. Of all the people who hadn't believed she'd get through the vigorous training to become a federal agent, Gus Winter was at the top of the list. "Never going to get used to saying that, are you?"

He laughed. "Not a chance. So long as you're happy—"

"I am," she said, quickly grabbing her backpack from behind her seat. "Good luck finding your hiker. Did you want to talk to Carine?"

"No—she'd call if she ran into the hiker. I plan to be back in time to pick up the baby. You two just relax and have a good time." He scrutinized Mackenzie for a moment. "You look stressed. When you were a college professor, you never looked stressed."

"I did. You just never noticed."

"Maybe because you weren't carrying a gun."

As soon as she climbed out of his truck, Gus took off. Mackenzie carried her backpack along a stone walk to the front of the house, its cedar shingles in need of a fresh coat of dark brown stain. Its shutters, a deep evergreen, were so nicked and scarred they probably should be replaced altogether. As with almost everything else in Bernadette Peacham's life, money wasn't the issue. She had ample funds to do whatever she wanted. Time, inclination and a tendency to overcommit were another matter.

The lake sparkled in the bright afternoon sun, and Mackenzie welcomed the cooler air, the familiar sights and sounds. She headed to the screen porch. A drop-leaf table she knew Bernadette meant to paint was there, in the same condition as when she'd brought it home from a yard sale two years ago. She often said that her life was so filled with deadlines, she appreciated having a project with no firm end date. She'd get to the table when she got to it.

The door into the kitchen was unlocked. Feeling herself begin to relax, Mackenzie found a note from Carine indicating she was off for a quick walk with Harry, her eight-month-old.

Which meant, as Gus had predicted, she was looking for any sign of the missing hiker.

Carine had left paper bags stuffed with groceries on the table, enough to feed two women for a week, never mind twenty-four hours. Mackenzie ripped open a package of marshmallows and popped one into her mouth as she headed down a short hall to a linen closet. In her haste to get out of Washington, she hadn't packed a swimsuit, but the closet, overflowing with a mishmash of towels, facecloths, sheets and extra blankets, yielded a fuchsia two-piece tankini and a beach towel—pink dolphins against a turquoise background—from her pre-law-enforcement days.

She ducked into the bathroom, which, like the rest of the house, had changed little over the years. Bernadette fixed things at the lake as needed. She didn't renovate.

Once she'd changed into the swimsuit, Mackenzie locked her 9 mm Browning in a small safe in the pantry. Then she headed back out to the porch and down to the water. She passed the shed her father had built for Bernadette, where the bloody accident that had almost killed him had occurred, and walked out onto the wooden dock. He'd been cutting wood for the new dock that day.

But she pushed the images back and stood at the end of the dock. Even in August, the lake would be cold.

With an ease that surprised her, Mackenzie dived in without hesitation, trusting herself to remember that the water off the dock was deep enough. She wouldn't risk smashing her head on a rock or scraping a knee on the rough bottom of the lake.

She surfaced almost immediately, squinting up at the clouds as she took in a breath and tried to stay focused on her surroundings, the feel of the breeze on her wet face and hair.

Don't think about Washington.

About Rook.

In a few moments, she adjusted to the cold water and flipped onto her back. The nearly cloudless sky was all she could see as she floated, going still, tilting her head back the same way she had as a girl, when the lake had been her refuge, and her keenly intelligent, eccentric neighbor had been her salvation in the tense, frantic months of her father's long and uncertain recovery. He couldn't return to the carpentry work he knew and loved. She'd later learned that money was tight. Her mother, who'd worked part-time as a teacher's aide, had turned to full-time work, every ounce of her energy going to keeping food on the table and helping her husband get back on his feet.

Mackenzie dived again, remembering telling her parents not to worry about her, that she'd be fine. She'd always loved roaming the woods, catching frogs on the lakeshore, watching the loons. With her father needing so much of her mother's attention, Mackenzie had figured her propensity to wander could finally be a help instead of an annoyance and a cause for concern. She'd relished her time alone in the woods.

Eventually, though, she'd decided to hitchhike into town, and Nate Winter, then a teenager, had picked her up and taken her to his uncle at his store, where she'd promptly stolen a jackknife and a couple of packs of waterproof matches.

Almost twenty years later, she couldn't remember the emotion that had driven her to pocket things that weren't hers, only the deep shame and anger—at herself, at everyone—when Gus had caught her.

And Bernadette's talk. Mackenzie remembered that. The law, Bernadette had explained, wasn't about seeing what you could get away with. Red lights weren't to be obeyed just when a police car was in sight. They were there for the welfare and safety of everyone.

She'd never mentioned Mackenzie's parents and how preoccupied and overwhelmed they were. In retrospect, Mackenzie understood that was why Gus had taken her to Bernadette and not them.

Blunt and straightforward, their neighbor had offered Mackenzie use of her library of books at the lake. She could take them home with her, or she could sit out on the porch or the dock and read to her heart's content. When Bernadette was in Washington, she allowed Mackenzie to let herself into the lake house for a fresh supply of books.

As she swam back to the dock now, Mackenzie felt the tension of the past two days fall away.

She climbed out of the water, shivering when the breeze hit her wet skin. She grabbed her towel, quickly drying her arms.

The door to the utility shed off to the right

of the dock had blown open. Bernadette often didn't bother with the padlock. There was nothing of great importance in the shed—canoes, kayaks, paddles, life jackets, swimming noodles, lawn mower and garden tools.

Even so, it wasn't Mackenzie's favorite place.

Its wide door, stained the same dark brown as the house, creaked in a gust of wind.

She draped the towel over her shoulders and stepped off the dock onto a path of gravel and sharp stones that she'd avoided on her run down from the house. As a kid, she wouldn't have even noticed the stones under her bare feet.

She heard a rustling sound in the brush between the shed and the shoreline and stopped, peering into the tangle of small birches and pines, thigh-high ferns, blackberry vines and invasive Japanese barberry so thick with thorns, nothing could get through it.

Wild turkeys? A squirrel?

Behind the shed were woods laced with paths that led to favorite spots along the lake, connected with trails that eventually snaked up into the mountains.

Mackenzie listened for a few seconds, but when she heard nothing more she draped her towel over one shoulder and reached for the shed door.

A guttural sound—a low growl—came from the brush. She turned quickly, just as something leaped out of the bushes, coming at her.

A man. Dark hair, a beard.

Mackenzie jumped back, but he was diving for her, slashing at her.

A knife.

She reacted instantly, adrenaline flooding her senses, and hooked her beach towel around her right arm to block another slash of his knife. Quickly, she grabbed his wrist, pointing the knife to the dirt path, and simultaneously locked his elbow in place with her other hand. She gave his wrist a sharp, hard twist away from her.

He groaned in pain, but still gripped the knife.

With the side of her foot she delivered a quick, hard kick to the inside of his knee.

The knife dropped from his hand, and he screamed in pain, sinking to the dirt.

Maintaining her hold on his forearm, Mackenzie kicked the knife into the brush.

Her attacker smelled of rancid sweat, and his beard was unkempt. His hair was wild, dirty, streaked with gray. He wore scarred hiking boots, lightweight khaki-green pants and a sweat-stained tan T-shirt.

White-flecked pale eyes stared up at her.

Those eyes . . .

She'd seen him before.

She felt something warm oozing down her left side but didn't let herself look.

"You're bleeding," he said, grinning at her. "I cut you."

He wasn't lying. She could feel the pain now, searing, overtaking the adrenaline that had protected her in the first seconds of injury. But the wound couldn't be deep. Her counterattack had prevented him from stabbing her in her kidney, killing her on the spot. Instead, he'd cut a five-inch gash in her side, just above her hip.

Spit formed at the corners of her attacker's mouth and sparkled on his beard. "You're going to pass out, Deputy Stewart. Think about what I'm going to do to you then."

He knew her name—he knew he'd just assaulted a federal agent.

Pain pierced through her. She needed to

disable him, make sure he didn't get up even if she did pass out. *Just one good chop to his neck.* But she could feel the warm blood from the slice on her side mingling with the cool lake water on her skin. Her grip on him slackened, and her towel slid off her arm onto the ground.

He seized the advantage and surged up, pushing her backward. She blocked his move, and managed to stay on her feet as he grunted, spun around and ran, crashing through the brush, swearing like a madman.

Did he have another weapon hidden in the woods?

Mackenzie knew she couldn't charge after him. She was barefoot and injured. She'd had one chance to nail him, and she'd failed. She needed to get to her gun, a telephone. Put on some dry clothes.

Her heart jumped. *Carine.*

Her friend was up on the road with her baby. What if she ran into this bastard?

What if she already had?

Mackenzie pressed her forearm against the wound on her side to provide compression. She didn't want to pick up her towel and risk passing out.

The shed door was still open. Had her attacker come out of there? Or had he been on his way into it, but saw her emerging from the water and ducked into the brush?

She had to check the shed for any other victims. If her attacker had an accomplice, he'd have surfaced by now. In her pink tankini, she was an easy target for two men.

Nothing was out of place in the shed. There was nowhere for a person to hide—the old canoe was upright, the lightweight kayaks leaned against a wall. Mackenzie grabbed a crowbar from among the tools hanging on hooks and nails, planning to use it as a makeshift weapon. But its weight pulled on her cut side, the resulting pain dropping her to one knee. The crowbar clattered to the cement floor, landing inches from an old stain—her father's blood, still there after twenty years.

Forcing herself to stand up, she chose a hammer—it wasn't nearly as heavy as the crowbar—and stepped out of the shed, squinting in the bright sunlight. The breeze made her teeth chatter.

I can't pass out.

"Mac."

What?

She blinked, trying to focus, trying to keep

her head from spinning. She had to be hallu-
cinating. She just couldn't be this unlucky.
Attacked out of the blue, stabbed, humili-
ated . . . and now Andrew Rook, special
agent of the Federal Bureau of Investigation,
black-haired, black-eyed and humorless,
had materialized in front of her?

His gaze narrowed on the blood dripping
down her side. He was controlled, focused.
"What's happened?"

"I was attacked. Not by a shark, either."
She pointed behind the shed with her bloody
hand. "The man who sliced me is in the
woods. He doesn't have a big head start. You
can catch him."

"You need a doctor."

She shook her head. "My friend Carine is
up on the road with her baby. I can't go after
her myself." She coughed—a mistake; the
pain was so intense, she saw white and almost dropped her hammer. "Go, okay?"

Rook reached into his jacket pocket. "I'll
call the police."

"Your cell phone won't work out here.
There's a phone in the house. I'll call, you
go." Mackenzie raised her eyes as she held
her bloodied side and tried to keep from
shivering. "Why are you here, anyway?"

He sighed through clenched teeth. "Later."
He drew a pistol from his belt holster and
held it out to her. "I'll go after your friend.
Take this."

"It's not necessary." She raised her hammer. "I'm all set."

"Take the damn gun, Mac." He plucked the
hammer from her and pressed the 9 mm into
her hand. "I've got another."

She didn't argue and straightened, suddenly aware again that she was in pink, a
bright pink tankini.

Hell.

She started toward the house, but after
two steps her stomach lurched. She went
still, feeling dizzy, her thoughts jumbled. How
had this happened? She'd been swimming
on a beautiful summer day, and now here
she was, woozy, knifed and arguing with the
man she'd come to New Hampshire to get
out of her mind.

"He knew my name," she said, letting the
wave of nausea pass.

She thought she heard Rook swear under
his breath. "Keep compression on your wound
and get warm. Don't risk hypothermia."

She glanced back at him. "Are you trying
to piss me off or are you just oblivious?"

Rook ignored her and took off into the woods.

Hanging on to his Browning, Mackenzie staggered to the porch and into Bernadette's kitchen. She found the land line and dialed 911, pushing back her pain—her concern for Carine—as she told the dispatcher everything she knew.

"Notify the teams hunting for the missing hiker that the man who attacked me could have found her first."

"Ma'am, you need to get off your feet and find a safe place—"

She'd forgotten to identify herself as a federal agent. She did so now and provided Gus's name as a contact.

When she hung up, she found a clean dish towel and pressed it to her wound, which was still bleeding freely, as she pushed around bags of hamburger buns and chocolate bars in search of Carine's car keys. She would drive up the road, go after Carine herself.

She was shaky and sweating, and her knees were unsteady beneath her. "I hate this," she said under her breath, slipping into her flip-flops, the dish towel pressed against her wound.

With Rook's gun in her free hand, she charged back to the porch. She wouldn't pass out and drive into a tree. She refused.

But when she reached the gravel driveway, Mackenzie knew she wasn't getting into Carine's car. She wasn't driving anywhere. Never mind the risk to herself—she'd end up running over someone. Rook, maybe.

She tensed to keep her teeth from chattering. Based on what she'd told the dispatcher, she had a fair idea of the array of cops that would be en route to the lake. She couldn't have them show up while she was standing there with chattering teeth. No cop would get away with it, not with a relatively superficial wound like hers.

And no one with any sense—cop or not—would get behind a wheel, dripping blood and clad only in a cold, wet swimsuit.

She had to trust Rook to get Carine and her baby boy back safely.

Six

Jesse Lambert hocked a loogie onto the side of the quiet, narrow dirt road that encircled the picturesque lake. He wondered if the cops would swab it for their forensics lab, or if it'd be dry before they got out here. No matter—he'd be long gone.

Would Mackenzie Stewart pass out before she could call for help? He didn't know how badly he'd cut her.

What if he'd just nicked her and she was after him now?

He liked that idea. Being back in the mountains exhilarated him. A few weeks of hiking would sharpen his mind, body and spirit, dulled somewhat by result of the lifestyle he led in Washington, D.C. He'd be back in top-notch shape in no time. But he didn't have a few weeks, not right now.

His knee ached where the freckled girl deputy had kicked him.

Bitch.

But he'd been energized by the conflict between them, her fight, her spirit. He hadn't expected her. It must have been fate, he thought, that had brought her there.

"New Hampshire . . . it's the only place I can think of where Cal might have stashed your money . . ."

Poor Harris, trying to make good on one last gamble. But New Hampshire was a reasonable answer, and Jesse had flown in late last night, crafting a bold but well-structured plan. He'd considered Cal and Harris both associates—they'd profited from their relationship with him. How had they returned the favor? They'd double-crossed him.

First thing this morning, he'd set out into the mountains.

His mountains. They comforted him, soothed him. He was never more at peace than when he was in the White Mountains. He would never live here; to do so would diminish their power to restore him. But after a violent outburst, he would always return to them.

The gurgling cry of a baby snapped him out of his thoughts.

A woman came around a bend in the road, a baby in a little red hat bouncing in a pack on her back. She gave a start, then smiled. "Oh, hello. I didn't realize anyone was out here."

This, Jesse thought, was crap. Seeing how she held a fist-size rock in one hand. She had to have heard him or spotted him. *These women up here.* She must have heard him in the woods. Meeting her eyes, he felt recognition dawn.

"Nice afternoon for a walk," he said conversationally.

She drew a shallow breath. "Definitely. I'm meeting a friend—"

"You're Carine Winter, right? The photographer?"

Her hand tightened visibly on the rock. What was she going to do, bash him over the head with it? She had a baby with her, and she was thinking about beating a man to death. *Him.*

But she gestured vaguely up the road. "I'm running late."

"Sure. No problem." Jesse stepped into the shade of an oak on the edge of the road, letting her pass. "I ran into Mackenzie Stewart a few minutes ago. She scared the hell out of me. I was just hiking, and all of a sudden, she was *there*."

Without saying a word, Carine picked up her pace. She had to have all sorts of questions about him, but wasn't going to linger and ask any of them. Jesse watched the baby's red hat bob up and down as his mother hurried on, moving as fast as she dared without hurting her son or drawing attention to her fear.

She was a Winter, and all Winters in the White Mountains were legendary hard-asses.

Mackenzie Stewart was the one who'd shocked him.

Jesse kept his tone mild as he called to Carine, "Tell your redheaded friend that I didn't mean to hurt her. I was scared. Just scared."

The marshals, the FBI, the state cops, the local cops—they would run everything he said and did past their experts, and they'd figure he was some kind of a head case.

That was all part of his plan, and suited him just fine.

He raised his voice a notch so Carine could still hear him. "I bought one of your calendars. Really like the picture of the loons."

In fact, he *had* bought one of her calendars. It hung in his house in Mexico. She was an accomplished nature photographer who knew the White Mountains as well as he did—and had captured their soul in her pictures.

He thought he heard a car engine down the road, and quickly ducked under the oak, revived now, a fresh surge of adrenaline pumping through his bloodstream. He knew every inch of the maze of trails that snaked into the mountains. Within the hour, he would be a needle in a haystack. Even with search dogs, the police would never find him.

He pictured Mackenzie Stewart's dark red curls, her compact, sexy shape and the crimson blood running down the smooth, creamy skin of her upper thigh.

She was so damn pretty.

Barefoot and soaking wet in her pink bathing suit, she'd still managed to disarm him and come damn close to kicking his ass. He'd had to use every bit of his willpower to get back on his feet and bolt into the woods.

His attraction to her was unexpected, as

potent and as visceral as his urge to stab her. In that split second of decision followed by action, when he'd jumped out of the brush at her, he had fully meant to kill her, not just cut her. If she hadn't stopped him, disarmed him, she'd be dead right now.

From the moment he'd spotted her at the Washington hotel with Judge Peacham the other night, Jesse had known he would have to hurt Mackenzie Stewart one day.

Today just happened to be the day.

Seven

The sound of a baby's cry drew Rook out of the cover of a trio of white pines and onto the sun-washed dirt road above the lake. A fair-haired woman with a baby on her back gasped and jumped back a step, a rock in her raised hand.

"FBI," he said quickly. "Andrew Rook. You're Carine?"

She nodded, lowering her arm. He had his weapon drawn, a .38 caliber Smith & Wesson he sometimes wore on his ankle, but she seemed to relax slightly. "He ran up into the woods." She motioned vaguely be-

Abandon

hind her. "The man—you're looking for him, right? He said Mackenzie—" Out of breath and obviously shaken, the woman looked to Rook for answers.

"Mackenzie's okay." He didn't need to go into detail about the attack now. "Are you or your baby hurt?"

"No." Carine squeezed her eyes shut and inhaled through her nose, holding the breath a moment before exhaling through her mouth. She opened her eyes again. "I'm sorry." Her voice quavered. "I'm a little upset."

"The man you saw, is he on foot? Does he have a vehicle?"

"He's on foot as far as I know. I didn't see a car. The road dead-ends. If he had a car, he would have to double back this way, and no one has passed me yet." She paused, calmer now. "He has enough of a head start that he could be on any of a number of trails. Maybe you can catch up with him. Feel free to go after him."

Rook had no intention of leaving her. "Let's get you back to your friend. I'll walk with you. You can tell me what happened."

Carine paled even more, but she seemed steadier. "Mackenzie isn't all right, is she?"

"She'll be fine. Mac's tough."

Unexpectedly, Carine smiled. "She lets you call her Mac?"

"No, but I do."

"She's told me about you."

Carine left it at that, and Rook could imagine what her friend had related about him. All of it true, no doubt.

Incongruously, Carine's baby grinned at him, showing two top teeth, two bottom teeth and a lot of drool. His dark eyelashes were clumped together with tears. Rook smiled back. "You're safe now, fella." He looked at his mother. "Boy, right?"

"Harry." She sniffled, adjusting him on her back. "That man. Do you know who he is?"

"No."

"I heard something scrambling in the woods. I thought it might be an animal. I picked up a rock." She reached behind her and touched her son's foot, tucked into a red sock that was half-off. "I've had encounters with rough types before, but it's different—" She took in another breath, obviously fighting to control a fresh wave of emotion. "It's different when you have a baby to protect."

"I'm sure it is. You did fine, Carine. You're safe now."

In measured words, as they continued down the dirt road, she related every detail of what she'd experienced, finishing just as they arrived back at Bernadette Peacham's house. Rook knew he had to tell Carine about Mackenzie's injury, but as he started to speak, Carine shot out ahead of him.

"Mackenzie!"

She was sitting on the gravel driveway, shivering as she leaned against the sedan Rook had rented at the airport. Carine hurried down to her, quickly lifting off the pack with her baby and setting it upright on the grass. He sucked on his little fist.

"Harry's getting big," Mackenzie said, obviously biting back her pain.

"You're bleeding—"

"It's under control. My liver's not going to fall out or anything."

Rook stood over her. "You're white as a sheet, Mac. Is an ambulance on the way?"

"I don't need an ambulance." She leaned her head against the car. Most of her red curls were matted to her skull, but a few sticking out, he noted. "I see you rented a black car. Very FBI of you."

"Mac—"

"It's just plain in-your-face cheekiness for

you to turn up here, Rook. You're in a suit. You're armed to the teeth. You weren't planning to climb Cold Ridge or join Carine and me toasting marshmallows, were you?"

He didn't answer her. Her eyes had a glassy, pain-racked look to them, and her lips were purple as she struggled to keep herself from shivering. "You're freezing," he said instead. Rook pulled off his sport coat and draped it over her. She made a face, but didn't object. "I'll take you to the damn E.R. myself if I have to."

"I told the dispatcher I'd been sliced. I know they'll send an ambulance even if I don't need one." Pressing the bloody towel she held to her side, Mackenzie shifted position, then winced. "If I pass out, just leave me here in the dirt. I'll come to in a few seconds."

Carine seemed relieved at her friend's stab at humor. "Is there anything I can do?"

"I'd love some dry clothes. My backpack's in the kitchen. I'd rather not go to the hospital in a pink swimsuit and G-man sport coat."

"I don't blame you. Back in a sec." Carine scooped her half-asleep baby out of the pack and headed off to the house, eager to help her friend.

Rook glanced down at Mackenzie. "I take it you don't own a suit in marshal's black."

"Black washes me out."

Her irrepressible humor had drawn him to her that night in Georgetown in the rain, even before her blue eyes, her quick smile, her intelligence. "Anything I can do?"

"Find this guy." Beads of sweat had formed on her upper lip, in spite of the breeze. "If he gets enough of a head start, he could be anywhere. There are a lot of hikers this time of year. He could head in any one of a dozen directions. If he decides to blend in, we'll be lucky if anyone remembers seeing him."

"Just rest, Mac. The woods will be crawling with search teams soon enough."

"I've been trying to remember where I've seen him. Nothing's coming." Her head fell back against the car with a thud. "I shouldn't have let him get away."

"You disarmed him and kept him from killing you. So you got a little scratched in the process—"

"Bastard. You, I'm talking about. 'A little scratched.' Easy for you to say."

He smiled. "Brought some color back to your cheeks."

And she would have to admit the slash in her side was nothing compared to what could have happened—even if she did let her attacker get away. An ambulance and town police cruiser arrived within seconds of each other. Rook moved to go and meet them, but Mackenzie reached up and touched his hand. "You know Bernadette Peacham owns this place, right?"

He didn't answer her.

"If she's in danger—"

"I'll take care of it."

Mackenzie studied him. "I'm guessing you're not here because of me."

"Mac—"

Her eyes cleared, and he could see the focus and intelligence that made her a good law enforcement officer. "Beanie's turned up in one of your FBI investigations, hasn't she?"

"Never speculate."

"I'm not speculating," Mackenzie said. "I'm asking a direct question."

"I don't know anything about the man who attacked you," Rook replied.

She sighed. "I believe you, if only because you straight-arrow, G-men types make lousy liars."

Carine returned with a pair of yoga pants

and a flannel shirt for her friend, and Rook took the opportunity to ease out of Mackenzie's line of vision and identify himself to a local cop. More police cars descended on the scene, lining the dirt road.

Mackenzie addressed all the cops and paramedics by their first name and tried to tell them what to do. "No stretcher," she instructed two paramedics. "If you even try to put me on a stretcher, we'll have words."

One of them, a red-faced, burly man about her age, rolled his eyes. "We're putting you on a stretcher, Mackenzie, so just shut up about it."

"You never did like me, did you, Carl?"

He grinned. "Are you kidding? I was a freshman in high school when you were a senior. We all had a crush on you. Those cute freckles of yours—"

"Okay. Where's my gun?"

He laughed, and a moment later he and his partner had her on a stretcher.

After the ambulance pulled out, Rook walked down to the lake. The shed door swayed in the breeze. Two local officers were already taping off the scene, carefully avoiding any contamination of forensics.

He spotted blood that had seeped into the

rocky, sandy soil and splattered the grass and nearby ferns.

Mackenzie's blood.

She'd lost more than she wanted to admit, and every drop clearly annoyed her. Rook didn't recognize the description of her attacker. It wasn't Harris—and Harris, his missing informant, Rook reminded himself, was the reason he was in New Hampshire. He wasn't there because of his relationship with Mackenzie. Maybe he should be, he thought. But he wasn't.

Rook averted his gaze from her blood. What if he'd just gone ahead and had dinner with her? Made love to her? Neither of them would be in New Hampshire right now.

Across the lake, which was choppy in the stiff breeze, he spotted a small house, presumably where her parents lived. Carine had given him the rundown of who was who on the lake, in case anyone else might be in danger. He pictured Mackenzie out here as a child and wondered what forces had taken her into the Marshals Service.

He was late learning about her background and her relationship with Judge Peacham.

Three weeks late.

The state troopers started to arrive. With a federal judge's property involved and a federal agent attacked, the FBI and the U.S. Marshals would be on the heels of the troopers, joining the investigation.

Rook had his own job to do.

Eight

Bernadette Peacham hated that her ex-husband had caught her eating a frozen lasagna for dinner. She hadn't even bothered to put it onto a plate or make a salad. She'd simply stuffed the single serving into the microwave, peeled off the film cover and dug in, and there was Cal, as handsome as ever, standing in her kitchen doorway.

And it was *her* kitchen. Not his. Despite their divorce, she'd hung on to both her house here in Washington, just off stately Massachusetts Avenue, and her lake house in New Hampshire. Her first marriage had smartened her up about protecting her financial interests, if not about improving her taste in men.

"I just heard about Mackenzie," Cal said. "An FBI agent stopped in my office. I came straight here. Have you talked to anyone?"

"The FBI just left."

He looked truly upset. "Bernadette— thank God you weren't at the lake this weekend. The police say the man who attacked Mackenzie might have camped on your property."

She shoved the lasagna container into the trash. Cal had always been disdainful of her benevolence. "For the record, I didn't let him."

"Do you have any idea who it was?"

"No."

Cal ran a finger across the round, white-painted table, a habit of his when he was stressed and trying not to show it. He'd taken off the ten pounds he'd put on in the last six months of their marriage, and he looked good. His hair was a little thin on top, and what he had left was all gray now, with no hints of the dark blond it used to be. Bernadette had met him three years ago, and it was as if she'd waited her entire life for him. Now, she could hardly stand the sight of him.

The feeling, she was quite sure, was mutual.

He was getting ready to move into the condominium he'd bought in an expensive complex on the Potomac. In the meantime, she'd agreed to let him stay in a guest suite at the house they'd once shared. He was a successful corporate attorney who needed nothing from her, but he would never see it that way. Cal, Bernadette knew, was a man who always wanted more, more, more.

It hadn't always been like that, she recalled. When they'd first met, he had talked longingly of living out at the lake full-time. Fishing, kayaking, growing a garden. But their marriage had opened up new doors for him, and Bernadette had watched as his income, his stress level, his tolerance for risk, his love of action—the game—all skyrocketed. The lake had lost its appeal for him. For a brief time, he had viewed the lake house as quaint and charming. Now, he regarded her house and land on the lake a waste, when she could sell lots, make a fortune, tear down, rebuild. He had any number of plans for what she could do with the property that had been in her family for generations.

She simply hadn't seen him changing until it was too late and their marriage was beyond repair.

"You and your three-legged puppies," he said.

"I told you that I didn't let him camp—"

"I was talking about Mackenzie."

Bernadette gasped, taken aback. "I can't believe you just said that. What a callous prick you've become, Cal. Mackenzie barely escaped with her life today. At least let her heal before you start demeaning her."

"I'm not demeaning her. I'm just being truthful. Where would she be now without you?"

"I imagine she'd be doing exactly what she's doing."

"No, you don't. You know what you did for her."

"What did I do? I hired her father to build a shed and damn near got him killed. That's what I did."

Cal sniffed. "It was an accident. It wasn't your fault. He was careless, upset because of his wild daughter—"

"For God's sake, Cal, Mackenzie was eleven. She wasn't wild—she'd just wandered off. Later on, she got a little wild, but—*please*. Let's not do this. I know you resent the help I've given to people along the way, but it's just a part of who I am. I don't think about it. I'm not looking for anything in return. So just let it go."

"I'm not as good as you are." His tone held no plea for understanding, no regret, only condescension. "Living in your shadow has never been easy."

So much, Bernadette thought, for their mature, civilized divorce. It had gone the way of their mature, civilized marriage. She had finally come to realize that he believed she was lesser for her generosity. Weaker.

She leaned back against the counter, feeling the cool granite through the thin fabric of her skirt. "Don't blame me for your insecurities," she said, hearing the exhaustion in her voice. She was just so damn tired of sparring with him.

"I never asked you to be less than the good person you are," Cal said. "I just got tired of being reminded every day that I don't measure up—if not by you, then by your deeds, your friends, your colleagues. My own clients."

Bernadette checked her impatience. They were divorced; she didn't have to wear herself out trying to pump him up. "Let's not rehash our problems. What do you want, Cal?

Are you hoping to benefit in some way from what happened today in New Hampshire?"

"That's not fair."

She sighed. "No, it isn't."

"Are you happy as a federal judge?" Cal asked.

"What's that got to do with anything?"

"Just answer the question."

"I don't think about happiness anymore. I'm not sure I even know what it is. A good meal? A pretty sunset? The fleeting moments when life is good? I don't think happiness even matters in our lives. It's not something I strive for."

He looked away from her. "I'm a decent man, Bernadette. I'm not a perfect one. I hope you'll remember that."

"I never asked or wanted perfection, Cal."

"Maybe not. I'm glad Mackenzie wasn't hurt any worse today. I know how fond of her you are. I'm sorry I was insensitive. I didn't mean to be. She's done a lot with her life, more than anyone thought she would after what she had to face. She blames herself for her father, you know. It doesn't matter how much time goes by. She blames herself."

Bernadette nodded. "I know."

"She'll blame herself for not getting this

guy today, too. At least she wasn't hurt any worse." He walked over to Bernadette and touched her hair. "You're beat—you look as if you fended off a criminal with a knife yourself." He pulled his hand away. "We had some good times together, Beanie Peacham."

"We did, indeed."

"Are you planning to date once I'm out of here? I know it's none of my business, but if you're not, you should. You're still an attractive woman. You have a lot to offer a man."

She smiled coolly. "And what does a man have to offer me? I like my life right now. Don't patronize me by suggesting I need a man to be happy."

"God forbid anyone suggest you need anything. Maybe if you'd needed me even a little bit—" He stopped without finishing his thought. "Never mind. They'll catch whoever attacked Mackenzie. She's indestructible. I'll say that for her."

He retreated down the hall, and a moment later, Bernadette heard his footfall on the stairs. She flopped down at the kitchen table, picturing Mackenzie fighting off an attacker— and twenty years ago, at age eleven, angry, guilt-ridden, neglected and frightened. Her father's recovery had been long and painful and uncertain, consuming all of them. He still had terrible scars from his gruesome injuries.

And poor little Mackenzie had found him, mangled, near death, his blood splattered all over the shed.

If ever a child had needed a role model and a friend in those difficult days, it had been curly-haired Mackenzie Stewart, so ebullient by nature, so filled with humor and fun, but traumatized by her father's accident. Bernadette had never considered herself up to the task of helping Mackenzie. She was a workaholic with one divorce behind her and zero interest in children.

She wasn't nearly as good as Cal believed.

There was a knock on the side door. Everyone had been urging her to improve her security, both here and in New Hampshire, but she never had. She got up, her hip aching from fatigue and from years of sitting in a courtroom.

She saw Nate Winter standing on the steps. Her first thought was that he was looking more and more like Gus, his uncle, whom she knew would see to Mackenzie just as he'd seen to his orphaned nieces and nephew more than thirty years ago.

Nate would know that, too. He was one of the most respected federal agents in Washington and it was no secret he felt responsible for Mackenzie's decision to go into the Marshals Service.

Bernadette opened the door. "Nate, it's good to see you."

He had on a dark suit and must have come straight from work. Life was good for him right now, with a new wife, a new home and a baby on the way. But Bernadette could see the tightness around his mouth, the only hint of any emotion.

He stepped into the kitchen. "We need to talk."

Nine

The police had released the shed as a crime scene, after finding no clear evidence that the man who'd attacked Mackenzie had been inside, although, given the open door, he must have either been inside or on his way in. She stood on the threshold, the cool evening air on her back. The wind had died down, and she could hear crickets chirping in the nearby brush. Her girls' night out with Carine was postponed indefinitely, but it would have been a nice night for laughing and telling stories.

Rook returned her hammer to its spot among Bernadette's tools. The police hadn't found any obvious clues to the identity of her attacker. "I had to explain you to my chief," Mackenzie said. Inside the shed, the air was close, smelling of dust and grease. "I told him we saw each other a few times, and I don't know why you're in New Hampshire. He threatened to come up here. Not because of you. Because of the attack, although I suspect it and your reasons for being here are not unrelated."

"You talked him out of coming up?"

"Apparently, Nate did."

"Ah."

She crossed her arms on her chest. Even with pain medication, any abrupt move hurt. The E.R. doctor had sewn her up with a layer of absorbable stitches in the fat and a layer of regular stitches in the skin. She had to go back in twenty-four hours to get the dressing changed, and in seven to ten days to get the top sutures removed. She was prescribed antibiotics as a precaution against infection. Pain medication she could take as needed.

"Nate called, too," she said. "Having Carine in danger again scared him. She came upon a murder scene a while back, when she and Tyler North were still deciding whether or not they were meant for each other."

"Tyler is her husband?"

Mackenzie nodded. "He's a pararescue-man. He's deployed right now." She thought a moment. "Carine hasn't told him about to-day yet, but when she does, he'll want to know every detail. I'll probably have to ex-plain you to him, too."

"If it's any consolation, I've had to explain myself to people around here all afternoon. You have a lot of friends in Cold Ridge."

"How *did* you explain your presence?"

"I said I was here to see you."

"Rook."

He smiled mysteriously but didn't elabo-rate. He started toward the door, and she stepped back from the threshold. He joined her on the soft, cool grass. "Maybe you should call it a night."

"As I said, I wouldn't be surprised if the at-tack on me and your reasons for being here are connected," she said. "You're here be-cause of an investigation."

He didn't respond.

"I've been thinking. I was in Georgetown the night we met because of Beanie

Peacham. I had a drink with her before Cal got there, then I walked around outside, and it started raining and there you were." When she tried to latch the shed door, her head spun. "And now here you are again."

He pulled her hands from the door. "You're cold."

"I guess I got used to the heat in Washington more than I realized."

"Did the doctors want to keep you for the night?"

"Yes, but I talked them out of it. I told them I had to come back here and toast marshmallows." She found the padlock in the grass and started to pick it up, but decided she didn't want to risk passing out in front of Rook. "It's a little late to be locking the shed."

Rook swooped up the lock. "Can't hurt, in case our guy decides to double back here."

"Of all places," Mackenzie said quietly. "Beanie's philosophy is waste not, want not. She wouldn't have had this shed built if the previous one hadn't basically fallen apart. She hired my father to do the job."

"Mac—"

"He was working out here alone one day. His table saw malfunctioned. The blade—" She stopped, pushing back a wave of dizziness, then resumed. "I don't know what happened, exactly. I was eleven. I found him. I was supposed to be helping him, but I was goofing off, chasing this toad that had caught my eye."

"You were a kid."

"He lost an eye, parts of several fingers. He had severe internal lacerations." She cleared her throat, staring at the shed door. "It was a mess in there, I can tell you that much. I didn't want to leave him, but I remember thinking that if I didn't, he would die. I ran up to the house and called the police."

"Where was Judge Peacham?"

"She was in town. It was just my dad and me here most of the day. When I hung up after talking with the police, I didn't want to come back down here. I thought he was dead. I didn't want to see the blood."

"But you did come back, didn't you, Mac?"

She nodded. "I stayed with him until the ambulance arrived. I was so covered in blood, the paramedics initially thought I'd been injured, too."

"That's a tough memory to have."

"It could be worse. At least my father lived. He had a long, painful recovery, and he's never really worked again. But he and my mother have a good life. They're doing a house swap with an Irish couple—they're in Ireland right now. All's well that ends well, right?" She smiled. "That's one of Beanie's favorlte sayings."

"Today ended well, Mac. The police will find this guy—"

"I don't like the shed. I used to have nightmares that monsters lived in there." She snatched the padlock from Rook and snapped it into place on the latch. Dusk was coming fast now, and the lake was still, mirroring the darkening sky. "I should have nailed that bastard before he got near me."

"Do you think he intended to kill you?"

"I don't know. Maybe, maybe not. He didn't hurt Carine, but he didn't have his knife with him, either."

"Thanks to you. Carine—she was fully prepared to defend herself and her baby with a rock."

"That's Carine. The Winters are all like that." Mackenzie couldn't summon the energy even to smile. "If anything had happened to her, because of me . . ."

"Nothing did," Rook said.

"You don't recognize his description?" she asked.

"No."

Then maybe her attacker wasn't someone involved in whatever investigation had brought Rook to New Hampshire after all. Or Rook hadn't identified him yet as anyone of interest. Or Rook was lying, but somehow she didn't think he would be a good liar. "I know I've seen him before, but I can't pin down where, who he is. Maybe I just saw him in line at the grocery."

"He recognized you."

"I haven't been in Washington that long. More likely he knows me from here."

"He referred to you as Deputy Stewart."

"My career change has been a topic of conversation around town for several months. 'The college instructor who heads off to train as a deputy marshal.'"

Rook slipped an arm over her shoulder. "You did well today, Mac."

"I got in one good lick. Big deal."

"You also got his knife away from him."

"My training kicked in. If he'd attacked Carine, or if Bernadette had been up here and he'd attacked her . . ." But Mackenzie knew better than to spin off into what-ifs, and didn't go further. "Next time I go swimming, I'm wearing jeans and sneakers."

"Not as much fun as your little pink swim-suit."

"Rook, just because I've got twenty stitches in my side doesn't mean I can't elbow you in your gut." But she appreciated his humor and felt herself leaning against him as they headed to a trio of Adirondack chairs and Bernadette's open fireplace. Even if he'd dumped her and was a snake, at least he could be a friend. "The police have my swim-suit and towel. They're checking for trace evidence. Can you imagine if I have to testify in court, and they hold up my dolphin towel and slashed tankini? I'll never live it down."

"You never will, anyway."

"You're a big help."

He grinned at her. "Welcome to law enforcement. No one will criticize you for what you did today, Mac. If I'd been caught by a knife-wielding lunatic out here in my swim trunks—"

"Ouch, Rook. I don't need that image in my head."

"No? What kind of swim trunks do you have me in?"

"Baggy, snot-green plaid ones that hang down to your knees."

"Lovely."

Except it wasn't true. The swim trunks Mackenzie pictured him in fit him perfectly, and nothing about them—or him—was ugly. But she didn't dwell on the image. "I'm lucky. He didn't cut through muscle or nick any vital organs. I'll be fine in no time. I'm a fast healer."

"What about the next twenty-four hours?"

"I have to keep the dressing dry and I can't do jumping jacks. Why?"

Just then Gus's truck pulled into the driveway, sparing Rook from having to answer.

Carine jumped out of the passenger side and waved cheerfully. "We're here for marshmallows."

But there was something off in her voice, and Mackenzie slipped from Rook's embrace and narrowed her gaze on him. "What's going on?"

"I was getting to that," Rook said. "Gus Winter and his team found their missing hiker. Your instincts were on target. Your attacker got to her first. She'd been stabbed."

"Dead?"

Rook shook his head. "Doctors say she'll make a full recovery. She's lucky they found her when they did. A night out in the open wouldn't have been good."

Mackenzie visualized the assault knife, but forced back the image. "Her attacker fits the description of the guy who came at me?"

Rook nodded. "She said he seemed deranged."

"A deranged hiker slashing women in the mountains." Mackenzie bit off a sigh of frustration, her earlier dizziness gone now. "I should never have let him get away."

"Which brings us to the next twenty-four hours."

"What?"

"Carine and her baby are staying at her uncle's house in town tonight. She needs time to pull herself together. You're welcome there—"

"I'm not staying at Gus's."

Rook gave her a faint smile. "That's what he said you'd say."

"I'm staying here. Honestly, Rook. First I get knifed. Then I let the guy who knifed me get away and scare the living daylights out of my best friend. *Then* I have to face a million cops while I'm wearing a pink swimsuit, which is confiscated as evidence along with my dolphin towel." She wanted to stop herself, but was on a roll now. "So don't try to talk me out of staying here, because it won't work."

"You're drugged. Once you hit a pillow, you'll be out for the night."

"I hope so."

"What if this guy comes back? I'm not trying to talk you out of staying here. You have a choice."

"What—" She snapped her mouth shut and studied Rook, noted the spark of humor in his eyes. He had killer eyes, a killer smile. "Why do I feel as if I just painted myself into a corner?"

"Because you did."

"You're staying here tonight?"

He smiled at her. "That's the plan."

All Mackenzie could think was that with Rook under the same roof, it was just as well she had twenty stitches in her side.

Ten

Gus Winter stabbed a fat marshmallow with one of the half-dozen or so sharp sticks Bernadette kept at her outdoor stone fireplace, and handed it to Mackenzie, then sank into an old, comfortable Adirondack chair. Gus had built the fire, as if the simple ritual was what he needed to put the events of the day into perspective.

Mackenzie sat forward and held her marshmallow over the flames, careful not to let it get too close. She liked a gooey center and a crisp exterior, which required a certain level of patience and marshmallow know-how.

"Beanie's helped a lot of people over the years," Mackenzie said. "I wasn't the only one."

"Not by a long shot. And you're a neighbor. She's helped perfect strangers." Gus reached for another stick. "Are you suggesting this nut today was someone she helped?"

"I'm not suggesting anything. I'm just casting a wide net."

"Are you supposed to be casting any net? You're one of the victims."

As if she needed reminding, with her bandages, her wooziness from medication. The cool air and the familiarity of the fire, the marshmallows, the sounds of the dark night, all helped center her. She could feel her fatigue, even as her mind spun with the images of the day, the scraps of information she had, the possibilities they presented.

"I don't mean officially. It's not my investigation, but that doesn't mean I can't speculate. Everyone in town is speculating."

"Point taken," Gus said.

She glanced at him as he picked up a second stick for himself. "Overkill?"

"Always with you, kiddo."

She smiled. "I thought I might irritate you less now that I've been knifed."

He took two marshmallows and impaled them on his stick. "Nah." He grinned at her. "You're the same Mackenzie I've always known and loved. At least you haven't lost your sense of humor."

"Hey, someone around here has to have a sense of humor." This reminded her of Rook, who was either in the house or else off with other FBI agents—she didn't know which. He wasn't by the fire toasting marshmallows. "The attack on the hiker this morning suggests this man wasn't here specifically because of Beanie. The lock on the shed wasn't broken. She probably just didn't bother with it."

"So he seized the moment and ducked in there to hide, or planned to?" Gus asked.

"Maybe. Carine left the house unlocked when she and Harry headed up the road. If this guy was looking for a place to rest, or stuff to steal, you'd think he'd go into the house."

"He might not have had the chance. We don't know how long he was here. He could have stumbled into the brush right from the woods while you were underwater."

Mackenzie felt the heat of the fire on her face as her marshmallow browned. Her eyes felt as if they'd been rolled in sandpaper. Sitting close to the flames probably wasn't helping. "Just as well he didn't crawl out from under a bed in the middle of the night."

Gus plunged his two marshmallows into the blaze. "This FBI agent, Rook. What's his story?"

"I don't know. He just showed up."

"Uh-huh. Friend of yours?"

"Someone I know."

"Who is he?"

She could tell Gus was growing impatient. Understandably. "Well, when I first met him, I thought he was a Washington bureaucrat."

"But he's not," Gus said unnecessarily.

"Seems so obvious now."

"You let him call you Mac. Last time I called you Mac, you told me in no uncertain terms it's Mackenzie."

"I told Rook the same thing."

Gus's marshmallows caught fire. He let them burn for a few seconds, then blew them out—his own ritual. "Anything personal between you two?"

She didn't hesitate. "No."

"You're not working a case together or something, are you?"

"Nope. Nothing."

"So there *is* something between you two."

Mackenzie bit into her marshmallow, testing to make sure it was soft throughout, but not so gooey it would fall off the stick. She had a tendency to lose marshmallows in the fire if she wasn't careful.

Gus continued to char his. "Does Nate know this Rook?"

"I don't know. Why don't you ask him?"

"I'm asking you."

The marshmallow was perfect, and she popped the whole thing into her mouth, enjoying the sweetness. She sat back in her chair and debated whether she had the energy to roast another.

"Nate's been decent to me since I moved to Washington," she said. "He's so well respected, I doubt anything I could do would have an impact on him—"

"That's not what I'm asking."

She sighed. "I know, Gus. Okay. Rook and I went out a few times. That's it. Story over."

"How'd he manage to show up here just minutes after you were stabbed?"

"I don't know—and I wasn't stabbed. Stabbing is when the knife goes straight into you." She looked over at him, silhouetted against the fire and dark night. "This was a cut."

The missing hiker, on the other hand, had been stabbed in her lower abdomen. She had come out of surgery, and her prognosis for a full recovery was excellent. Everyone—Gus, especially—would hate seeing a woman who'd come to the White Mountains to hike with friends end up stabbed, fighting for her life. That she'd survived the attack was a miracle, but the profilers, Mackenzie knew, would add it to the mix. Why hadn't their perp stabbed the woman repeatedly? Why had he done so once, and run?

Was he deranged?

Mackenzie thought of his eyes. The eyes of a man in the midst of a psychotic breakdown?

She set her stick in the grass. "Have you talked to Beanie?"

Gus pulled his blackened marshmallows out of the fire. "No, why would I?"

"Because you've known her since kindergarten."

"Before that. I didn't go to kindergarten."

He ate the top marshmallow, his prickliness more pronounced than usual. Gus and Bernadette both had deep roots in Cold Ridge, and as different as they were, they each planned to spend their last days there.

Mackenzie stared up at the starlit sky. If

she sank any deeper into her chair, she'd become a part of it. "You and Beanie are going to end up in the same nursing home, you know. It'd serve you right."

He gave Mackenzie a quick grin. "Probably would."

"The police and the FBI don't think this guy had anything to do with her."

"What's your gut say, Mackenzie?" Gus leveled his gaze on her. "Think it was random, him showing up here?"

"No," she said. "I don't."

He turned back to the fire and lowered his remaining marshmallow into the flames once more, presumably to char the one square millimeter he'd missed. "Wishing you'd stayed in academia right now?"

"I'm wishing I'd worn a black swimsuit today."

He laughed, but Mackenzie couldn't summon the energy to respond in kind. She closed her eyes, trying to listen to the crickets and the soft lapping of the lake against the rocks. Instead, she heard the rustling in the brush from this afternoon, and chastised herself for thinking it was an animal, harmless, normal.

She felt the smooth edge of the assault knife cut across her skin. She hadn't done so at the time—somehow, her mind hadn't let her feel it—but she did now.

Had her attacker meant to kill her?

Had he just wanted to scare her, humiliate her?

Had she stopped him, or had he *let* her stop him?

Her mind drifted, and she saw herself diving into the lake, swimming underwater, recalled the feel of the sun and wind on her face when she'd surfaced. Then climbing back onto the dock. Hearing the rustling sounds. Her utter lack of any sense that she was in danger.

Wild turkeys, squirrels. That was what she'd thought she'd heard.

"Time for you to call it a night."

She opened her eyes, realized that she'd zoned out. It was Rook who'd spoken. He was sitting in the Adirondack chair next to hers.

"Where's Gus?"

"He left ten minutes ago. You're done in, Mac."

He was right. The adrenaline and meds had drained her, more than any loss of blood or the brief, futile fight with her attacker had. "Yep, bedtime." But she smiled at Rook. "I'll toast one last marshmallow and head in."

She thought he would argue with her, but he took Gus's abandoned stick and stabbed a marshmallow. "I've never been much on marshmallows."

"What? How's that possible? Everyone likes marshmallows."

"Too sweet."

"Ah. Now that makes sense. Nothing too sweet for our Special Agent Rook." She handed him her stick, and he skewered another marshmallow and returned the stick to her. "You want to tell me what you're doing up here?"

"Mac, you know I can't."

"Anything to do with J. Harris Mayer?"

He looked at her. "Cal Benton stopped by your place last night and asked if you'd seen him."

She sat up straight. "How the hell do you know—" She broke off, shoving her stick straight into the fire Gus style. "Nate Winter told you. So that cinches it. You're looking for Harris, too."

"You know him well enough to call him Harris?"

"Not necessarily. I just do."

"Have you had any contact with him since you came to Washington?"

She shook her head. "No." She yanked her marshmallow out of the flames just as it was about to catch fire, and turned to him, trying to summon the strength and focus to figure him out. "Rook, are you interrogating me?"

"I'm toasting a marshmallow." He let it puff up with blackened blisters, then winked at her, pulled it out of the fire and ate it in one bite. "Perfect."

"Bet the inside was still hard."

Her marshmallow fell off the end of her stick into the fire.

Rook got to his feet. "I'd say that's a sign."

She looked up at him from her chair. He was so damn good-looking. And his eyes . . . In the dark, with the stars sparkling overhead, they seemed to see right into her soul.

He was probably just trying to decide if she was holding back on him.

The man was in Cold Ridge because of his work. Not because of her. She had to remember that, regardless of how attracted she was to him.

"You don't have to stay with me, you know," she said.

"It's me or the local cops, or one of your fellow marshals. You're not in any shape to defend yourself if this guy comes back. You'd be lucky to wake up."

"And if you're investigating Beanie's connection to J. Harris Mayer—if Harris is up to no good—then you can sneak around in the middle of the night and search her house."

"Not without a warrant."

Without a warrant, anything he found while deliberately searching Bernadette's lake house would be subject to suppression in a court of law.

Although he didn't exactly deny that he wouldn't like to take a look around.

The police had checked the house for any sign of an intruder, but that was as far as they could go, too, without any evidence to justify a wider search.

Of course, Mackenzie was Bernadette's houseguest and friend. She could poke around in the house without a warrant. But Rook would never ask her to, and she wouldn't know what to look for without his help.

What are you thinking? She gave herself a mental shake. Bernadette was a respected federal judge who happened to have known

J. Harris Mayer for decades, long before his downfall.

"Need a hand getting up out of that chair?" Rook asked.

"Nope. Thanks. I can manage." But Mackenzie reeled slightly as she stood up. Rook had the grace—or the good judgment—to let her steady herself, and she blew out a breath. "Not one of my finer days."

"See how you feel about that tomorrow."

She started to argue with him, but saw he was serious and wasn't patronizing her because she was less experienced in law enforcement. "I'll do that."

He waited for her to take the lead back to the house, but she turned to him, the darkness and the dim light from the screen porch casting his angular face in shadows. Sexy shadows. "Thanks, Andrew. For helping out today. For staying tonight."

"Not a problem."

"All in a day's work?"

"Mac—"

"You could have just told me that our relationship was interfering with your work. At least you could have thought up a good lie. Told me there was someone else."

"There isn't." His gaze on her was unwavering. "I shouldn't have left that voice mail. I should have at least stopped by to explain things."

"Then you might have caught Cal Benton knocking on my door, and could have asked him why he was looking for Harris Mayer. He thought I'd seen him at a fund-raiser I attended with Beanie—Judge Peacham—on Wednesday." Mackenzie frowned at Rook. "Ah-hah. Now it makes sense. Cal saw you and Harris together at the hotel, didn't he?"

Rook stepped up onto the porch with her. "None of that matters. I cut things off with you because I didn't want to put either of us into a situation we'd regret."

She surprised herself with a laugh. "Hard for me to think I'd regret sleeping with you, even if you dumped me ten minutes later. I might kick myself on a certain level, but another, no way."

He smiled. "Still feel that way?"

"I rarely change my mind."

"Mac." He brushed a few stray curls off her forehead and let a knuckle drift across her mouth. "I'm glad you weren't hurt any worse today. I'm sorry I didn't get here sooner to back you up."

She tried to smile. "You're not making it

any easier for me to think you're a snake in the grass."

He kissed her softly. "Good. I'm not big on snakes."

He didn't wait for her to respond, and moved past her, opening the door to the lake house. Mackenzie walked in, grateful that she didn't fall flat on her face, and he didn't end up carrying her, after all.

Eleven

Jesse washed the dried blood off his hands in the brown-stained sink of a gas station bathroom more than an hour's drive from the lake where he'd slashed Mackenzie Stewart. He'd taken a little-used trail out to a side road before the cavalry could hunt him down. An organic farmer who supplied area restaurants with fresh produce picked him up. Jesse got the spiel about eating organic.

The blood mixed with the hot water and the crud in the sink.

"Hey, at least blood's organic."

His voice sounded hollow, and his reflection in the dirty mirror made him look like a cadaver. Violence wore him out, drained him in a way nothing else did. The level of brutality he could summon at will shocked him every time. He didn't know where it came from. His well-to-do, respectable family in Oregon had seen the propensity for violence in him early, how a violent outburst would settle him down, calm him. He hadn't had anything to do with them—or they with him—since he'd dropped out of high school and headed east.

Until today, he'd never hurt anyone in the mountains. But the conniving Harris and Cal had left him with no other choice. Jesse was so pent up with anger, he needed to blow off some steam. He wanted his money, along with their little insurance policy to get him out of their lives and never to return—whatever it contained. Pictures, DNA, fingerprints, bank accounts, addresses of properties he owned, names. His *life.*

If he was caught searching Judge Peacham's property for the money and materials, he had to be sure no one linked him with her, her ex-husband or her no-account friend Harris.

There were easier ways, perhaps, to accomplish that mission than by attacking the

female hiker that morning, but he'd succeeded in throwing off the police. They were
hell-bent on finding a scary, unhinged lowlife
who struck women at random.

He hadn't gotten any of his first victim's
blood on his hands. But she hadn't kicked
him, either.

He dried his hands with a stiff brown paper towel, crumpled it up and tossed it into
an overflowing, filthy trash can. Too late to
worry about leaving behind DNA. One speck
of blood in the sink, and the cops would
trace it back to Miss Mackenzie, figure out
he'd been there washing up.

But he'd planned for that in the hours after
confronting Harris Mayer.

J. Harris Mayer.

J for *Jackass, J* for *Jerk* . . .

Actually, the *J* stood for John. How anticli-
mactic was that?

Jesse pushed back the uncomfortable reality of just how close he had come to mess-
ing up today with the redheaded marshal,
and focused instead on the task at hand.

It was past ten, dark and chilly. He un-
zipped the backpack he'd hidden in a cluster
of rocks off one of the trails above the lake,
after he'd attacked the hiker. She'd come

damn close to tripping over it—as good a reason as any to pick her to stab. He could have killed her on the spot, but alive, she'd be able to confirm any description of him if he had to attack again.

A shrink might call that a rationalization to commit violence, but whatever. It had worked.

The backpack was filled with supplies, although there was nothing the police could trace back to him should they have managed to get to it before he had. His decision to head down from the hills to the lake carrying only his assault knife had paid off. Agile, not weighed down by gear, he'd made a quick getaway.

He pulled out clean hiking pants, a clean shirt and clean socks. Horn-rimmed glasses with plain lenses. A Red Sox cap. He was in Red Sox country—when people saw his cap, they wouldn't think, *Oh, that must be the man who stabbed those two women today*.

The beard was a problem, but he figured dealing with it now would only draw more attention to him. Go into a gas station bathroom with a beard and come out with one, no one would notice. Come out without one, everyone would notice.

Once transformed into a respectable-looking, inexperienced hiker—not the fit, half-mad hiker police were looking for— Jesse slung his backpack over one shoulder, exited the bathroom and bought a Coke and a bag of Frito's, with silent apologies to his organic farmer, and left the gas station.

He noticed splattered blood on his right hiking boot.

Deal with it later. Stay focused.

He walked down the pitch-black road, the scattered houses near the gas station giving way to impenetrable woods. He heard animals rustling in the brush. Bats swooped across the starlit sky. The air was cool now, but the wind had died down and the mosquitoes hadn't yet found him.

After a half mile, he came to a trailhead and indulged in a moment's relief when he saw that his rented BMW was still there. An expensive car parked at a trailhead this far from the crime scene shouldn't be suspicious, but even if police checked out the BMW, they would discover it was rented to a small, law-abiding Virginia consulting firm.

Fifteen minutes later, a chubby couple in their late forties welcomed him into their bed-and-breakfast, a Victorian gingerbread house just off a tiny village green.

Not exactly where police would expect a deranged slasher to spend the night.

Jesse was in no mood for good cheer, but when the couple smiled at him, he smiled back. "Great day to be out in the mountains. I hope I'm not too late?"

"Not at all."

Nothing in their manner indicated they'd heard about the knife attacks and the search for the man responsible.

The husband, who sported a beard of his own, led Jesse upstairs to a cottage-style room with its own bath. "Breakfast starts at eight," he said, "but if you want it earlier—"

"Eight's perfect. Thank you."

"Are you hiking tomorrow?"

"I'm climbing Mount Washington."

The man nodded with approval. "Good for you. I used to climb it once a year, but I have a bad knee. Got to keep going while you can, I always say. Your first time up Mount Washington?"

No. He'd climbed it at least a dozen times. But Jesse smiled and tried to look humble, even a little nervous. "It's my first visit to the White Mountains."

"Mount Washington's a challenging climb. People often underestimate it. Tomorrow's supposed to be decent weather, although you never know. You can start out in sunny, seventy degree weather, and by the time you're on the summit, the fog's rolled in and you're fighting seventy-mile-an-hour wind gusts."

"I hope that doesn't happen to me."

When he was finally alone, his door shut and locked behind him, Jesse poured a bath, making the water as hot as he could stand. He dumped in half a bottle of a fancy bath and shower gel. It didn't smell too girlie, and it foamed up nicely.

While the tub filled, he trimmed his beard. He'd shave in the morning. If his hosts asked, he'd just say it was for good luck climbing big, bad Mount Washington.

He rinsed out the sink and turned off the tub faucet, then lowered himself into the hot water. He sat in the bath until his skin was fiery-red and wrinkled and his mind was clear. He returned his focus to where it belonged, on betrayal, on men who would cut deals with him and then try to double-cross him.

J. Harris Mayer.

Calvin Benton.

Jesse conjured up their faces and recognized how much he had come to hate both men, and he didn't back off from that surge of raw emotion, the sheer violence that churned inside him.

"Bastards," he whispered. "Who do they think they are?"

When he climbed out of the tub, he used two thick, white towels to dry himself off, then slathered on the entire contents of the little bottle of body lotion that came with the room. His skin was soft and pampered looking—not that of a man who'd just stabbed two women and made a mad dash over hill and dale to avoid the police.

He wiped the steam off the mirror with a corner of his towel and gazed at his reflection, less cadaverous now. He could acknowledge what he hadn't been able to for the past hours.

"You failed, ace." He leaned in close. "You didn't complete your mission. Whatever ol' Harris and Cal have on you, they still have."

That and his money.

They still had the million dollars he was owed.

Jesse stood back from the mirror and dropped the towels onto the floor. For forty-two, he looked good. Hard. Fit. Mackenzie Stewart was fit and knew a few moves, but luck and luck alone had spared her today.

Don't think about her.

But he pictured the shape of her breasts in her pink swimsuit, and he had to exhale to release some of the tension mounting inside him again.

"Stay on task."

Something had happened to his voice. It wasn't as strong, because he was thinking about the girl marshal, the water dripping from her hair, the vibrant blue of her eyes.

Jesse tightened both hands into fists, kept his gaze on his own reflection.

A nice, cool, even million wasn't chump change. It was real money. *Damned* if he was going to let those two bastards blackmail him. It was his money, and he wanted it now. On his terms.

His identity, his money.

He needed to center himself, regroup, figure out what to do. If he didn't cooperate with Cal Benton, would the cagey SOB keep the money and his insurance policy? Or would he go to the FBI? Would he try to use the information he had on Jesse to get *more* money?

Anything was possible. Jesse knew he had to press forward, and so he would.

In the meantime, he thought, turning from the mirror, he would give himself tonight to indulge in his fantasies about his redheaded girl marshal.

Twelve

Rook produced a dented aluminum percolator from a lower cabinet in Bernadette Peacham's simple kitchen and set it on the gas stove. He needed coffee, and soon. He'd passed a bad night in a small upstairs bedroom just big enough for a double bed and chest of drawers. It adjoined the room where Mackenzie had slept. He'd heard every move she made, every soft moan of pain—and a loon. The bird's plaintive cry had woken him after he'd finally dozed off. It was a long time before he'd gone back to sleep.

Mackenzie yawned in her seat at the rectangular table alongside a shaded window.

Behind her was a picture window with a view of the lake, where the rising mist was slowly burning off in the morning sun.

She pointed at the coffeepot. She'd pulled on shorts and a sweatshirt, but looked as if she could crawl back to bed. "Beanie's had that pot for as long as I can remember."

"It must be a hundred years old."

"Fifty, anyway."

The percolator required dismantling. Rook pulled it apart and set the pieces on the scarred Formica counter. Sunlight streamed through the windows. It was a beautiful summer morning—a good day for canoeing and a long walk on a lakeshore trail.

He added water to the stained line, then set the pot on the stove and found a can of inexpensive coffee in the refrigerator. Using the scoop inside, he dumped some of the contents to another stained line, inside the filter basket.

Mackenzie yawned again. "You forgot to put the cover on the filter. Once the coffee starts to perk, you're going to end up with a mess." She stretched out her legs, wincing, but not, he noticed, going as pale as she would have just twelve hours ago. She gave him a cheerful smile. "I don't like grounds in my coffee."

Rook pulled off the pot lid, put on the basket cover, replaced the top and turned on the gas stove. The burner came on with a *poof,* and he adjusted the flame. "It'd be a lot easier to run to a doughnut shop."

"There are no doughnut shops around here. Closest one is . . . I don't know. Fifteen, twenty miles, anyway." She pushed back her hair, the curls more pronounced this morning. "You'd never make a good caretaker. Just as well you're a mean SOB FBI agent."

"I'm not mean."

"I meant to say professional. A professional federal law enforcement officer."

"How long do I let the coffee perk?"

"Exactly eight minutes, according to Beanie. If it boils, we'll end up with rotgut. I can't drink rotgut. I'm injured."

He cast her a skeptical look. "You're not *that* injured."

She grinned at him, unrepentant. "What have I been saying?"

But she *was* injured, and Rook could see that fact had her more off balance than she wanted to acknowledge. She'd had an encounter with her own mortality yesterday. Her training as a marshal had helped her survive the attack, but it would only help so much in dealing with the emotional aftermath.

And she was new to law enforcement, he remembered.

He hoped her relative inexperience would help her deal with yesterday's trauma rather than make it more difficult, but he realized he didn't know her well enough to gauge her reactions. Maybe Gus Winter did. Or Carine. Or, back in Washington, Nate.

Rook was well aware he was the outsider among the people of Cold Ridge.

Mackenzie rose stiffly and pulled open the refrigerator. "Have you ever been in a knife fight?" she asked without looking at him.

"No. Not a knife fight."

She glanced back at him. "Other kinds of fights?"

"None I didn't walk away from."

"And not all on the job, I'll bet." She reached into the refrigerator and pulled out a glass bottle of milk from a local dairy, setting it on the table. "I don't like knives. The idea of stabbing someone—anyone—bothers me. But this guy yesterday? He likes knives. He likes being up close and personal." She returned to the refrigerator for orange juice. "He liked seeing me cut."

The coffee bubbled and Rook turned down the heat even more. "He stabbed the hiker and ran. He didn't stick around to make sure she was dead or to savor the moment. With you, he had no choice but to run."

"I don't know, I got wobbly after I kicked him," Mackenzie said. "He could have found his knife or grabbed a hammer from the shed—I'm not sure I could have stopped him."

"You'd have found a way. He probably realized that."

"I just don't think I looked all that scary."

Rook wasn't fooled by her matter-of-fact tone. Now that she was safe, the stark reality of what had happened was starting to hit her. "Maybe you should talk to someone," he suggested.

"Maybe we should find this guy."

"No argument from me, but you're hurt, Mac. At least give yourself today to rest."

"I do better when I stay busy."

He didn't respond. She poured orange juice into a small glass and drank half in a single gulp. He remembered how he'd noticed her red curls on that rainy night in Georgetown. Then her blue eyes. Her freckles. And her shape, he recalled. She worked at her conditioning—running, weights, martial arts—and was at a high level of fitness, but she'd never carry a lot of muscle.

Not for half a second had he pegged her as a marshal. On that warm summer night, chatting while the rain pelted on the sidewalk outside the coffee shop, he'd just thought the pretty redhead across from him had been destined to cartwheel into his life. In some ways, he still did.

"I have a tentative doctor's appointment this afternoon." She sounded barely resigned to the idea. "When's your flight back to D.C.?"

"Tonight." He could easily reschedule, but she'd know that. "It was supposed to be an uneventful, quick trip up here."

"Feel free to go about your business."

He checked the clock above the stove. Another two minutes before the coffee was done. "Trying to get rid of me, Mac?"

"There's no point in wasting more of your weekend up here, and if you still want to find Harris—well, he's obviously not hiding out here at Beanie's."

"What about the man who attacked you?"

"If he's mentally unbalanced, he could

have forgotten he stabbed me by now." She looked out the side window, the shade shifting in the light morning breeze. "I'm not as woozy as I was yesterday. If he has anything else in mind for me, I can defend myself."

When the coffee was ready, Rook filled two mugs, handing one to her. She thanked him, then headed out to the screened porch, hesitating a moment before making her way down to the dock.

He debated his options. Give her space? Follow her?

It was a beautiful morning, and she needed a few days to rest and get back on her feet. But she wouldn't want to take them. She'd want to get out into the woods and find the man who'd attacked her and the hiker, and who'd scared the hell out of her friend.

Carrying his coffee with him, Rook walked out onto the porch and down through the cool, dew-soaked grass to the dock. He hadn't slept well, and he needed a shower, not to mention at least a half a pot of coffee.

"Nasty stuff, this brew," he said as he joined Mackenzie at the end of the dock.

She squinted at him and smiled. "It is pretty bad."

"Any snakes in this lake?"

"Not poisonous ones." She drank more of her coffee, shifting her gaze back to the water. "Rook, am I part of some FBI investigation?"

"Mac . . ."

She looked at him again. "I'm serious. Am I?"

He shook his head. "No."

"Bernadette?"

He took another sip, wondering how old the can of coffee was.

Mackenzie sighed audibly. "Not answering. Okay, fine. I understand. Thanks for sticking around last night, but you can go on back to D.C. Take an earlier flight." Her tone wasn't harsh. "There's nothing for you to do here."

"I have a few people I should see while I'm here."

"FBI buddies?" She dumped the last of her coffee into the lake. "Maybe it should only have perked for six minutes. I forget."

Taking her mug with her, she walked back to the porch, stumbling on the steps. If he pointed out her unsteadiness, Rook figured she'd just tell him she needed a second cup of coffee. Or breakfast. Or more marshmallows. Anything to keep him at bay.

But she'd be like this anyway, he realized. He had nothing to do with it. She was independent, determined, impatient with her own vulnerability and her reduced capacity to get out there and hunt their fugitive—a frustration he could well understand.

When he returned to the kitchen, she was cracking eggs into a cast-iron frying pan on the stove. "Carine brought enough food for a week, never mind a weekend. If there's one positive about yesterday, it's that I was here, not her." She grabbed another egg, cracked it, tossed the shell back into the carton. "And Harry. Nothing happened to him."

"I can finish up breakfast."

"My turn to wait on you."

She rinsed her hands at the sink and dried them on a dish towel hung on a drawer handle. Rook eased in behind her and grasped her right wrist, avoiding her injured left side. "Mac." He didn't know what else to say. "I'm sorry. I was a damn heel."

She sucked in a breath, which made her wince in pain. "Apology accepted." She angled a look up at him and grinned suddenly, a flash of pure mischief in her very blue eyes. "Bastard. So, where were you and Harris on Wednesday? I figure you were in the hotel bar, and you saw Bernadette and me together, realized we were friends and decided then and there you had to dump me."

Rook kissed the top of her head. "You're going to burn the eggs."

"I'm going to burn *you*," she replied. "Am I close to describing what happened? If I hadn't gone to that damn party, we'd have had dinner together. I probably wouldn't even have been here yesterday to get sliced."

"You're speculating."

"So? I'm on pain medication. I'm entitled. And you're not going to confirm or deny that you canceled dinner because you found out that Beanie and I are friends." She flipped the eggs, which were fast turning to rubber. "So, are you going to reschedule your flight and leave early?"

"Not going to let up, are you?"

She just smiled at him.

Rook made toast to go with the eggs, which were at least as bad as his coffee. He wasn't leaving early. He'd check with the investigators for any new lead on their fugitive slasher. He'd told them yesterday to let him know if J. Harris Mayer turned up anywhere. But it was a long shot, and they had to look at the evidence. Harris wasn't their priority.

Rook wasn't even sure if his missing judge was *his* priority. But Harris had left many loose ends, and the timing of his disappearance was, if nothing else, provocative. Rook's job wasn't to investigate the attacks yesterday; it was to locate Harris.

Time to get back to Washington and step up the search for his AWOL judge.

Mackenzie ignored the pull of pain in her side as she pushed through ferns to a narrow trail her attacker must have followed yesterday. The police had already been here with search dogs. But she wanted to satisfy herself; she couldn't just sit on the porch and swat mosquitoes.

Rook, of course, was right behind her. He hadn't left for Washington yet. And he still hadn't explained his reasons for being in New Hampshire. "I knew you were tight-lipped even before I realized what you did for a living," she said without looking back at him. "A straight-arrow type. Not a rule breaker."

"Are you a rule breaker, Mac?"

"I haven't been in law enforcement long enough to know."

"I'm talking about personality."

She glanced back at him at last. If there was a sexier man on the planet, she didn't want to meet him. But if Rook wasn't on her heels, Gus Winter would be. He would pester her nonstop about overdoing—and he wasn't as good-looking. "I'm creative and results-oriented. How's that?"

Rook smiled at her. "Sounds like an academic's spin."

Was *that* why he'd dumped her? Because he'd heard she wasn't a by-the-book type? But she hadn't gotten into hot water in her six weeks in Washington . . . Nate. Had he suggested to Rook that she might not be his type? Which would mean her connection to Bernadette *wasn't* the reason for the breakup by voice mail?

If only Rook was just some sexy guy she'd dated a few times who'd decided it wasn't going to work out. But it was worse than that. She liked him. She enjoyed his company.

Over and done with.

What she wanted now were answers. Why was he in New Hampshire, why was he looking for Harris Mayer and who was the man who had attacked her yesterday?

Would he attack someone else because she'd failed to take him down?

Mackenzie pushed her way through another patch of knee-high ferns growing in the light shade of the birches and beech trees along the lake. Her side ached, but she was doing much better than when she'd rolled out of bed, thinking she'd have to face Rook with dark circles under her eyes and her hair sticking out. Breakfast had helped. She wasn't going to collapse in front of an FBI agent, especially not one she'd almost slept with.

The trail became soft and damp as they came to a trickling stream that emptied into the lake. She paused as Rook came up beside her, then pointed across the rock-strewn creek. "There's a clearing on the other side of that hill. Thought we could check it out."

"Need a hand crossing?"

"No."

She jumped over the narrow stream as she answered, but one sneaker landed in a squishy, near-black stew of dirt and rotted plant matter. Normally she'd have cleared the mud by a good eighteen inches. She jerked her foot out of the muck, prompting a jolt of pain from her cut, and bent forward, hands on her knees, teeth gritted as she bit back a curse and waited for the pain to subside.

"There." Mackenzie straightened slowly and smiled at Rook, who'd cleared the mud easily. "Stitches are all intact. I'm rusty on crossing streams."

"You didn't take any pain medication this morning, did you?"

"None of the stuff with the codeine. I took a couple Tylenol."

"You don't have to be out here. It's not your job to find the man who attacked you."

"Not yours, either."

She continued through a patch of invasive Japanese honeysuckle and barberry that Bernadette had been battling for years. Walking helped clear her head. She'd looked at dozens of mug shots yesterday at the police station after her trip to the E.R. She'd done dozens of different computer searches for her fugitive, using different sets of criteria. Beard, no beard. Blue eyes, no eye color. Restricted geographic location, virtually unrestricted geographic location.

Looking at too many faces wasn't a wise idea. She needed to stick to shots of real possibilities. She didn't want the faces on the computer screen to start to blur with the one in her mind of the actual perpetrator. She was trained to recognize features that could be plugged into a database or help with a sketch, but eyewitness accounts, including hers, were notoriously unreliable.

But she'd seen this man before, somewhere. She was sure of it.

Last night, she'd found a pad of paper and a pencil in her nightstand, and had jotted down everything she could think of about the attack. She didn't censor herself. Whatever came into her mind went on paper. Colors. Thoughts. Smells. Tastes. Where she'd felt the breeze. How she'd thought it was wild turkeys she'd heard in the birches.

The exact moment she'd realized she'd been cut.

When she'd felt the blood. The pain.

The lapping of the lake water on rocks and sand, and the chirping of birds in the distance—and nearby, too. Something else. Not birds—a red squirrel, chattering in one of the hemlocks.

She wrote down a description of the spit on her attacker's beard. The touches of gray in his dark hair.

His eyes.

Had he guessed he seemed familiar to her?

Did he know where they'd seen each other before?

Mackenzie had a good memory, but nothing she did helped place the man who'd jumped her with an assault knife. She understood that the investigators suspected her attacker had seemed familiar to her because of some kind of life-and-death defense mechanism.

In other words, that she'd unconsciously made up any recognition.

But she hadn't.

As Mackenzie reached the clearing, the lake sparkled through the trees, a view she'd always loved. "I used to camp out here."

Rook stood next to her. "On your own?"

"Sometimes. I was never afraid. I don't know why, because I'd hear animals out here at night." She smiled. "Of course, my parents and Beanie weren't far away."

"Did you always want to go into law enforcement?"

"Never, actually. That came later, when I was working on my dissertation and realized I yearned for something different for myself. You?"

"Always."

"I can go back to academia if the Marshals Service kicks me out." She started to pick up a small stone and flip it into the water, but her bandaged side reminded her that probably wasn't a smart idea. She sighed. "There's nothing here. He's probably hiking in Wyoming by now."

She turned back. When they reached the stream, she didn't try to cross it in a single leap, but jumped to a rock in the middle, then to the bank. Rook again made it across in one long stride.

Gus and Carine were waiting for them on Bernadette's porch. Carine had Harry, who was cooing to himself, tucked on her hip. She seemed more herself after their recent scare. Rook quickly excused himself and ducked inside.

"Just checking on you," Gus said. "There's nothing new. Beanie called last night. She didn't want to disturb you. She said to use the house as long as you need to."

"I appreciate that, but I'll be getting back to work as soon as I get the okay from the doctor."

He didn't argue with her. "Rook's leaving?"

"He has a flight tonight. Mine's not until tomorrow—"

"You won't be ready to fly tomorrow," Gus said.

Carine grinned suddenly. "You two. I swear you've been arguing since Mackenzie could talk. We can't stay, but if there's anything you need, just let me know."

"There isn't right now, but thanks."

After they left, Mackenzie sat in a comfortable wicker chair on the porch, closing her eyes and smelling the clean air, enjoying the relatively low humidity. She could have had this life: a house on a quiet lake, a job that would allow time there. But she'd walked away from it, and now she wondered if the attack yesterday meant that her new life had intersected, somehow, with her old one.

That was a problem for another time, she thought, unable to stop herself from drifting off.

Thirteen

On his way to the airport in his rented car, Rook took a detour to the small private college where Mackenzie had taught before she'd headed to FLETC, the Federal Law Enforcement Training Center in Georgia. Its secluded campus was typical New England, with ivy-covered brick buildings and lush lawns that were relatively quiet in these weeks before the start of classes. A huge handmade sign welcomed incoming freshmen for orientation.

Of all the people in Cold Ridge, New Hampshire, who could have followed Nate

Winter into federal law enforcement, Rook suspected Mackenzie Stewart hadn't been on anyone's short list of candidates.

He lingered in the shade of a giant oak. Why give up this life? What had compelled her? He pictured her on one of the pretty walkways, rushing to class, smiling at students who weren't that much younger than she was.

"You're crazy," Rook muttered to himself. "Go home."

Less than four hours later, Rook was back in Washington. T.J. met him at the airport, and Rook filled him in. But T.J. already knew all about the events in New Hampshire.

"Other than walking into the middle of a knife attack on a federal agent, how was it up in the woods?" T.J. asked. "Any sign of our missing informant?"

"Harris can't even qualify as an informant. He's been playing games for three weeks. I've got nothing." Rook stared out the window. Even from the air-conditioned car, he could tell the Washington heat wave hadn't let up. The city looked hot and steamy. "New Hampshire's one of the safest states in the country, and a knife-wielding lunatic just happens to turn up at Bernadette Peacham's lake house the day I show up looking for Harris. Never mind Mac and why she was there."

"It's a curious world," T.J. said.

Rook laughed in spite of himself. Nothing ruffled T. J. Kowalski. When he pulled into Rook's driveway, T.J. shook his head. "Another thirty grand, and this place will look like a hard-ass FBI agent lives here instead of a sweet little old grandmother."

"Shut up, Kowalski."

"Used to stop here for homemade cookies after school, didn't you?"

"I'm armed."

But what T.J. said was true. Rook had grown up within walking distance of his grandmother's house, and as a kid he'd stop by for cookies, to help her with chores, to tell her his tales from school. When he joined the FBI, he'd never expected to end up back in Washington, living in his old neighborhood— the Rook neighborhood. His seven years in Florida had given him distance from his tight-knit family, provided a perspective he'd never have if he'd stayed. When his grandmother died, he'd intended to fix up the house and sell it, but once he'd started working on it, he'd found himself staying. He added skylights on the stairs and in the kitchen, stripped the carpet to reveal hardwood floors. It was looking less grandmotherly, but the dogwoods and bird feeders in the garden still reminded him of her.

She knew he'd go into law enforcement. It was the Rook destiny. He couldn't see himself switching careers the way Mackenzie had, after all she'd invested toward earning her doctorate.

He noticed his nephew's car in the driveway. The kid was a casualty—with any luck a temporary one—in the ongoing battle between Scott Rook and his wife. To please one, he had to disappoint the other. To please them both was impossible—and not, they knew at some level, Brian's responsibility. They loved their oldest son more than life itself, but every day, they woke up thinking about how they could motivate him, focus him.

"I saw the sketch of this guy with the knife," T.J. said. "He could be anybody. If the police up in New Hampshire think he's a deranged hiker who slashes women for kicks, who am I to argue?"

"I don't like coincidences."

"Life is full of them. I asked around about

Deputy Stewart. Word is she's cute as a button, smart as a whip and could kick your ass—provided she got half a chance. She's hard on herself. Her fellow marshals are protective of her, which she hates, and word's getting around that some FBI asshole broke her heart." T.J. looked over at Rook. "That would be you. I could get good money for turning over your name."

"I didn't break her heart. We only went out a few times."

"One of them was dinner here."

"Almost. That's the date I canceled."

"There's discipline for you. If it'd been me, I'd have had dinner first, *then* dumped her."

"I'm not talking to you about Mackenzie anymore. It's Harris I'm after." Rook shoved open the car door and got his bag from in back. "Harris is a bitter, entitled old man who drinks too much, T.J., and I don't know if he's on the level or spinning bullshit. If he's on to something—"

"Then he needs to start talking and stop with the bullshit. He's a smart man. If he's serious, he'll know telling us what's going on is his only option. Ten to one he got cold feet and bailed on us."

"I hope so."

Rook shut the door and headed inside, straight upstairs to the computer room. His nephew barely looked up from the flat screen. "I'll be off in a sec."

"You have to work tomorrow?"

"I gave my notice, and my boss said not to bother to come in."

"You gave your notice? Why?"

"I don't like to work weekends."

Rook kept his irritation to himself. It was the second job of the summer Brian had quit—a retail job with irregular hours. His mother had wanted him to study abroad over the summer. His father had wanted him to get a job and at least pay for his car insurance. But Brian had flunked out of college instead.

"Put in any applications?"

"Nah." Brian tapped on the keyboard. "I don't think I'm going to work anymore this summer."

"That must mean you've decided to go to college this fall, after all."

"Maybe. I don't know. I'm still thinking about it."

"You'll need to get applications in." When his nephew didn't respond, Rook sighed. "Brian . . ."

The kid looked up at him. His features were so like his father's, but he didn't have Scott Rook's self-discipline and hard edge. "If I take the year off to work, I can afford not to work for a few weeks now."

The logic in that statement was typical Brian. "We can talk about it tomorrow," Rook muttered.

"Yeah. Okay. How was New Hampshire?"

"You'd have hated it. No computers, no cell phone service—I didn't even bring an iPod with me."

The kid grinned awkwardly. "What'd you do, listen to the mosquitoes buzz in your ear?"

"Loons," Rook said.

His nephew gave a mock shudder. "Even worse."

Fourteen

Jesse loved to fly, especially alone. All his problems fell away. He felt free in the air, un-encumbered by his obsessions. He was apart from the world. There was no past or future, only now. As he looked down at the sprawl of greater Baltimore and Washington, D.C., he welcomed the sense of superiority and peace that overcame him.

He'd gotten out of New Hampshire with-out so much as a second glance from the couple at the bed-and-breakfast, the other guests, the people at the airport.

The police had no idea where their perpe-trator was, who he was. Nothing. Their sketch didn't look anything like the upscale hiker he'd become after the organic farmer had dropped him off.

Jesse had spent Saturday and Sunday roaming the famous Presidential Range, its peaks named after U.S. presidents—Washington, Jefferson, Madison, Adams, Monroe. At night, he'd regaled his hosts with stories of his mishaps, his fascination and appreciation of the White Mountains. There was no way—none—that they'd think he was the fugitive slasher.

Today—Monday—he had slept late, focusing on the work that lay ahead. It was midday now. His time in the mountains had helped center him. He'd thought about Mackenzie Stewart a lot. And Cal. That corrupt bastard must be beside himself at this point, wondering where Jesse was, debating whether he'd call from Mexico in surrender, turn up in Washington again or just disappear.

Disappear.

Just keep flying. Refuel, continue on to the Caribbean.

Start over.

But he didn't want to start over. He had a life in western Mexico—a home in Cabo

San Lucas, on the tip of the Baja Peninsula, with stunning views of the Sea of Cortes. It was everything he wanted. There, he was a successful American business consultant, with no ties to New Hampshire or Washington, D.C.

Cal and Harris had found out about Cabo.

Jesse knew he couldn't go back without dealing with their treachery. He'd had to stretch his finances to buy his Mexican dream house. He needed the million he was due, but he could find a way to replenish his accounts if he refused to cave in to Cal's demands. He had been putting together deals since his parents ran him out of the house.

He'd learned the hard way to rely on no one, trust no one, but himself.

If he kept on going now—if he didn't dig back into the lives below him—he would have to give up Cabo. With no control over his own identity, Jesse couldn't trust Cal Benton to hold up his end of the deal—to send the money and keep quiet.

Never.

And with that idiot Harris sneaking off to the FBI, Jesse wasn't willing to risk having Cal's "insurance policy" end up in the feds' hands.

He had two choices. Disappear and re-build his life from scratch. Establish a new identity. Find a spot that he loved as much as Cabo. Give in to blackmail and thievery.

Or . . . not.

He was the one who turned other peo-ple's lives into nightmares. People paid him to go away. Cal and Harris had turned the ta-bles on him, threatening to become *his* nightmare. Jesse drove a hard bargain, but if they had cooperated and kept up their end, he'd be back in Cabo by now, investing his profits and enjoying his life.

Leaving behind the money those two weasels had stolen from him was possible but not desirable. It would be annoying to have to replace it. Very annoying. But he could. There were always people with se-crets who would pay not to have them ex-posed to the world.

Jesse had secrets of his own. Cal and Harris hadn't unearthed all of them.

It was almost as if they'd ripped out his soul and were holding it hostage. How could he just leave now, without putting things right? He wasn't going to return to Cabo and look over his shoulder for the foreseeable fu-ture. He had no intention of giving up his life there out of fear of what they had squirreled away on him.

On the other hand, if they hadn't betrayed him, he never would have seen Mackenzie Stewart. He never would have attacked her.

That's changed everything, hasn't it?

A silver lining in his dark cloud. How could he just fly away without seeing his red-headed girl marshal again?

A sudden bump from a shift in air pressure brought him back to the present. Flying required concentration. It anchored him. He couldn't let his thoughts drift for very long or he'd crash.

A simple enough equation.

He landed at a small, private airstrip northwest of Baltimore. Another rented BMW awaited him. As he disembarked from his plane, Jesse visualized Deputy Mackenzie. She was self-reliant, too. Her ability to fight, her gritty determination and her work as a federal agent were incongruous with her delicate appearance and soft, heart-melting eyes.

She didn't belong in the violent world she'd chosen. Jesse wasn't at all sure that he approved.

He caught his reflection in the side mirror

of the BMW. He didn't appear hunted or out of control. It was a steamy, hazy Monday afternoon in the Washington area, and he looked good in his expensive, casual clothes. Nothing of the deranged mountain man remained.

Within the hour, he unlocked the door to the expensive condominium he'd leased in the same complex where Cal Benton had bought his post-divorce home. Cal's condo was one floor below. But of course, he had no idea who his upstairs neighbor was.

Using his cell phone, Jesse dialed Bernadette Peacham's number in New Hampshire. He knew it by heart, because he was a planner. He doubted she had caller ID, but it wouldn't have mattered—his was a private number.

"Hello."

Mackenzie. His throat tightened. He pictured her, her big blue eyes staring out at the beautiful lake. Was she healed enough to wear her gun? It was wrong, her and guns. So wrong.

He heard her inhale.

"Sorry," he said. "Wrong number."

He hung up and looked out at the Potomac River, calm and still in the hot afternoon sunlight. He was no longer a knife-wielding lowlife. He was a wealthy Washington consultant home from an important meeting.

His transformation was complete.

Fifteen

Mackenzie pulled her backpack out of the small plane's overhead compartment and slung it over her right shoulder. The tight quarters and the rough skies had jostled her just enough to make her feel every millimeter of her wound, but she'd resisted reaching for pain medication. She hadn't taken any since Saturday. It was late Tuesday now, four days since the attack that had slit open her left side.

Four frustrating days, she thought as she disembarked, trying not to look too grouchy in front of the flight attendant, pilots and her fellow passengers.

Time to return to her ghosts, fall into her own bed and get back to work in the morning. Her attacker's trail was stone-cold dead. The search teams hadn't turned up any evidence of his identity or whereabouts in the mountains, and prints the police got off his knife didn't match anyone in the system. Mackenzie had done what she could to help with the search, but she'd been too optimistic about diving right back into work.

She melted into the line exiting the Jetway. Her side ached, but as much as she wanted to go straight home, she had one stop to make first.

Bernadette Peacham had asked to see her.

A taxi was in order tonight, Mackenzie thought as she made her way into the crowded terminal. She could have called any number of people for a ride, but she'd kept her flight arrangements to herself. She was bedraggled and wobbly. If she had a good night's sleep, she was confident she could be her usual kick-ass self by morning.

But as she stopped to figure out which way to turn to reach the terminal exit, Andrew Rook eased in next to her, catching her totally by surprise. He was in jeans and a lightweight jacket, and he was heart-stoppingly sexy, looking neither bedraggled nor wobbly.

"Allow me." He took Mackenzie's back-pack from her shoulder. "All those pink swim-suits and dolphin towels get heavy, don't they?"

"Rook, if you told anyone it was a pink suit—"

"I didn't have to."

"It's all over Washington, isn't it?"

"The suit. Not as many people know about the dolphin towel."

Small comfort, she thought. "What are you doing here? How did you find out what flight I was on?" She stopped herself and sighed. "Damn FBI."

He smiled. "We aim to please."

Although he was dressed casually, it was a Washington crowd at Reagan National Air-port. Anyone paying attention would peg him as an FBI agent. That she hadn't the night they'd met still stuck in Mackenzie's craw. No one would see her and think, *Deputy U.S. Marshal.* Certainly not tonight, with her hair yanked back in a loose ponytail and her baggy, casual attire covering up her ban-dages for the flight. She had dark circles under her eyes from pain and four nights of near sleeplessness as she'd tried to figure out who her attacker was, and rehashed all she'd done wrong.

Free of the backpack, she picked up her pace and said good-naturedly, "I liked you better when I thought you worked for the IRS."

He ignored her. "My car's in the parking garage. Do you want me to get you a wheelchair?"

"Since you have zero sense of humor, I assume you're serious. No, I do not want you to get me a wheelchair. If you want to do something for me, flag me a cab."

"Not a chance, Deputy." He glanced at her, his eyes darker than usual. "If I let you take a taxi and you tripped in the dark and loosened a couple of stitches, I'd be in big trouble."

She stopped abruptly. "Who put you up to this? Gus? Did he call and tell you I was on the way?"

"I called him."

"Why?"

"To check on you."

Her mouth snapped shut, and she resumed walking, telling herself not to expend any energy trying to figure out Special Agent

Rook. "Maybe that was your cover story with Gus, but you have an agenda that has nothing to do with my health and well-being."

With his free hand, Rook dug his car keys out of his jacket pocket. "Were you this cynical when you were a college professor?"

"Instructor. I was never a professor. And I'm not cynical. I'm realistic."

When they reached his car, Mackenzie was out of breath, which irritated her. But four days of a downsized workout or none at all had taken its toll. She'd get up early and do some kind of exercise before she went into work, stitches or no stitches.

Rook tossed her pack onto the backseat of his car. "If it's any consolation, Gus didn't suggest I pick you up. He said if I did, I should treat you right."

"He raised two nieces—he has a good eye for men like you."

"Men like me? Carine's married to a pararescueman. Antonia's married to a U.S. senator and former rescue helicopter pilot."

Mackenzie frowned at him. "You've done your research. Do you know Antonia? She lives in Washington."

"I think she might have checked me out for a concussion once."

Mackenzie wasn't sure what to believe. Antonia, the middle Winter sibling, was an emergency room physician. She and her husband, Hank Callahan, the junior senator from Massachusetts, had invited Mackenzie to their house in Georgetown twice since her arrival in Washington. Had Rook checked out all the Winters because of his investigation? Because of the attack? Because of *her?*

"I'm in good company, if you ask me," Rook added. "And Nate's a decent guy—"

"Thanks to Gus, or so he'd say."

"You stayed at his house after I left?"

She nodded. "Just at night. It was easier than having him on my case or, worse, insisting on staying up at Beanie's with me. He's a fabulous cook. That helped."

"They treat you like one of the family."

"But I'm not," she said, stepping past him to the passenger door. "I have both my parents."

Rook pulled open the door for her. "You were a hellion as a kid, pretty much on your own after your father was hurt. Your sense of humor and red hair and cute freckles must have kept you from getting throttled on a regular basis."

She hustled in front of him and got in the car. "You *have* been talking to Gus." She looked up at Rook, who might have been grinning, but it was difficult to tell in the dark. "Were you questioning him as part of your investigation?"

Without answering, Rook shut the door and walked around to the other side of the car.

When he got behind the wheel, Mackenzie, eyes focused straight ahead, said, "I have one stop to make."

"Mac—"

"Bernadette summoned me to see her. She's not someone easily put off. It's up to you whether or not you want to drive me there."

She thought she saw the muscles in his forearm tense as he stuck the key in the ignition. "It's not a problem."

"She lives off Embassy Row."

"I know where she lives."

Mackenzie sank back into the comfortable seat. "Of course you do."

Bernadette Peacham's elegant 1920s house on a quiet street off Massachusetts Avenue always made Mackenzie think of garden parties with its ivy-covered brick and lush landscaping. Rook parked under a massive oak, and when she climbed out of the car, the humidity almost took her breath away. The night air and massive shade trees hadn't cut the stifling heat.

An outside light came on as she and Rook took the moss-lined brick sidewalk to the side entrance. Bernadette, still in a wrinkled, gray suit she'd obviously worn to the court-house, opened the door and gave Macken-zie a sweeping, critical once-over. "You don't look as bad as I expected. A little pale. I'm so relieved this lunatic didn't stab you to death."

"Me, too," Mackenzie said, then motioned behind her. "Beanie, I'd like you to meet—"

"Special Agent Rook." She stood to one side and smiled coolly, eyeing him. "Am I right?"

"A pleasure to meet you, Judge Peacham," he said, his tone neutral.

"Yes. Well, come inside."

She led them past the kitchen and down the hall to the family room. Her Washington house was the polar opposite of her simple lake house in New Hampshire, and if Mackenzie hadn't known better, she'd have thought this was the wrong Bernadette Peacham. Expensive antiques from various periods mixed with traditional fabrics and colors, and artwork from her travels all over the world. Cal had taken his favorite pieces from Peru and Japan, but most were from Bernadette's life before their brief marriage.

"I can't wait to be out of here," she said. "It's so damn hot!"

Mackenzie remained on her feet. She didn't plan to stay long. "I don't blame you. When do you head for New Hampshire?"

"Friday. I know it gets hot there, but not like this. And if it's hot, I have the lake right outside my door."

"Are you worried about being there—"

"With this lunatic on the loose? No, of course not. He'll be long gone by then, or in custody, one would hope. I've never worried one second when I've been at the lake on my own, and I don't intend to start now. You needn't fret. Gus will check in on me, no doubt. He's like a mother hen sometimes."

Of all the images that came to mind when Mackenzie thought about Gus Winter, a mother hen wasn't among them. Not even close. "I left some food in the refrigerator. Nothing that would spoil before you get there. There's a half bag of marshmallows in the bread box—"

"Marshmallows? Mackenzie, you know they'll attract ants."

"I wrapped a rubber band around the bag. It's so tight an ant can't possibly get in."

Bernadette waved a hand, dismissing the subject of marshmallows and ants. "You're the one who was attacked. We should all be worrying about *you*." She softened slightly, sinking into a wingback chair. "How are you? I heard you were lucky the knife didn't penetrate deeply."

"It's a superficial wound. Painful, but it'll heal. Every day's better."

"I'm sure it wasn't just luck that you weren't hurt worse. You've always been a good fighter."

Mackenzie was aware of Rook lingering in the doorway, but he didn't seem eager to jump into the conversation. "I had him, Beanie," she said, "but I couldn't hold him."

"You'd been stabbed. Even more experienced officers have faltered in similar situations." Bernadette's tone was matter-of-fact more than reassuring. "Give yourself time to heal. Don't push yourself, or you'll end up delaying your recovery."

"That's why I didn't head back here until tonight."

"Good. Now, this man—you recognized him?"

"He seemed vaguely familiar."

"Vaguely? That's not the kind of thing one wants to hear in a courtroom."

The state police detectives, FBI agents and deputy marshals investigating the two attacks in New Hampshire hadn't wanted to hear it, either. They wanted specifics, and Mackenzie couldn't provide them. The eyes, she'd said. They'd solidified the sense that she'd seen him before. She hadn't been very helpful—and she was convinced they'd all downplayed, if not totally disregarded, her statement because of her knife wound and initial round of pain medication.

"Would you recognize him if you saw him again?" Bernadette asked.

"I'd know it was the same man. I'm not sure it'd help me figure out where I've seen him before."

Mackenzie didn't flinch as Bernadette studied her with a frankness that anyone who knew the exacting judge got used to. Bernadette was blunt and straightforward, but also unfailingly generous, intelligent and fair-minded. Finally, she sighed, shaking her head. "I'm sorry. I wish this attack hadn't happened. I wish I could at least help find the perpetrator. I've seen enough lowlifes come through my courtroom. But I'm clue-less. I'm not good with sketches. I don't think I'd recognize myself in one."

"What about Cal?"

"Cal?" An edge came into Bernadette's voice at mention of her ex-husband. "Why would he know anything?"

Mackenzie gave Rook a sideways glance, but he remained impassive. She turned back to Bernadette, shrugging. "No reason."

"I hardly ever see him anymore, although he's still living here." She added quickly, "He has the downstairs guest suite."

Mackenzie had stayed there often enough herself on her visits to Washington over the years. Bernadette had always been a wel-coming hostess, although less so after her marriage to Cal Benton. Mackenzie wasn't sure if he didn't like company or didn't like her; perhaps he'd just sensed she didn't like him.

"When's he moving out?" she asked bluntly.

Bernadette seemed to take no offense. "This weekend. When I get back from New Hampshire in September, he'll be out of my life for good."

"Did you talk to him about the attacks in New Hampshire?"

"Of course. He suggested your assailant could be someone I've helped out at some point."

"One of your 'three-legged puppies'? Isn't that his phrase?"

Mackenzie's cool tone drew a glance from Rook, but he didn't comment. Cal, who hadn't known her as a child, nonetheless had made it clear he considered her one of his wife's "three-legged puppies."

"Cal doesn't realize how offensive he is sometimes," Bernadette said. "I think it's just his way of trying to be funny. He doesn't recognize this man, from the sketch or the description, either. The police seem to think he's a deranged drifter, and I tend to agree. Maybe you just saw him buying something at Gus's store one day." She gave Mackenzie a pained look. "Or an assault knife."

"Gus doesn't carry that kind of knife at the store."

"I didn't mean that literally." Bernadette rose, kicking off her flats and standing in her stocking feet. "I can see you're tired. I wish I knew something that could help you find this man."

"The police aren't giving up yet," Mackenzie said. "Are you okay here? I don't want to scare you, but the man was on your property."

"Your marshal friends swing by from time to time. I hate having anyone at my elbow day and night. In any case, you're the one who was knifed, even if it was on my property. Do *you* have round-the-clock protection?"

Mackenzie almost smiled. "I'm not a federal judge who can't shoot."

"I hate guns. Your point's well taken, but I'm not worried."

Mackenzie wanted to ask her about Harris Mayer but resisted because of the FBI agent standing in the doorway. Let Rook ask if he wanted to. She didn't have enough information, but if she barreled her way into an ongoing investigation, she would be back in Cold Ridge and out of the USMS before she got a scratch on her badge. Even Nate Winter wouldn't be able to help her.

Bernadette walked past Rook and into the hall. Mackenzie noticed how closely he was observing the judge, but he continued to maintain his silence. She followed Bernadette, brushing by him. "Where's Cal now?"

"I have no idea." Bernadette's mouth tight-

ened as if she was trying to hold back un-
wanted emotion. "Why all your questions?"

"Just making conversation." But that
wasn't entirely true, and Mackenzie wondered if both the federal judge in front of her
and the FBI agent behind her realized she
was holding back. Yet blurting what she
knew about Cal Benton and his final affront
to his wife and their marriage would do no
one any good. Mackenzie said carefully, "Cal
will miss the lake, don't you think?"

"If he had his way, he'd cut up the land
into lakefront lots and tear down the house
and build a new one. He says it's only a step
above camping."

"When was he in New Hampshire last?"

Rook said something under his breath,
and Mackenzie realized she'd pushed too
hard. Bernadette reached the side door off
the kitchen and spun around, arms crossed
on her chest. "Mackenzie, I'm a judge. Before I was a judge, I was a prosecutor. I know
when I'm being grilled. I'll make allowances
because of the circumstances, but otherwise, enough with the questions."

"Sorry. Long day. Enjoy the lake. It was
beautiful there this past weekend."

Bernadette smiled wistfully, her irritation

fading quickly. "It always is. I didn't let what happened to your father stop me from appreciating it. I won't let what happened to you stop me." She gasped, obviously horrified by her own words. "That didn't come out the way I meant it to. Not at all. Mackenzie, I'm sorry. I'm not unfeeling."

"I know, Beanie. Forget it. I'll see you later."

"I don't know anything about the man who attacked you. Neither does Cal. He takes care of himself. I know he does. From what I've learned about him these past three years, he always has. And he's very good at it."

"I've no doubt."

Her pale green eyes leveled on Mackenzie. "What do you know that you're not telling me?"

"I only have questions, Beanie. No answers."

She didn't respond right away. "I know the feeling," she said finally. She opened the door, the hot night air immediately oozing into the cool interior. "Special Agent Rook, it's good to meet you."

"Likewise, Judge Peacham."

"You're very disciplined, keeping your mouth shut all this time."

He smiled at her. "Good night, Judge."

Mackenzie started to speak, but Bernadette held up a hand. "I've kept you long enough. Take care of yourself. Thank you for stopping by."

"Always good to see you, Beanie."

Rook's car was still relatively cool when Mackenzie returned to her seat, but she could feel fatigue gnawing at her—and his gaze on her, probing, as if she'd tried to hide something from him, too.

"Where'd she get the nickname Beanie?" he asked, starting the car.

"I think Gus gave it to her in first grade, and it stuck."

"But she's beloved? She's known for her kindness and generosity?"

"That doesn't mean she's a pushover. She's smart, and she's dedicated to her work as a judge."

"No kids?"

Mackenzie shook her head. "She was married for a few years after law school, but it didn't work out. No kids."

"Just you," he said.

"I have a mother. Beanie knows that. People might say I got lost in the shuffle after my father was injured, but we all cared about each other. That was never a question. And everything turned out all right."

"How did Judge Peacham help you?"

"She kept Gus from hanging me by my thumbs, for starters. Mostly, she let me into her library and let me use her house as a refuge. I never went into the shed, though. I'd sit on the porch and read—just that break from the difficulties at home made a difference. My father didn't need me underfoot when he was in such pain."

"Tough times."

"People have faced worse."

Rook was silent a moment. "We're not talking about what other people faced."

Mackenzie decided to change the subject. She didn't want Rook picturing her as a lonely, troubled eleven-year-old. "Anything new on Harris Mayer?"

"He hasn't turned up yet."

"Are you actively looking for him?" she asked.

"Yes."

She let Rook drive a couple miles without pressing him further, hoping he might take the initiative and elaborate. But he didn't. Finally, she gave him a sideways look. "Talking to you is like getting blood out of a stone sometimes."

"Only when you ask about matters that are outside your area of concern."

"I should expect to get shut down. Got it, Rook. Nate Winter gave me the same lecture."

"Smart man."

When they arrived at her borrowed quarters, Rook didn't ask if she needed help, he just climbed out of the car and opened the back door before she'd gotten her seat belt unhooked. He grabbed her backpack and walked to the porch, the heat apparently having no effect on him.

Mackenzie joined him, feeling drained. Before she'd left New Hampshire, she'd retraced her assailant's path through the woods and up to the road above the lake, not so much looking for clues the search teams had missed but hoping for something— anything—that jogged her memory. She'd probably pushed herself a bit too far.

"Thanks for the ride," she told Rook. "I mean it. It was decent of you, even if you had ulterior motives."

But he didn't make a move to head back to his car. He nodded toward the porch. "I want to make sure your place is secure before I leave."

"It's not secure. It's a leaky haunted house. Who knows what I'll find in there?"

He didn't laugh. Mackenzie gave up and mounted the steps to the porch, fumbling in a pocket of her backpack for her keys. She unlocked the door and motioned him inside. "Help yourself." She followed him in and switched on lights as he checked the windows and closets. "I'd give anything for Abe Lincoln to pop out from under a bed right now."

"The Rooks are Virginians."

"Bobby Lee, then."

"Mac . . ."

They were in the small kitchen, and she fought an image of him getting up with her in the morning. He sighed through his teeth, his eyes dark, his body tensed as he visibly repressed all emotion. But he cupped her chin, catching her by surprise, and traced one finger along her jaw. She didn't pull back, and he kissed her—not lightly, either. She responded, grabbing his arms and steadying herself as her mouth opened to his tongue, the heat of him.

But he was a man of supreme willpower, and he pulled back. "You make me crazy, you know that?"

She smiled, a little breathless. "It's good for you."

"Probably is," he said, straightening. "If you didn't have twenty-five stitches—"

"Only twenty."

"Sleep well, Mac. If the ghosts bother you, give me a call."

That'd be the day, she thought. She watched him head out, trotting down the steps as if he had all the energy in the world. When he was out of her driveway, she went into the living room, with its cozy, antique furnishings. Except for the loud ticking of an old grandfather clock, the house was quiet. No ghosts, no Andrew Rook, no deranged hiker with a knife.

Mackenzie's eyes felt scratchy with fatigue. She hoped being back in Washington would help her remember where she'd seen her attacker before. She was convinced, still, that she hadn't just conjured up a sense of familiarity because of fear and adrenaline.

But whoever he was, she wouldn't be satisfied until he was in custody, unable to hurt anyone else.

She suspected it was one goal she and Rook shared.

As she headed to her bedroom, she touched a hand to her mouth where he'd kissed her. *Damn.*

The man made *her* crazy, too.

Sixteen

Mackenzie poured herself a cup of coffee and headed to her desk at the district U.S. Marshals office in Washington, D.C. After less than two months, she didn't feel settled in yet, but it was her first duty assignment and she was committed to a three-year stay. She had managed to get up early and lift a few free weights and stretch, avoiding any doctor-forbidden moves that would pull on her stitches. Every day was an improvement, but that didn't mean she was patient with her progress.

On her way downtown, she'd touched

base with a New Hampshire state trooper working on the investigation into the attack on her and the hiker.

He'd had no news. It was as if her attacker had crawled out of a cave in the White Mountains with his assault knife and gone hunting. Members of the public were being urged not to hike alone, but not to panic, either. There'd been no other attacks, and any sightings of black-bearded, solitary men hadn't panned out.

Maybe their guy was back in his cave, Mackenzie thought, setting her coffee on her desk and noticing a Saks Fifth Avenue box. There was no card on top. She opened up the box, unfolding tissue paper with a mixture of dread and amusement.

Inside was a new pink swimsuit. A *very* pink two-piece.

She quickly replaced the top. "Smart-asses."

Nate Winter materialized next to her. Since he worked at USMS Headquarters in Arlington, Mackenzie assumed he was in D.C. because of her. Impending fatherhood, she noticed, hadn't made him any less cut-to-the-chase.

"Hey, Nate," she said, hoping he hadn't seen the swimsuit or heard her muttering. "Here on business?"

"Here to see you, Mackenzie. I couldn't get away or I'd have flown up to Cold Ridge." He nodded to the Saks box with the barest twitch of a smile. "You'd have to worry if you got here this morning and *didn't* find a little present on your desk."

"I'm never living down the pink swimsuit. Never." She tucked the box under her desk. "I'm going to exchange it for a solid black one-piece. One with a high neckline and a matching skirt."

"You don't think they really bought that suit at Saks, do you?"

She should have thought of that one. She laughed, shaking her head. "I get sliced, and these bastards pawn off a cheap swimsuit on me." She sat down, spinning her chair around to face Nate. "So, what can I do for you, Deputy Winter?"

"How's the wound?"

"Healing. I'm not on any pain meds. It was just one of those things. Stupid."

"Not stupid. Give yourself a little credit."

She sighed. "At least I wasn't attacked while I was on duty, not that I'd ever go swimming on the job. I'd been telling all my doubters—of which there are many—that I'm more likely to get hurt off the job than on, and now we have the proof. If I'd been working at the college and gone for a swim at Beanie's on Friday afternoon, this guy would have attacked me. I just wouldn't have had a prayer."

"I don't know. You were feisty as a college professor."

"But not as well trained," she said.

Nate shifted slightly. He wore a dark gray suit, a contrast to the street attire of most of the field agents filling up the office. Mackenzie had rummaged around in one of her unpacked boxes for stretchy pants and a dark, lightweight pullover—and her shoulder holster. Carrying her weapon in a belt holster pulled on her stitches.

"This guy didn't kill the female hiker," Nate said.

"She says he told her he wanted her to suffer. If Gus hadn't found her, she would have died of exposure." Like Gus's brother and sister-in-law, Nate's parents, Mackenzie thought, then added, "I don't know what he had in mind for me."

"Maybe nothing. Maybe you just surprised

him and he reacted. My point being we don't know, and until we do—"

"Beware of speculating," she finished for him.

"Stick to the facts. How's Gus? I've talked to him, but it's hard to gauge his state of mind. He wasn't happy about seeing you bloodied—he made that clear."

Mackenzie leaned back in her chair, comfortable with Nate Winter despite his senior status, his seriousness, his notorious impatience. With the attack in Cold Ridge, more people would become aware of her connection to him, and their mutual connection to Bernadette Peacham. Mackenzie didn't know how Nate would react. Find a way to send her to Alaska, maybe?

"Gus is Gus," she said. "He tried out a new recipe on me while I was up there. Some kind of marinated, grilled fruit over couscous. He says it's Beanie's influence. She was at the lake earlier in the summer and had him and Carine and little Harry over for dinner, said she'd been taking cooking classes here in Washington."

"Beanie Peacham's taking cooking classes?"

"I know. Worrisome." But Mackenzie

couldn't maintain her humor, and seeing Nate brought the reality of what had happened on Friday—what *could* have happened—to the surface. "Nate, if anything had happened to Carine or Harry because of me . . ."

"It wouldn't have been because of you. The worst thing you can do right now is let your mind spin around what might have been. What happened is bad enough in its own right." His gaze rested on her, critical, appraising. "Are you sure you should be back here?"

"The doctor said it'd be fine. I just have to avoid heavy lifting for a bit." She paused to give Nate a chance to reassure her that she was absolutely right, she'd be up for field-work in no time, but he didn't. She got up, relieved there was no tug of pain to cause her to wince in front of him. "Coffee?"

"No, thanks."

She frowned at him. "Nate, what's up? You didn't come here to check on my stitches, and you're not the one who snuck in this pink swimsuit."

He looked uncomfortable, a rarity for him, and finally sighed. "Do you still believe the man who attacked you looked familiar?"

"Yes." It didn't surprise her that Nate knew.

He could have found out from Gus or Carine, never mind law enforcement. "I keep trying to remember where I've seen him. I've checked my student records, fugitive cases I've worked on, everything I can think of. So far, no connections."

"It's not your job to find this guy. If the investigators in New Hampshire want your help, they'll ask." Nate regarded her more with the authority his job afforded him than with brotherly affection. "You understand that, right?"

"Did someone complain about me?"

"No one's complained. I just know you, Mackenzie. You need to be smart," he said bluntly. "Be patient."

Mackenzie grabbed her coffee, trying to resist a surge of defiance. But she knew she wouldn't. She gave Nate a cool look. "How smart and patient were you after you were shot?"

Almost a year and a half ago, he and a fellow deputy—his wife's twin brother—were shot sniper style in New York's Central Park. Nate's bullet wound, a graze to the shoulder, was relatively minor, but he hadn't left the investigation to the FBI and his colleagues in the Marshals Service. He'd bulldozed his way into the middle of it. He'd met Sarah Dunnemore as a result and given up his solitary life, opened himself up to having a family of his own and all the risks that came with it, as he, orphaned at seven, understood more than most. But as far as Mackenzie could see, he had no regrets.

He said stiffly, "We're not talking about me."

"That's for damn sure." Mackenzie's urge to stand up to him dissipated, and she grinned. "You weren't wearing a pink swimsuit when you were shot."

She thought she detected a spark of amusement in his eyes. "I remember that suit. It's one bright shade of pink. Tough to miss you in the water."

"I don't think our knife-wielding fugitive ever saw me in the water. The shed door was open. I suspect he was on his way out or on his way in while I was underwater or something—I didn't see him, anyway—and I surprised him. He tried to hide, but ended up attacking me."

"Could he have slipped away without being seen?"

"If he'd waited until I went back into the house, he'd at least have had a better chance. He crouched in the brush alongside the shed. I heard him before I saw him. It's filled with Japanese barberry—he could have gotten stuck with thorns. It had to be buggy there, too. Maybe he saw a snake. Whatever. He decided to jump me."

"His thinking might not have been that organized."

"The prevailing wisdom still is he picked the hiker and me to attack at random. He looked wild, but he also seemed in control of himself. I can't explain it."

"Gut feeling?"

"If you want to call it that." Mackenzie was suddenly aware of Nate's nearly two decades of experience in law enforcement compared to her months of training and mere weeks at her first assignment. "I need to figure out where I've seen him."

"Adrenaline can do strange things to people."

"So why not me? I know I could be imagining I've seen him before, but, honestly, I don't think so."

"It could just be a simple mistake. Mackenzie—" He broke off. "Never mind. I need to get rolling." He nodded to her holster. "How're you with a shoulder holster?"

"Terrible. That fraction of a second extra it takes to reach across my body for my weapon—I don't know. I'll try not to shoot myself."

"Were you as big a pain in the ass as a professor?"

"Bigger."

She'd known Nate and his two sisters for as long as she could remember. In those awful months after her father's accident, Gus would bring them by the house with food, and they'd help with repairs that she and her mother couldn't manage on their own. Harry and Jill Winter had died up on Cold Ridge before Mackenzie was born, but she knew that their children—Nate, Antonia and Carine—had faced a tragedy far worse than her own. She'd looked up to them, let them show her the route to survival.

But they'd never imagined her as a federal agent. Not one of them.

"No, don't go," she said. "Tell me why you're really here."

"Just to check on you."

"Nate. I know you think I should have stayed at the college, finished my dissertation. But I got through training. I didn't have your help or support there. I did it on my own."

"I know you did, kid." There was a measure of tenderness in his expression now. "I keep thinking of you as that little curly-haired redhead sitting in your father's blood. Mackenzie, we all want what's best for you."

"What's best for me right now is that you be straight with me."

He started for the elevators, but she followed him.

"You know why Andrew Rook was in Cold Ridge, don't you?" she asked.

Nate banged the down button, sucked in a breath through his teeth and regarded her with a big-brotherly impatience that was entirely familiar to her. "You're relentless, Deputy Stewart. Always have been. I put that in my report about you."

"Relentless is just another way of saying pain in the ass."

"So it is."

"Nate—what about Harris Mayer?"

He glanced away from her. "He's late for a meeting with the FBI."

"Rook?"

The elevator dinged. "You want to play with the big guns, Mackenzie? Here's your chance." The elevator doors opened, and Nate stepped inside, turning to her. "Rook's all yours."

Seventeen

J. Harris Mayer owned a white-painted, black-shuttered brick house on a narrow, prestigious Georgetown street. As Rook stood in the front room, he could see the overgrown rhododendron that grew past its first-floor window.

Harris's neighbors probably wished he had moved or gambled away the house. Rook and T.J. had checked with them, and they clearly hoped the FBI or the local police—someone—would find Harris dead of a heart attack. His disgrace wasn't the issue so much as the shabby condition of his house. It needed paint, extensive repairs and a couple of guys with trimming shears and chainsaws to tackle the out-of-control greenery. The windows hadn't been washed in years. Bees had built nests in various cracks and crevices.

But Rook and T.J. and two other agents hadn't found Mayer dead in his bed or passed out on his kitchen floor. They'd arrived an hour ago, in the heat of the afternoon, having obtained a warrant to check the house for him. The scope of the warrant limited them to searching places where a person could have fallen ill or be hiding—a closet, a shower, not a desk drawer.

"He's skipped," T.J. said, joining Rook from the foyer. "He's not here."

Rook concurred. They'd gone through the house from attic to basement, alert to anything in plain sight that would lead them back to the judge for permission to conduct a more thorough search.

T.J. eyed a slender, curve-legged desk in a corner of the threadbare but elegant room. Everything needed dusting. The house smelled musty; the central air-conditioning hadn't been turned down low enough to keep up with the heat and humidity. The family antiques throughout the house just emphasized that Harris's was a life squandered. He'd gone off the tracks a long time ago, well before his public downfall. It had just taken a while for him to crash.

"Wish we'd found a receipt for a plane ticket to Fiji sitting on a desk," T.J. said. "That'd get us in here going through this place with a fine-tooth comb. I don't have a good feeling about our friend J. Harris, Rook."

Rook sighed. "I don't, either. We'll just have to keep looking for him. I don't know if a soup-to-nuts search here would help us, but I'll see what we can do to get an extension on the warrant."

"If Mayer had given us more to go on . . ."

"I should have pushed him harder."

T.J. shrugged, taking the setback in stride. "For all we know he was blowing smoke and got tired of it, just pulled out and headed for the beach—or he decided he didn't want to face you once you figured out he was engaging in fantasy."

"Maybe," Rook said, determined to keep an open mind.

They left the house. Outside, uniformed Washington police officers provided scene security, in case the neighbors got curious about strange men bursting into the discredited judge's house. A crowd hadn't gathered. It was too damn hot, or people were just busy, or not at home, or didn't want to be obvious about their curiosity.

"Whoa," T.J. said. "Is that your redheaded deputy?"

"That's her," Rook replied through gritted teeth.

As a federal agent herself, Mackenzie had made her way through security, and stood at the bottom of the steps, her curly hair frizzing slightly in the heat. Rook remembered kissing her last night. What the hell had he been thinking?

T.J., who was known for his good looks, trotted down the steps to the brick sidewalk. "Deputy Stewart, right? I'm T. J. Kowalski."

"Special Agent Kowalski—nice to meet you. Andrew's told me about you. All good, of course."

Using his first name, Rook knew, wasn't intended to have an affect on him, but to charm T.J. Obviously it worked, because T.J. smiled at her. "Nice to meet you, too, Deputy—"

"Mackenzie," she corrected. "I didn't expect to find the FBI here. Did something happen to Judge Mayer?"

"Not that we know of," T.J. said. "What's your business here, Mackenzie?"

She glanced up at Rook, still on the steps, then shifted her gaze back to T.J. "Harris Mayer and Judge Peacham go way back. I don't really know him."

"That doesn't explain why you're here."

"No, it doesn't." She gestured broadly toward the house. "No sign of him?"

T.J. hesitated a moment, as if he expected Rook to intervene—but Rook had no intention of diving into the middle of their exchange. Let Mackenzie wriggle her way out of this one. T.J. could handle her. "No," he said. "No sign of him. The house is secure. He's not in it. You know where he is?"

"Not a clue." She squinted at him. "Well. I guess you answered my question for me. Again, T.J., nice to meet you." She made a point of looking up at Rook on the steps. "Mind the heat, you two. It sneaks up on you."

She walked back across the street and got in her car.

T.J. glanced up at Rook. "Want me to find a reason to cuff her?"

"Tempting." Rook joined him on the sidewalk, a slight breeze stirring up the street smells. He just felt hotter. As she pulled out into the roadway, Mackenzie waved at them, then hit the gas and took off. "Think she knew we were here?"

"Hard to say. She didn't look too beaten up from this past weekend."

"Says she heals fast."

"Deputy Stewart's a wiseass," T.J. said with some amusement. "I've always seen you ending up with a wiseass, Rook."

"Yeah. Whatever. Let's go."

"You know, your redheaded marshal didn't exactly shake in her shoes talking to me. Then again, people *like* me. I have a sense of humor."

Rook ignored him, leading the way back to their car.

T.J. didn't take the hint. "You're not going to let yourself trust her, are you? I can't say I blame her for wanting to know what we're up to. She's not a suspect. She's not under surveillance. She's just friends with Bernadette Peacham, our new favorite federal judge. Who is also not a suspect. Her ex-husband—"

"Isn't a suspect," Rook finished.

"Officially."

"Harris Mayer isn't, either, but we can't find him."

"Yeah. I don't like that one." T.J. opened the driver's door and looked across the steaming roof of the car at Rook. "Deputy Stewart moves well for someone with a knife wound in her side. I wouldn't want to underestimate her."

"I haven't," Rook muttered, getting in the car. He and T.J. had a long day yet ahead of them. Time to get on with it.

It was dark when Rook finally quit work and drove out to Arlington, detouring to the historic house where Mackenzie was living. He parked behind her car and got out, remembering his optimism the first time he'd stood in that same spot a few weeks ago. He'd picked her up for dinner in Washington—nothing fancy, just an evening out to get to know each other better.

A light shone on the back porch, and a misting rain had begun to fall, forming a fine film on the steps. Rook debated turning around and heading on home. What could he do here but get himself in deeper with a woman he'd met for all the wrong reasons?

The porch door opened, and Mackenzie stepped out, her hair pulled tight into a curly ponytail, as if she'd tried to tame it once and for all in the high humidity. She was barefoot, wearing shorts and a T-shirt that, somehow, made her seem even smaller than she was.

She tilted her head back, eyeing her visitor. "I could have winged you, Rook, and nobody would have said boo. Here I am injured, alone in a haunted, isolated house, and you know it, yet you sneak up on me anyway."

"Did I scare you?"

"No. I thought you might be a ghost for a second."

"You don't believe in ghosts," he said.

"Stay here a couple nights. You'll believe in ghosts." She took in a breath, putting up a hand as color rose in her cheeks. "Alone, I mean. Stay here a couple nights alone, and then talk to me about ghosts."

"Nate and his wife didn't seem to mind the ghosts."

"Sarah wouldn't. It'd take a lot for Nate to believe he was in the presence of any ghost, never mind the ghosts of Abraham Lincoln and Robert E. Lee." Mackenzie crossed her arms over her chest, her shirt rising just enough to reveal the bandages on her left side. "Would you like to come in for a minute?"

Rook took a step toward her. "I won't stay long."

He followed her into the cool kitchen. The small table was crowded with dishes and odds and ends, as if she'd just unpacked one of the boxes stacked along the wall. He wondered if she had plans for the evening, or if she would stay here, alone with her ghosts.

"Mac, about this afternoon at Harris's house—"

"Not much to say, is there?"

"We want to find him."

"Understood. If I knew where he was, I'd tell you. If I even had a clue, I'd tell you. I take it New Hampshire didn't pan out, and you didn't find him there." She yanked out a chair at the table and plopped down. "He's not wanted, officially. Is he providing you with information? He's such a bottom-feeder. I can just imagine what all he knows."

"We have no reason to believe he had anything to do with the attack on you."

"Glad to hear it." She didn't seem to make any effort to hide her sarcasm, but bitterness wasn't in her nature. She sighed. "Damn it, Rook. What's going on?"

He noticed a six-inch length of spent packing tape on the floor and scooped it up, dropping it into an empty box set against the wall, next to the full ones. "Last night at Judge Peacham's . . . Mac—you were holding back on her. She knew it. She just didn't want to pressure you in front of me."

"You FBI mind readers."

"If it's something I need to know, I want it. Now would be a good time."

Mackenzie jumped to her feet, but gave a small moan and reached for her side. "Okay, so I can't do sudden moves to throttle FBI agents just yet. Give me a couple more days."

"Mac—"

"Whatever I told or didn't tell Beanie last night is *personal.*"

"Are you sure?"

It was a simple, pointed question that made her snap her mouth shut. "Cal stopped here and asked me about Harris before I left for New Hampshire. Have those two cooked up something that's got the attention of the FBI?"

"Mac," Rook said, then sighed. "I shouldn't have come."

An awkward silence descended between them.

She started for the door, presumably to see him out, but Rook touched her arm, felt the same spark of attraction he'd experienced when they'd first met, and acted on it. He curved his fingers under her chin and traced her lower lip with his thumb. "Mac." He sighed once more, shaking his head. "Damn. I wasn't going to kiss you again."

She didn't resist or tell him no or shove him out the door when his mouth found hers. Instead, she kissed him back. He could feel her eagerness—the spark of desire in her. If not for her bandaged side, he'd have slipped his arms around her and drawn her closer to him, let her feel his reaction to her, her touch, the taste of her.

"You're complicating my life, Rook," she said, then kissed him again.

He felt a shudder of arousal. "You're not exactly simplifying mine."

As she stood back from him, her very blue eyes met his. "I don't like setting myself up to be hurt."

He smiled. "That didn't hurt, did it?"

She opened the door for him. Outside, the rain was steady now, falling softly, without wind, thunder, lightning. There was no front moving through to push out the heat and humidity. The light from the porch hit her face, bringing out the dark smudges under her eyes. It had only been five days since Mackenzie Stewart had found herself in a fight for her life—not enough time, Rook thought, for anyone to expect her to be back to normal, especially with her attacker still out there.

He walked past her and stepped onto the porch.

She remained in the doorway. "I've known Beanie Peacham all my life. I don't trust many people, but I trust her."

"What would you do for her?" Rook asked.

"She's never asked anything from me."

"Maybe she knows she doesn't have to ask."

He expected a hot reaction, but Mackenzie didn't rise to his bait. "You mean because I anticipate her wishes? That's not the case. It just isn't. I'm not being defensive, and I'm not in denial."

"Fair enough."

"You don't like her."

Rook smelled earth and some kind of flowers on the rain, and he thought of ghosts, wondered if they ever ventured out across the plush grounds, among the tall, old trees. *Man. What's wrong with you?*

He shook off thoughts of ghosts and focused on the woman in the doorway. He hated to abandon her—but what the hell else could he do? When Harris Mayer had pointed her out at the hotel last week, Rook had expected backing off from her wouldn't be difficult. But he was wrong, and in the days since he'd left her the voice mail canceling dinner, he'd only found himself more attracted to her.

And yet he knew better than to underestimate this woman—to take her bandaged side and her response to him as vulnerability.

"I think Judge Peacham looks at you and sees the eleven-year-old, traumatized and guilt-ridden about her father's accident," he said. "And maybe the academic she'd hoped you'd become."

"I did become," Mackenzie said.

"Did she approve of your career change?"

"No one did. Beanie's not alone in that one."

"Why . . ."

"Why did I become a marshal?" Mackenzie grinned so suddenly, so unexpectedly that Rook felt gut-punched. "Because I didn't want to write my dissertation."

"Did your students always laugh at your jokes?"

"Always. You law enforcement types—not so much." But her eyes turned serious, and she said, "I wanted to catch bad guys and help keep people safe. That's it. That's why I filled out my application."

"It's as valid a reason as any I've ever heard."

"Why did you become an FBI agent?"

He shrugged. "It never occurred to me to do anything else. Mac—"

"I can't make love with these damn stitches," she said quietly, quickly. "So, just say good-night."

Rook didn't move. He could see what she was thinking. "Mac, making love to you isn't just unfinished business that I need to take care of and then move on. I'm not that big a cad." He stepped closer to her. "We can go a little further, even with the stitches. I won't hurt you."

"What?"

But she took his hand and backed into the

kitchen, and he brought his palm to her breast, her eyes on him, liquid, certain, stripping away his reserve. "How could I have thought I could just walk away?"

She smiled, moving against his palm. "Don't think about that now."

He raised her shirt and heard her breath catch as he unclasped her bra and skimmed his fingertips across her hardening nipples, the soft skin of her breast. His senses flooded with the smell of her, the feel of her. She reached a hand into his hair, moaning softly as he teased and tantalized, then, careful of her bandaged side, lifted her bra and shirt over her head and cast them onto the floor.

"Rook," she whispered, tightening her fist in his hair, then letting go. "Andrew . . ."

He gazed at her, taking in the milky skin, the curve of her breasts, the flat stomach, the flare of hips, wanting her, aching for her, his need a jolt to his system.

"Mac."

His voice was strangled, and he gave up, slipped his hands around her, high, avoiding her injury. Her skin was cool now, creamy under his touch. Everything about her aroused him, absorbed him. He kissed her neck, moving lower, lost in the scent of her, the taste of her, as tongue and teeth explored, lingered, pushed her to soft moans of pleasure. He felt her falter slightly, but they both stayed on their feet.

Her skin heated, and she dug her fingers into his shoulders, giving a small cry, a gasp of need and frustration. When he rose up, her lips were parted, and he plunged his tongue into her mouth, letting her know just how aroused he was. But she found out for herself, dropping a hand between them, skimming her fingers across him, locating his zipper, lowering it. She slipped her hand inside. He was hard, throbbing against her touch.

He growled into her mouth. "Mac—hell."

She smiled boldly. "Do you want me to stop?"

But his body answered for him, and she gulped in a breath, her smile gone now, her mouth on his again as she reached deep and took the length of him. He fought for air, kissing her, teasing her nipples with his thumbs in the same rhythm she used on him. When she quickened her pace, he eased one hand down the smooth skin of her back and into her pants, along the curve of her buttocks.

His urgency mounted, but he forced a pause, looked into her eyes, which were a dusky blue now, brimming with need and desire. "I don't want to hurt you."

"You're not . . . oh." She moved against his hand. "Trust me."

His fingers reached her hot, moist center, and her grip on him faltered slightly. He didn't stop. He flicked, pushed, circled his fingers around her, into her, probing, as she responded, moving against them, onto them. She worked her own magic and torture with her hand, capturing, stroking, faster, then faster yet.

"Mac, I can't hold on." He could hardly breathe, never mind talk.

"Then don't, because neither can I."

Her body shuddered and she cried out, her grip slackening. But she didn't let go. She stiffened against him, and he could feel her willpower as she regained her hold. With her next brutal stroke, he used every ounce of self-control to keep himself from exploding.

Not now. At the moment, he thought, it was enough for him to pleasure her.

His time would come.

He thrust his fingers deep into her, as insistent and brutal as she'd been with him, watching her eyes close as she gave in to the sensations. She grasped his shoulders, bracing herself as her body rippled with release. Slick with perspiration, she collapsed against him, breathing hard into his neck.

Finally, she stood back, utterly spent and as unembarrassed as he was.

She scooped up her shirt and bra and grinned at him. "You really are a bastard, you know. Honestly. Making me be the only one who . . ." She didn't finish.

"Regrets?"

She slapped him lightly with her shirt. "Not hardly."

"Your stitches—"

"Intact. All intact. You didn't hurt me, Andrew." She slipped on her shirt, not bothering with the bra, and smiled at him. "I was never in pain."

He believed her. "I've been thinking about this moment for a long time."

She raised her eyebrows. "So when we were having coffee that night in the rain, you were thinking—"

"Not then."

"You are *such* a bad liar."

He pulled himself together, then kissed her—softly this time, romantically. "Now," he said, smiling, "we have unfinished business."

She let out a breath. "I think we just might."

On his way home, Rook drove too fast and was so agitated he almost missed his own damn driveway.

His nephew was reading a gaming magazine and listening to his iPod at the kitchen table. Rook pulled out the chair across from him and sat down. "How can you read and listen to music at the same time?"

"What?"

"How . . ." He sighed. "Take the damn headphones off and you'll be able to hear me."

"Oh. Yeah." Brian grinned, removing the earbuds and hitting the pause button on his iPod. "Bad day?"

"It had its moments. What about you?"

"Just hanging out here. I ran the dishwasher and picked up my room." He nodded toward the microwave. "I've got leftovers heating up."

Rook decided not to push him about his future plans. Brian's father could tackle that problem. "What leftovers?"

"I don't know. I dumped a bunch of stuff I found in the fridge into the microwave. There's enough for two, if you want."

In a brief flash, Rook saw his nephew's loneliness and uncertainty. His friends from high school were off to college or had jobs, and Brian was in Arlington, eating leftovers with his uncle.

Rook suddenly didn't feel that great about his own life, either. He'd let his emotions get away from him with Mac, and he didn't know what the hell came next. He was worried about her—but he was worried about himself, too, because tonight proved he had no self-control at all, not with her. Spotting her with Bernadette Peacham last week and seeing a potential conflict between his professional and personal lives, he'd thought he'd put on the brakes in his usual efficient, objective manner.

But he hadn't. He was in a free fall.

He got to his feet and took a pitcher of iced tea out of the refrigerator. At least it was fresh. If it'd been stale, he'd have felt damn pathetic.

When he filled two glasses with tea and turned back to the table, Brian had already stuck his earbuds in place and tuned into his music again.

Eighteen

Jesse entered the small campus auditorium just as a panel discussion on current issues in legal ethics—he liked that—let out. Four middle-aged men rose from chairs at a cheap table. Calvin Benton was on the left end, facing the audience of about fifty law students and professors. He shook hands with his fellow panelists, the polite applause fading quickly as people started filing out.

Despite the intense police search for him in New Hampshire, Jesse had done nothing to conceal his identity. Beardless, clean, dressed in expensive clothes, out of context, he doubted even Mackenzie Stewart would recognize him, at least not from a quick glance. Up close, the way she'd been on Friday, was another matter. He could still see her now, in her bright-colored swimsuit, water dripping down her face as she'd tried to figure out what had caused the noise she'd heard.

Stop, he told himself, pushing the image from his mind.

He stiffened, shielding himself against any further intrusions of the redheaded marshal. She'd captivated him, but Deputy Stewart would love to put him behind bars, a fact that no amount of wishful thinking on his part could change.

He walked down the center aisle and crossed in front of the stage to a side entrance. Cal, visibly pale, reluctantly joined him.

"You've got nerve." Benton's voice was a low hiss, and he glanced behind him, as if making sure no one could see them together. "What are you doing here?"

Jesse shrugged, enjoying Cal's discomfort. "Sorry I missed the discussion. All finished now? No book signing?"

"I don't have a book."

"Your fellow panelists do."

"We're not here to sell books." Cal's biting sarcasm and unrelenting arrogance were, Jesse figured, a fairly transparent attempt to conceal his fear. "You shouldn't have come."

"Caught you by surprise, did I? I just want five minutes of your time. You and I have unfinished business."

Another panel member squeezed past them, saying good-night and complimenting Cal on his portion of the talk. Cal managed to return the compliment, but when the other man was out of earshot, he growled to Jesse, "Not here."

Amused by his discomfort, Jesse walked down the corridor to a corner and stood in front of a window overlooking a courtyard, where students, divided into small knots, ran through the rain. "Decent crowd for a hot summer night," Jesse said mildly. "They're all summer students?"

"Not all—most. They're participating in a special six-week program. As if you give a damn. Where's Harris? I haven't seen him in a week."

"Missing him, are you?"

"He's a coward. He's probably gone into hiding until you and I have sorted things out ourselves. Unless you . . ." Cal narrowed his eyes. "Perhaps I should just call the police and let them find Harris."

Jesse withdrew his cell phone from his pants pocket and held it out. "Go right ahead. I'll wait."

Cal took in a breath, held it, then exhaled with a huff. "Bastard. You'd better hope no one with a cell phone is taking a picture of us right now. A stranger coming up to me. Tempting."

"You have to love Washington," Jesse said. "Afraid you're under surveillance?"

"By whom? I've done nothing."

"You know Harris went to the feds."

The last color drained from Cal's face. He cleared his throat and looked out the window evasively. "I don't have any control over him. He's as slimy as you are. I want to be rid of you both."

"We make a nice trio, don't we? Our mutual friend met with the FBI last week. With a Special Agent Andrew Rook."

"If Harris gave the FBI anything, they'd be on us by now."

"I heard the feds searched his house today."

That got Cal's attention. "*Harris's* house?"

"Apparently, they're getting worried about him."

"Fine," Cal said, rallying. "If he got cold feet and took off, that buys us more time to conclude our arrangements. The feds can spin their wheels looking for him all they want. They have no cause to dip into my affairs. And they don't even know you exist."

Jesse pressed a fingertip to the window, as if trying to touch a raindrop.

Cal gulped in a quick breath. "Go to Mexico, Jesse. Don't risk Harris ratting you out to the FBI—never mind what I have on you. I can't put you in prison. They can. Get out of Washington." He was on a roll now, almost arrogant again. "Once I'm confident you're holding up your end of our deal, I'll hold up mine. I'll wire you the money. I'll stay out of your life."

"What about my identity, Cal? Can you wire me *that?*"

"Your 'identity,' Jesse, is my insurance policy that you don't ever darken my door again." Cal gave him a cold look. "Did you have anything to do with the attack on Mackenzie Stewart in New Hampshire?"

"What attack, Cal?"

His face reddened, anger mixing with the

arrogance now. "The police say a deranged drifter knifed her and another woman, in two separate attacks."

"Do I look like a deranged drifter?"

Cal's shoulders seemed to slump, as if he couldn't maintain the arrogant-Washington-insider act another second, and he shook his head. "If Harris is playing games with the FBI, why don't you and I just back off and leave each other alone? Call it a draw, Jesse. You have your leverage against me. I have mine against you—"

"I don't believe in draws." Jesse made himself sound almost bored. "I believe in winning. You should know that, unless you haven't found out everything about me, after all."

For a split second, Cal seemed ready to wilt, but then his experience and discipline clicked into gear, and he straightened, squaring his shoulders. "I wish I didn't know anything about you. I want you out of my life. That's all." Cal kept his voice low, but he was visibly shaken, tense. "I don't even want to know everything about you. Just drop out of Washington and go live your damn life. I'll get you the money—trust me. I have no reason not to get it to you."

"It doesn't work that way. I don't like to be leveraged."

"You have a vivid imagination," Cal said. "It's one of the reasons you're good at what you do. Me? I'd never imagine that some of the people I've helped you 'leverage' over the past few months would be capable of doing the things they've done." Cal maintained his outward self-control. "You give me more credit than I deserve."

Jesse didn't let himself be distracted. "I want whatever evidence you have on me. Computer files, hard copies of files, accounts, recordings, videotapes. Whatever it is, I want it. All of it."

A fat old man was making his way up the hall with a push broom. Cal stepped back from the window, but said nothing. He was overestimating his power. If he believed that Jesse *was* the man who'd attacked Mackenzie and the hiker last week, the nonfatal outcome worked in his favor. Cal would mistake it for weakness and inefficiency.

Jesse went on calmly. "And I want my money. Now. Not later."

A muscle worked in Cal's jaw. "How many times do I have to say it? You'll get your damn money once you're out of my face. When I'm out of any danger that this entire mess is going to backfire on me. I don't want your million dollars—it's not worth it to me to risk not holding up my end."

Probably true, but Jesse was unmoved.

"If Harris decides to come out of hiding and talk to the feds—"

"I'm not worried about Harris," Jesse said.

"Fraud, bribery, blackmail, extortion, conspiracy. Those aren't light charges. Be smart. Get out of Washington now while you can. I've profited from other people's sins. I'm not even disgusted with myself. Some of the dirty politicians, bureaucrats and lobbyists you and I squeezed saw themselves in a new light and stopped what they were doing. Some of them have reformed out of fear. They're looking over their shoulders, scared of what comes next—who else might know their secrets?"

Jesse almost laughed. "Oh, so noble, Cal. You helped me because you had no choice. I had your balls in a vise."

Sweat erupted on Cal's brow, and he stank of it. "And so we blackmail each other. What I have on you is more damaging than what you have on me. So I had an affair while Bernadette and I were technically still married. Who's going to care now that we're divorced? Even she wouldn't."

"You had your affair at her house in New Hampshire."

"It's not anything I'm proud of, and I don't want it to get out—but it's nothing compared to the material I have on you. If the feds had to choose between nailing your ass and nailing mine, they'd choose yours."

Jesse reached into his inner jacket pocket and withdrew a color printout of a digital photograph. "Take a close look. You'll notice that's you with the hairy legs and the saggy ass."

Cal frowned, as if confused. "What are you talking about?"

"You think I only know about the brunette you humped in New Hampshire back in June. Take a close look, Cal. That's not your brunette. That's your blonde, a high-level congressional aide who had a weekend of wild sex with you at the summer home of a respected federal judge. But you tell me. What do you think?"

Cal crumpled up the picture, sweat pouring down his temples. "You're disgusting."

"You can see her face. You recognize her, don't you? I believe we blackmailed her boss."

"Not we—you."

"Oh, you helped. You and Harris got me the information, the access. Rich SOB he is, too. You'd think you'd have stayed away from New Hampshire after I already caught you with the brunette."

Cal didn't say anything, just looked sick.

"What was the blonde doing—having sex with you in exchange for you keeping quiet about her? Or did she give you the information about her boss in the first place?"

"Stop—"

"She came to a bad end about two weeks ago. I guess you know that."

"Jesse, don't. She overdosed on pain pills. She had a problem back. Her death was an accident."

"There are whispers it was suicide, because she was upset about a man."

Cal took a sharp breath. "You're disgusting!"

"*I'm* disgusting? I like that." Jesse yawned. The Washington heat made him sleepy. If only he could have stayed in the mountains longer. "The police are still investigating the accident."

"How many pictures do you have?" Cal asked.

"Pictures *and* a recording. If I leave them with the feds, they'll dig deeper, and they'll hang you high. Even if they can't prove you were blackmailing her."

"I *wasn't.*"

"Look at our friend J. Harris Mayer. He was never prosecuted. You'll be ruined, Cal. Judge Peacham will be ruined, too. Even if people believe she wasn't involved in your treachery, they'll wonder how it could happen under her nose."

"Bernadette doesn't deserve that. We were separated—"

"That'll matter? You'll go down and your ex-wife will go down. And your girlfriends." Jesse paused deliberately, for effect. "The media will trot them out one by one."

More than angry, Cal looked tortured, but he straightened, sniffed like the high-powered lawyer he was. "Threatening me doesn't change anything."

"I'm not bluffing," Jesse said.

"Drag me down and I drag you down. That's the way it is."

"Double-crossing me wasn't a smart move."

"Ditto. I won't go to the feds with what I have on you. You won't go to the feds with what you have on me. You've done worse, Jesse. You attacked a federal agent."

"Good night, Cal. I'll be in touch." He tapped his pictures. "Just wanted you to know the score."

Cal opened his mouth as if to speak, but instead marched down the hall, the crumpled photo of his blond lover in bed with him still in his hand.

Jesse waited in the dim light until Cal disappeared. The janitor pushed his broom toward the supply closet, and Jesse smiled at him, then went on his way, back to the parking lot, the heat, the smells of the city. His BMW was still faintly cool. He sat behind the wheel, remembering the night he'd taken the picture of Cal Benton and the very attractive, very corrupt aide. It probably hadn't occurred to Cal that anyone would ever catch him in bed with her—that it was that big a deal, a little sex in exchange for him doing good by her. Sneak up to his soon-to-be-ex-wife's place in the country, and not worry about the prying gossips in Washington.

Even if he couldn't be tied to the blond aide's death or blackmail, the scandal would sink Cal Benton, and it would sink Bernadette Peacham.

The man was a fool, but Jesse hated seeing the tight control he'd once had over their operation unravel.

The car cooled to a temperature more to his liking. He glanced in his rearview mirror and thought of Mackenzie Stewart in her pink swimsuit. The curve of her breasts, the shape of her legs. *Would* he have killed her last Friday?

Oh, yes.

Jesse glanced at his watch. Ten o'clock. Plenty of time, he decided, for a quick trip out to Arlington. Mackenzie was back in town. He wondered if she'd gone to bed yet, or if she'd be up, staring at his sketch and trying to figure out where she'd seen him before.

Nineteen

With just her desk lamp on in her darkened living room, Mackenzie peered at the eyes of the man in the police sketch. She couldn't sleep. She kept thinking about Rook and how she should have just waved goodbye in the rain and distracted herself from her desire for him with a stiff drink.

Except she didn't have any liquor in the house.

She had regrets, she decided. Not for herself—she'd be fine. She *was* fine, her body still humming, suffused with the after-effects of their near lovemaking. Whatever it was that had gone on in the kitchen . . .

Her regrets—her fears—were for him. He was obviously in the middle of a sensitive investigation that involved people she knew. He was ambitious, driven, good at his work.

With a hiss of frustration, Mackenzie shook off that line of thinking, and said aloud, "Rook knows what he's doing."

That was what she should keep in mind.

She turned her attention back to the sketch. The drawing didn't capture the strangeness of her attacker's eyes. She tried to understand why she'd focused on them. Did they truly hold the key to why he seemed familiar to her?

Why had he attacked her and not Carine? Was it, at least in part, because he'd known Carine *wouldn't* recognize him? But he hadn't seemed concerned that Mackenzie would. He'd even taunted her, using her name.

Why?

The telephone rang—the house's hard line. Since she was there only temporarily, Mackenzie hadn't bothered getting a line in her name, relying instead on her cell phone for personal calls. She picked up.

"Burning the midnight oil tonight, are you?"

It was a male voice, hoarse and unrecognizable. "Who is this?"

Click.

Did he *know* she was up late, or had he just dialed her number at random? But she remembered the wrong number she'd received at Bernadette's lake house over the weekend. Another coincidence she didn't like.

She grabbed her gun and ran out to the porch. Was her caller watching her, stalking her? The air smelled of rain and wet grass, and the cloud cover made for a dark night. She walked down the steps, slick from rain, and out to the driveway, listening for the sound of a car—or a man hiding in the shrubs. She wouldn't be thinking about squirrels and wild turkeys tonight.

She walked to the end of the long driveway. Streetlights cast eerie shadows, and nearby houses had living-room lights on, their residents, no doubt, enjoying a normal evening at home. The only cars visible were parked in driveways.

Was this man watching her from a hidden, darkened car?

She returned to the house, her slip-on sneakers soaked by the time she sat at the table in the kitchen. She kicked them off and reached for her cell phone, dialing Nate Winter's number.

"Did you and Sarah ever get crank calls here?" she asked when he picked up.

"No. What's going on?"

She told him about the call, skipping any mention of Rook's visit. Nate didn't interrupt. When she finished, she decided she didn't want to sound paranoid, and added, "It could have been anyone. I'm not suggesting it was the man who attacked me."

Nate was silent a moment. "Do you want me to come over?"

"And do what? There's nothing to be done tonight. The caller didn't use my name. On most occasions I wouldn't have given it a second thought."

"Mackenzie . . ."

"It's okay. Sorry to disturb you."

"Anytime," he said softly. "You know that. But you've had a rough week. You need to give yourself time—"

"I just want to figure out where I've seen the man who attacked me. We need to find him before he hurts someone else. Because he will, Nate. I know he will."

"If he does, it won't be your fault. It'll be his doing and his alone."

"I had him. I had him, and he got away."

"Then you didn't have him, did you?"

She sat back, stung. And yet, she thought, she appreciated Nate's clarity—his blunt honesty. "No, I guess I didn't."

"Don't be afraid to ask for help. You're not in this thing alone. Understood?"

"Yes, understood." Still, she knew—as did Nate—that raising the alarm over as dubious and amorphous a call as the one she'd just received wouldn't inspire confidence. "Say hi to Sarah for me. She's doing well?"

"She's heading over there tomorrow to mark out a new dig."

"Alone?"

Nate didn't answer right away. "No," he said finally. "She won't be alone."

When Mackenzie hung up, she realized her wet feet were cold—surprising, given the relentless heat. She headed to her bedroom, wondering if she'd overreacted to the call. She'd been in the middle of studying the sketch, reliving the events of last Friday, and, admittedly, was a little off balance.

Not just a little.

Maybe it was the ghosts, she thought, pulling back the covers on her bed, and imagining Rook with her in the process.

Damn near making love to him hadn't exactly helped her get centered. What should she make of their relationship?

She sighed. "Nothing. That's what you make of your relationship."

Because to do otherwise was to distract her, distract him and risk another axing by voice mail. Too much was up in the air. Tonight they'd let their hormones and emotions get away from them, but so be it. It was time to be sensible. She needed to stay focused on her work, on healing. And on assisting investigators in any way she could to find their knife-happy guy in New Hampshire.

Without, of course, crossing too many lines.

Not that showing up at Harris's house in the middle of an FBI search had crossed any lines. She hadn't realized the search was under way—why would she? Cal Benton had turned up asking about Harris *before* she'd left for New Hampshire, and Rook had gone there looking for him. And Mackenzie knew Harris, if not well.

Stopping by his house after work made perfect sense.

Nor, she thought as she undressed, mindful of her stitches, did she regret letting Rook back into her kitchen.

"Letting? You all but dragged him," she said aloud.

But she didn't laugh or even smile at her attempt at humor as she fell into bed. She liked being around him. She had since they'd ducked out of the rain together.

He was here because he's working an investigation.

A point to remember. Andrew Rook was a tough-minded, focused law enforcement officer. If he thought she had information the FBI had a right to, it'd be under the hot lights with her.

Cal.

But Cal's illicit weekend was a personal matter unrelated to Rook's investigation.

Mackenzie's feet finally felt warm. She kicked off the covers, feeling a dull ache in her injured side. Maybe she should rethink her decision to keep quiet about Cal sneaking off to Bernadette's lake house for a fling. The facts were what they were. She hadn't created them—and just who was she protecting by staying silent? Was telling herself that she was just minding her own business and being discreet a rationalization?

If it was her investigation, she'd want to know *all* the facts about any parties involved, and decide for herself what was material and what wasn't.

Probably Rook would, too.

On her way to work in the morning, Mackenzie checked in with Gerald Mooney, her state police contact in New Hampshire. "An organic farmer came forward," he said. "He thinks he might have picked up our guy hitchhiking."

"Where?"

"Sorry, I can't give you any details until we have more solid information."

Meaning until they'd checked out the farmer and where he'd picked up and dropped off his hitchhiker, followed any trail the hitchhiker had left and all the spokes off that trail. In other words, they wouldn't tell her more until they were satisfied they wouldn't jeopardize their investigation. Above all, Mooney wouldn't want to say anything that could get out and end up alerting the attacker and causing him to hurt someone else.

Mackenzie was the "victim," and she didn't like it.

"Is news about the farmer out?" she asked.

"Partially. Let's just say it's a strong lead. He doesn't own a television. He didn't see the sketch until he was in town to pick up supplies and happened to notice It up on a community bulletin board."

"What about the other victim? How's she doing?"

"She's out of the hospital. She has a long recovery ahead of her. What about you?"

"I get my stitches out tomorrow. I'll be doing jumping jacks before you know it."

She thought Mooney might have chuckled. "I'll keep you posted as I can," he said.

An organic farmer. A hitchhiker who fit the description of her attacker. Mackenzie debated thinking up an excuse to fly to New Hampshire, but when she got to her desk, Joe Delvecchio, her chief, a stocky, no-nonsense man in his early fifties, dumped a stack of files on her desk.

"What's this?" she asked.

"You're a Ph.D., Stewart. Go through the files and see what you make of them. Meeting at one."

"ABD."

"What?"

"All But Dissertation. I don't have my

Ph.D. I joined the service to get out of writing my dissertation—"

His glare stopped her. "Meeting's here. Happy reading." He took two steps, stopped and turned back to her. "Next time you get a weird phone call, you call me. You don't call Nate Winter."

Ah. So that was it. "Got it, Chief."

But he wasn't finished. "And if you get an itch to go visit some old friend the FBI happens to want to talk to, don't scratch it."

"Harris Mayer isn't a friend—"

"We work *with* the FBI in this office. We don't work against them."

Mackenzie started to speak, then decided to keep her mouth shut.

The chief softened slightly. "If I didn't think you weren't smart, I'd have given you more time to go through those files."

"Thanks, Chief. I appreciate that. Did you hear about the organic farmer and the hitchhiker?"

"Is this like a knock-knock joke or something?"

She rocked back in her chair, wondering if he'd add another fifty files to her stack if she told him about her contact with the detective

in New Hampshire. But she hadn't done anything wrong, and neither had Mooney.

Delvecchio stared at her, apparently expecting an answer—or maybe a funny joke.
She gave him the rundown of what Mooney
had told her.

"Progress in the investigation," he said.
"That's good news."

"It's gutsy for this guy to hinge his freedom on getting someone to pick him up
hitchhiking."

"Think that's what he did?"

She considered the chief's question and
shook her head. "He had a plan B and a plan
C. He'd have hijacked a car, or stolen one—
and he probably had another knife squirreled away." She paused, but Delvecchio
didn't comment. "Which doesn't make him
sound like a deranged hiker to me."

The chief looked at her with something
approaching satisfaction. "We'll find him,
whoever he is." He pointed to the stack of
files. "You just do your reading."

"It won't take me until one," she said. "I
had to read four hundred books in five
months studying for my orals."

Delvecchio didn't respond to her humor,

although what she'd said was true. For a split second, she thought she might have gone too far, but he sighed. "See? Smart. That's what everyone says about you, Stewart. You're smart. You'll be running the damn show around here in ten years if you get your head screwed on straight."

"My head—"

But he walked away, and Mackenzie knew she'd been dismissed. She grabbed the top file. It was on a cold fugitive case. *All* the files were on cold fugitive cases.

Why wouldn't Delvecchio think her head wasn't screwed on straight?

"Gee," she said to herself, "let's think a minute."

She'd dated an ambitious, well-regarded, tough-minded FBI agent who broke all her rules about staying away from law enforcement types and happened to be investigating—on some level—a federal judge who was her lifelong friend. Even if Bernadette wasn't suspected of wrongdoing, Delvecchio wouldn't like having one of his new deputies in the middle of an FBI investigation.

And she'd found herself in a knife fight

while wearing a pink swimsuit. She'd blocked a slash of her attacker's knife with a beach towel.

She'd recognized her attacker, but couldn't place why or where.

To top off her bad luck, she'd received a creepy phone call in the middle of the night and hadn't called Delvecchio.

Lots of strikes against her, Mackenzie thought. Time to duck and cover. The best way to prove herself right now was to walk into the one o'clock meeting prepared, knowing every damn file the chief had given her to read.

The meeting lasted for an hour, but bled into another meeting that last for two hours. Mackenzie's eyes were rolling back in her head when she returned to her desk. But it was solid work—the start of a joint task force to pick up fugitives who'd been on the lam for way too long. If she hadn't wowed anyone with her expertise, insight and command of her particular stack of files, she'd at least held her own.

"Nice job in there," a senior deputy said as he passed her desk. He didn't even give her a chance to thank him. But she didn't want to get a reputation just for research and analysis—she wanted to do fieldwork.

She'd head to the firing range. She was getting her stitches out in the morning. Shooting a few rounds wouldn't hurt.

Like all her plans since her morning coffee, that one went out the window when Juliet Longstreet turned up. Just back from specialized training, Juliet was tall, blond and very fit, an experienced marshal who was also from northern New England—Vermont—and had experience with a case that had reached into her personal life.

She'd also worked with Nate Winter for a time in New York.

"Ethan and I want to take you house hunting tonight." Ethan Brooker was a former Special Forces officer, now a White House advisor; he and Juliet were engaged to be married in the fall. "We'll grab a bite to eat on the way."

"Is noncompliance an option?" Mackenzie asked.

Juliet grinned. "No."

"Then I'd be delighted."

"Good. We'll meet you back here in an hour."

Mackenzie realized she wouldn't even get

a chance to head home and change her shoes. She saw Nate's fingers in the house hunting idea. Had he put Juliet and Ethan up to it out of concern for her welfare—or out of concern over what she'd do next?

Maybe, Mackenzie thought, Juliet and Ethan were just trying to befriend a new deputy in town who'd just survived a knife fight.

Probably not.

But sooner or later, she'd have to find a place to live. The leaks would be fixed, and the house eventually would open to the public.

If the leaks *were* the work of the resident ghosts, Mackenzie didn't want to be around for what they cooked up next.

"I'll be ready," she told her new friend.

Juliet nodded, obviously satisfied. "Do you have enough to keep you busy for the next hour?"

"You bet. If I look the slightest bit bored, someone will shove a stack of files at me. Idle hands and all that."

"You're learning." Juliet grinned. "See you soon."

Twenty

Jesse looked out the impressive windows of his leased condo at the Potomac River reflecting the orange sunset and wished he'd paid more attention in his U.S. history classes. Washington was jam-packed with historic sites, museums, government buildings. Earlier in the summer, he'd been standing on a corner, debating where to get a bite to eat, and realized he was practically on top of Ford's Theater, where John Wilkes Booth had shot Abraham Lincoln.

Mackenzie was an academic. Political science. She would know the history of many of Washington's more obscure sites.

He turned away from the window. So far, the investigation into the tragic death of the congressional aide didn't seem to be leading detectives to Cal Benton. He and his blonde had been careful, just not so careful that Jesse didn't have pictures of them.

But the search for Harris was heating up. Jesse felt secure that he had bought himself time to pressure Cal, but was it enough time? He couldn't push too hard and risk having Cal take his chances with the FBI, go to them with his little insurance policy and cut a deal—Jesse in exchange for a reduced prison sentence or no prison sentence at all.

It was a delicate balancing act.

Jesse didn't have to remain patient, but he had to be deliberate, purposeful.

He headed down to the lobby and out to the parking garage, getting into his rented BMW. Cal's car was parked at the end of the row. Perfect. He would have seen by now that someone had been inside his condo.

And he hadn't called the police, because he wouldn't dare.

Feeling his spirits revive, Jesse drove out to Arlington and the historic house where Mackenzie was staying. He had driven past the place earlier and spotted a honey-haired woman in the driveway, conferring with two contractors in separate vans. Sarah Dunnemore Winter, no doubt. He'd done his research.

He liked the idea that he and Mackenzie both had temporary residences. It wasn't just something they could share—it meant that her future was as yet uncertain.

What if he and his pretty marshal were bound to be together?

What if that was why he hadn't killed her? Not because of her skill and luck, but because his subconscious had undermined his plans? On some level, he'd known he had to let her live.

Her car wasn't in the driveway. He considered slipping inside the house and waiting for her return, but that was too impulsive, too dangerous. If he was wrong and Mackenzie was on the premises, she'd have him. She was on alert these days and she was armed. He wouldn't get away a second time.

The house's security system was unimpressive—one of the improvements that would likely come in time. Right now, there were no surveillance cameras on the property. It was a simple matter for Jesse to park in the shade and get out of his car. He'd grabbed a knife just like the one he'd used in New Hampshire—a straightforward Ka-Bar.

He cut a fat pink hydrangea blossom and left it on her doorstep.

"From a friend," he said. "From someone who knows you better than you know yourself."

To be sure she knew it was from him, he left his assault knife with the hydrangea.

Twenty-One

The list of J. Harris Mayer's friends and associates wasn't as long as it once had been, but tackling just the top half of names had taken Rook and T.J. late into the evening, with little to show for their efforts. People were far more alarmed to find the FBI at their door, asking about the disgraced former judge, than they were at his absence. According to those who knew him best, the disappearing act he'd done last week wasn't unusual or out of character for him. He was long divorced, and his kids were grown. What was to stop him from taking off to the beach?

Or New Hampshire, Rook thought. He and T.J. were in heavy Beltway traffic, the perfect cap to their day. T.J. was at the wheel, just as frustrated.

When his cell phone rang, Rook had a brief urge to toss it out the window. He didn't want to talk to anyone.

He saw the readout. *Mac.*

He decided not to throw out his phone. "Hey, Deputy—"

"Rook," she said. There was something in her voice. "Andrew. Does anyone call you Andrew? You have brothers. They're all Rooks themselves. It'd get confusing at family gatherings."

"Mac?"

"Humorless, Rook. You are—"

"What's going on?"

"I'm at my house." She cleared her throat. "Someone left me a present. A wilted hydrangea and an assault knife. Cute, huh?"

"We're on our way." He looked over at T.J.

"I've called the police," she added. "Well. You *are* the police. So am I, but—*damn.* What's wrong with me? I know this guy, Andrew. I do. I just can't remember how. And now he's here, and he'll hurt someone else if we don't find him soon." She sucked in a breath. "All right. Get here. I'll—"

"You'll take cover and wait."

"Right. That's what I was going to say." She wasn't offended. "Thanks."

"Don't hang up. I'll stay on until the police get there."

"How far out are you?"

"Fifteen minutes. Where are you?"

"Behind my car door. Not in the vehicle." She sounded more herself now. "If he jumps me from the bushes, I'll nail him this time. But he's not here. He's a slippery creep who's trying to get under my skin. He left his little present and took off."

"Likes his knives, doesn't he?"

"Apparently. So, what does T.J. call you— Andrew or Rook?"

Rook wasn't fooled by her manner. The flower and knife had shaken her. "Sometimes Andrew and sometimes Rook."

"My deranged hiker—he links to whatever you're working on," Mac said. "It's no coincidence that you both turned up at Beanie's house at the same time." She paused a moment. "Maybe you need to talk to me. Let me in."

"Harris hasn't told us anything actionable, Mac." Rook heard the wail of sirens on her end of the connection. There wasn't one thing he liked about having to hang up, but he had no choice. "You've got to go, I know. We'll be there soon."

"It's a pink hydrangea," she said. "No more pink for me, I swear."

Even spooked, she drew on her sense of humor. She clicked off, and Rook loosened his grip on his cell phone. He filled in the gaps of his and Mackenzie's conversation for T.J., who'd hit the gas and was navigating the traffic with ease.

When they arrived at the historic house, an Arlington police cruiser had landed on the scene. Showing ID, Rook and T.J. walked over to the porch, where Mackenzie was speaking with an officer.

"When you send her flowers," T.J. muttered to Rook, nodding to the hydrangea and the knife on the porch step, "don't send pink. And no knives. Chocolate always works."

As Rook exhaled, he let out a soft curse. "The hydrangea's here in the yard. This son of a bitch waltzed right in here, cut the damn flower . . ." He swore again. "Bold."

"I'll go talk to the locals, see what I can find out," T.J. said.

Rook noticed that Mackenzie had extricated herself from the detective and was heading their way. "You don't have to make yourself scarce—"

"Yeah, I do."

He winked at Mackenzie as they passed each other. She stopped in front of Rook, her hair down, red curls hanging in her face. "I swear, I'd be less creeped out if he left me a severed squirrel's head or something straightforward like that. A flower and a knife? That's just bizarre." With both hands, she pushed back her hair, and he could see perspiration glistening on her forehead. "I'm trying to keep an open mind. It could have been anyone, really. The attack's been in the papers—"

"It wasn't anyone," Rook said.

"No. Probably not. I wish I'd been here and had another crack at him."

"Where were you?"

"House hunting with Juliet Longstreet and Ethan Brooker."

Rook knew them. "How long were you gone?"

"About two hours. He must have—I don't

know. My car wasn't here. He wasn't looking for a confrontation. He just wanted me to know he's been here, to throw me off balance." She looked back toward the porch. The crime scene guys would remove the flower and knife, test them for any trace evidence. "I'd like to hear what your FBI profilers have to say about this guy."

"He's a bold, calculating sociopath who's getting reckless," Rook speculated. "Does this incident help you remember him?"

"No. But we have a history. I just don't know what it is."

Rook touched her fingers, a subtle move that the other law enforcement officers in the vicinity wouldn't notice. "You okay?"

"Frustrated." She smiled suddenly. "Maybe it was my ghosts."

Joe Delvecchio pulled into the driveway, followed by Nate Winter and his wife, a stunning, visibly pregnant woman. Sarah Dunnemore Winter wouldn't blame ghosts for the "present" on the porch steps. Like everyone else, she'd look to the man who'd attacked Mackenzie in New Hampshire.

Rook stood aside and let Mackenzie deal with them. T.J. rejoined him, shaking his head. "I want this SOB," he said.

"Get in line."

Nate eased in next to Rook. Winter had a reputation as a serious agent, but tonight the senior deputy was at a crime scene for personal reasons. Because of his long friendship with Mackenzie, Rook thought.

"Nothing like this happened to me my first year on the job," Nate said. "Hell. She called you?"

Rook nodded.

"My uncle and I got to her father first when the saw went wild and cut him to pieces. She'd stayed with him. There was so much blood, at first we thought she was injured, too. We thought Kevin was dead. Gus found a pulse, and then we worried he wouldn't live until the ambulance got there. He's a great guy. Strong, decent. His wife Molly, too. He kept defying the expectations. Everyone was focused on him."

"Mackenzie slipped through the cracks."

"She's avoided blood and gore—her words—ever since. I thought that'd get her kicked out of the academy, if her authority issues didn't. She's not easily intimidated, in case you haven't noticed."

"I've noticed."

"She hasn't told her parents about the attack. They're in Ireland—she wouldn't want to upset them. She's not used to being on that side of things. Letting people in."

"Why are you telling me this?" Rook asked.

Nate looked out across the driveway toward his wife and Mackenzie, who were chatting together. "If Mackenzie knew where Harris Mayer was, she'd tell you. If Judge Peacham knew, she wouldn't necessarily tell Mackenzie. Or you, for that matter."

"I don't distrust Mackenzie, if that's what you're asking."

"I'm not asking anything," Nate said, then gave a polite nod. "I have to go."

Once Winter was out of earshot, T.J. gave a low whistle. "He may be a bigger hard-ass than you are, Rook."

"You want to translate what he just said?"

"He said if you break Mackenzie's heart, he's not going to forget."

Rook scoffed. "You're full of shit, T.J."

Unrepentant, his partner grinned. "I'll stick around in case you need a ride home."

"I'll need one," Rook said, half under his breath.

Within a few more minutes, most of the law enforcement officers left. T.J. gave a deliberate yawn. "My stomach's calling for a pizza with everything on it. Except anchovies. Anchovies and pepperoni just don't mix."

Rook sighed. "Two minutes."

He walked across the steamy driveway to the porch, where Mackenzie was arguing with a young uniformed officer about how she didn't need a cruiser making periodic checks on the place overnight. He didn't back down—he said they'd be checking on the property, not on her. She finally relented, likely because it was the only way she'd be rid of him. The officer took his victory and retreated.

"Kid's got a future if he can stand up to a marshal," Rook said.

Mackenzie gave him a dark look. "They're all creeped out about the hydrangea."

He had no idea if she was joking, but it was clear that no one liked the prospect of a stalker—and no one blamed the ghosts for the flower and the knife. "Everyone would relax better if you just weren't here tonight."

"Nate and Sarah offered me their guest room, but I declined. Bad enough Sarah has this place to worry about, with a baby on the way and me here attracting trouble. She doesn't need me underfoot at home."

"Come back to my place. T.J.'s starving. My nephew will be there—he's always starving. We're ordering pizza." Then Rook added, "You can have the upstairs bedroom all to yourself."

She squinted at him, clearly not sure about the idea.

"Look at it this way. Either I'm staying here or you're staying at my place. If it's not me, you know it'll be Nate, and why would you want that? He has a new house and a pregnant wife. He's a senior deputy." Rook smiled. "He's not as good-looking."

"I don't know, Rook, Nate's pretty good-looking. Of course, there's T.J. He's so good-looking he's been known to stop hearts." But she couldn't sustain her humor, and blew out a breath. "Honestly, there's no need for you to stay—"

"Then grab a toothbrush, Mac, because I'm not leaving you here alone."

She shoved both hands through her hair, then let them drop. "All right. Give me two minutes."

"Take all the time you need."

"And I'm taking my car," she said. "No way am I having Chief Delvecchio catch me getting dropped off at work in the morning by an FBI agent."

Rook could see her point. "I'll send T.J. on ahead to buy the pizzas, and I'll ride with you."

"Fine, but I'm driving."

The woman was relentless, but as Rook watched her head back into the house, he noticed a slight wobble in her steps. Tonight had gotten to her. From what he'd seen of the investigators, the hydrangea and the knife had gotten to them, too.

When they reached Rook's house, Mackenzie got to her backpack before he did, slinging it over her right shoulder and following him to the door. She'd said little in the car. He didn't know if she was more pre-occupied with what she'd found on her porch step or with the prospect of spending the night at his house.

Brian opened the door. "There you are." He ran a hand over his head, a gesture that suggested something was up. "I was just about to call you. Some guy stopped here looking for you."

Rook stepped inside, frowning at his nephew. "Some guy? Who?"

"I don't know. I asked him his name, but he wouldn't say. He just said to tell you he's sorry he missed you."

Mackenzie walked past Brian and set her backpack on the floor next to the stairs. "Can you describe him?"

"Late fifties, gray hair, well dressed." Brian shrugged, regarding her with the mix of nonchalance and curiosity only a nineteen-year-old could pull off. "What else?"

"Was he dark or fair—"

"Very fair."

"Cal Benton," Mackenzie said.

Brian obviously didn't recognize the name. "What's up? This some fed deal? Is he wanted?"

"Hang on a sec, Brian," Rook said. "Mac—"

But she'd already bolted out the door, and he charged after her, surprised she'd moved as fast as she had. She spun around to face him. "I can do more on my own. I'm not working a case."

"T.J. will be here in another minute. He'll stay with Brian. We'll go together—"

"I'm friends with these people," she said, climbing into her car.

"You're friends with Judge Peacham. Cal Benton—"

"I won't stay long." She smiled up at him. "Save me some pizza."

As she backed out of the driveway, Brian ambled out of the house and stood next to his uncle. "You can go after her if you want. I'll be fine here."

Rook shook his head. "I'll wait for T.J."

"We could always call Dad and have him intercept her."

Rook grinned at his nephew. "Now you're thinking." But he watched Mackenzie's car turn up the street, and sighed. "Mac knows what she's doing."

"You hope so," Brian said.

"Yeah. I hope so. Come on. Let's go inside, and you can tell me every word this guy said to you."

"I wrote it all down."

"No kidding?" Rook cuffed his nephew on the shoulder. "Good for you."

Twenty-Two

Mackenzie almost backed out of Bernadette's driveway two seconds after pulling into it. But the house was lit up, suggesting whoever was there—Bernadette alone, or Cal, or both of them—hadn't gone to bed yet.

By the time she climbed the steps to the side entrance, the door was open. Bernadette, barefoot in a flowing black caftan, stepped aside. "You can talk to me upstairs. I'm packing for New Hampshire. I leave in the morning." She turned, then stopped abruptly, glancing back at Mackenzie. "Stairs won't bother you, will they?"

"Not at all. Is Cal here?"

A coolness came into her eyes. "No."

Bernadette about-faced and headed down the hall, leaving Mackenzie to pull the door shut behind her and find her way to the front of the house. She took the sweeping staircase to the second floor, remembering how much she used to love to visit Bernadette in Washington—especially before Cal. Mackenzie had tried to be neutral about him, although none of Bernadette's other friends seemed to bother. Certainly no one in Cold Ridge did. He just wasn't a favorite. But everyone wanted Bernadette to be happy, and if Cal made her happy, who were they to criticize?

She had a suitcase open on the floor at the foot of her four-poster bed, the custom-made, champagne-colored comforter pulled back, as if she'd tried to sleep but had given up and decided to pack. "I'm going to drive," she said, grabbing a stack of lingerie out of the top drawer of an antique dresser. "I'd planned to fly. Gus offered to pick me up at the airport, but driving should help clear my head."

"Beanie, I don't know that driving is wise right now."

"Don't worry about me. For heaven's sake, I've been at this job for a while now, and I've never had a thing happen until . . ." She waved a hand in dismissal and dumped the lingerie into her suitcase. "Never mind."

"Until I became a federal agent, you mean."

"It doesn't matter. I'm not the least bit concerned about my own safety." She turned back to her dresser and pulled open another drawer. "But you're not here to talk about my travel arrangements, are you, Mackenzie?"

Mackenzie stood on the soft, cream-colored carpet, took in the champagne brocade drapes, the simple elegance of the room. Should she have come here, disturbed Bernadette's preparations for her vacation in New Hampshire? But Mackenzie knew better than to try to back out now. She'd never get away with it. Bernadette knew her too well and would insist on an explanation.

She didn't even try to be subtle. "Why would Cal stop at an FBI agent's house?"

"Why would Cal—what?" Bernadette spun around, cradling a trio of hiking socks. "You're talking about Andrew Rook, aren't you? Cal stopped to see him?"

"That's right. A little while ago."

She narrowed her eyes. "And why would this be of any concern to you, might I ask?"

"Beanie . . ." Mackenzie fought to find the right words. "Talk to Cal."

"I talked to Cal from the day we met three years ago until the day our divorce was finalized eight weeks ago. Now, I only talk with him when I have no other choice. I'm done, Mackenzie. I can't do it anymore. I married the man I thought he was—maybe the man he wanted to be. That's over now. We've gone our separate ways. When I get back here in September, at most I might run into him at a cocktail party."

"Talk to him, anyway."

"I'll change the locks on the house if that'll make you more comfortable."

"That's not it."

She tossed the socks into her suitcase. "Then what is it, Mackenzie? What would make you barge into my house at this hour? Do you *want* to upset me?"

"Harris Mayer and Cal know each other. Harris has disappeared—"

Bernadette straightened, adopted her courtroom manner. "Choose your words carefully, Mackenzie. 'Disappeared' is a rather strong one."

"Taken off, then." Mackenzie couldn't pretend that she could dismiss the friendship between her family and Bernadette and adopt some kind of manufactured objectivity. "I just don't want you to get hurt. You're one of the kindest, most generous people I know."

"And that makes me weak and stupid?"

It sure didn't make her easy, but Mackenzie kept to her point. "No, it makes people like me care about you."

Bernadette sank onto the edge of the bed, her eyes filling with tears. "I'm sorry." Her voice was barely a whisper. "I'm so sorry."

"Sorry for what? You haven't done anything wrong."

"I just know—oh, Mackenzie. I just know I've brought this awful mess onto your shoulders. That man. That disgusting man who attacked you . . ." She shook her head, using the back of one hand to wipe her tears. "I just know it's my fault that he was on my property."

"If you know anything specific—"

"*Damn* it, Mackenzie, I know what to do. I *don't* know anything."

Mackenzie almost smiled. "Okay."

Bernadette sighed through her tears. "I

swear you are the most resilient person I've ever encountered. I didn't mean to bite your head off." She got to her feet, waved a hand at her suitcase. "I'm not even sure what I've packed. Scarves and mittens, for all I know."

"I should go," Mackenzie said.

"If I see Cal before I leave, I'll talk to him. Promise. But right now I don't have a clue why he'd turn up at Andrew Rook's house."

When she returned to her car, Mackenzie fought an urge to head north, back to New Hampshire. She could fulfill everyone's expectations and just drop out of the Marshals Service. Go write her dissertation. Carine had offered her the use of her studio, a tiny place just up the road from the 1830s brick house where she, her husband and their baby lived.

"You're going to pass out, Deputy Stewart. Think of what I'm going to do then."

How long would she be looking over her shoulder for this man? Moving back to New Hampshire wouldn't solve anything. He'd still be out there, and she'd still have to wonder when he'd jump out of the bushes again, when he'd call her in the middle of the night, when he'd leave her some creepy present.

What she had to do was find him.

She took two wrong turns on her way back to Rook's house. *Denial,* she thought when she got there, raising her hand to knock on his front door. But it opened, and he stood there in jeans and a T-shirt, looking so damn handsome she had to give herself a mental slap. Falling for him all over again wouldn't help her find her attacker.

"Save me any pizza?" she asked.

T.J. was at the kitchen table with Brian Rook, who immediately excused himself and headed upstairs. He referred to his uncle as Andrew. Not Andy or Drew—just Andrew—and Mackenzie supposed she'd gotten herself into a bad habit, calling him Rook.

He put a slice of pizza on a plate and handed it to her at the table. "It's warm, not hot."

"It'll be fine. Thanks."

T.J. pushed back his chair but didn't get up. "We got hold of Cal Benton and talked to him. We'll talk more tomorrow. He apologized for not giving Brian his name."

"Did he say why he decided to stop here?" Mackenzie asked, taking a bite of her pizza. She hadn't realized how hungry she was. It seemed like a week ago that she, Juliet and

Ethan had stopped for a quick bite before checking out house listings in semiaffordable neighborhoods.

"He said it didn't occur to him that coming here would be a problem." T.J. shrugged. "He was married to a federal judge. He didn't think twice about knocking on Andrew's door."

"Was Brian unnerved?"

Rook came into the kitchen and shook his head, taking the chair between his partner and Mackenzie at the round table. "Brian doesn't have nerves, I swear. He could have called his father or one of his other uncles—or me—if he was scared. He wasn't."

"Cal's not a particularly scary guy. What did he want?"

The two men were silent. Finally, T.J. said, "Harris Mayer knocked on our door about a month ago insisting he could help us break open a case involving blackmail, extortion, fraud and bribery. Money exchanging hands illegally among rich Washington types. People threatened with exposure of secrets."

"Threatened with violence?" Mackenzie asked.

Rook answered. "Harris hasn't indicated violence is a factor. We've met a few times, but he's always vague. It's been hard to gauge whether he just wants to be part of the action again and is making up stuff to get our attention, or if he's for real."

"He likes pulling people's strings," T.J. added. "Pulling our strings—he knows we're not going to hurt him. That doesn't mean someone else won't."

"If whoever's behind the blackmail and whatnot realized he was talking to the FBI . . ." Mackenzie didn't finish; she didn't need to. "A good reason to disappear. What's Cal's involvement?"

"We don't know," Rook said. "He and Harris met through Judge Peacham and have gotten together a few times in recent months. By itself, that's nothing. Put it together with everything else that's gone on in the past week, and who knows."

Mackenzie thought a moment, pictured the man leaping out of the brush next to Bernadette's shed. His colorless, soulless eyes. "Do you think my guy—the man who attacked me and presumably left me the little gift on my porch steps—is part of this blackmail and extortion scheme?"

Rook's gaze stayed on her, but T.J. was the one who spoke. "We don't know."

"Bernadette?"

"The same," T.J. said.

"I've known Beanie Peacham all my life, and I can remember Harris coming to the lake with his wife and kids when I was nine or ten. I attended Beanie and Cal's wedding." Mackenzie sighed, no longer in the mood for pizza. "Well, Rook, no wonder you dumped me."

She thought she saw T.J. smile, but he quickly got to his feet. "I wish we could have happened along tonight just as this SOB was leaving that knife and flower for you, Mackenzie. Whether he's mixed up with our business with Harris or not, the guy's a creep. We'll get him."

"Damn straight." Mackenzie smiled. "Thanks, T.J. Maybe the neighbors saw something that'll help. The house is tucked back on the property, but—well, who knows. I'm just glad Sarah wasn't there."

At the mention of Nate's wife, T.J. visibly gritted his teeth, his look sober. "A bunch of crazy-assed vigilantes tried to take Sarah out in the spring. Something about that house, I swear. Time to improve security there, if you ask me."

Mackenzie remembered the uproar in the

spring. Nate, Juliet Longstreet and under-cover marshals from California had been in-volved. She'd just started her training and couldn't wait to get her first duty assignment. But she said, "I don't suppose security will help much with Sarah's ghosts."

T.J. rolled his eyes but managed a grin. "I'm out of here. See you two tomorrow."

After T.J. left, Rook poured Mackenzie a whiskey and set it in front of her. "You look like you could use a drink, Deputy Stewart."

"A couple sips, anyway." She picked up the glass, staring into the amber liquid. "I want to find the bastard, Andrew. And Harris. And Cal—"

"It's not your fault he showed up here. Just do your job, Mac. That's all anyone's going to ask of you."

She took a swallow of the whiskey, re-membering her attacker's colorless eyes. She set the glass down and looked at Rook, on his feet now, leaning back against the counter. It was a comfortable house, with homey remnants of his grandmother and the masculine touches he'd added.

And a nephew upstairs, she thought.

"Leaving the knife was this bastard's way

of telling me he could have killed me last Friday."

"He didn't kill you."

"Maybe he could have and was just—I don't know."

"Just letting you think you'd kicked his ass?"

"I disarmed him. If I'd kicked his ass, he'd be in jail right now instead of wherever he is." She took another swallow of the whiskey, then asked abruptly, "Where did you do your first assignment?"

"South Florida."

She kept her eyes on him. "Did you have doubts?"

"I come from a family of cops. Doubts were never my problem." He smiled at her. "The opposite. I was pretty cocky. I was always in a hurry, didn't like to question myself."

She drank more of the whiskey, pointing the glass at him. "You're still cocky, Rook."

"But I'm more measured. Mac, you didn't hesitate last Friday. If you'd hesitated, you wouldn't be getting stitches out tomorrow. Everyone who knows what you did realizes that you'll have their back in a fight. You won't run when the action gets real." He shrugged. "Armed and in your marshal's duds, you'd be tough to beat."

She got up and brought her glass to the sink, turning to him. "Thank you—and T.J., too. Calling you after I saw the hydrangea and the knife seemed like the thing to do."

"I'm glad." Rook touched her mouth, looked into her eyes and smiled. "You're beat, Mac."

He kissed her softly, without any of last night's hunger and fire. But the longing was there, she knew. She could feel it in herself, too.

He smiled. "Get some sleep."

The kiss, his touch—the few sips of whiskey—only added to her overall sense that she was on the verge of spinning out of control. She grabbed her backpack, grateful when Rook didn't follow her up to the guest room.

Brian Rook met her in the hall. "I put some towels out for you in the bathroom and, uh, cleaned up a little."

"Thanks."

He shrugged, heading off to his room. He was obviously shaken by Cal's visit and the reaction to it—and he had doubts. Tough to admit to doubts about anything to an uncle as confident as Andrew Rook. Mackenzie started to follow Brian and talk to him, but stopped herself. The kid was nineteen. Doubts, even for a Rook, were probably a good thing.

Twenty-Three

When she heard Cal stumbling into the house, Bernadette threw off her covers and ran downstairs, pleased she'd had the good sense to wear her L.L. Bean pajamas to bed.

She confronted her ex-husband as he poured himself a large glass of Scotch in the kitchen. She remained in the doorway, arms crossed on her chest, but she'd never been able to intimidate Cal. Whatever his faults, she'd always admired that about him. "Where's Harris?"

"Harris Mayer? I have no idea." Cal took a long drink, eyeing her with a frankness that she used to find appealing, sexy even. "He's your friend, not mine."

"He's taken off."

"So? He's a grown man. He can take off without telling anyone."

She could see she wasn't going to get anywhere asking Cal about Harris directly. "Why did you stop at Andrew Rook's house tonight?"

He faltered only slightly. "Nothing you need to concern yourself about."

"No? Where are you right now, Cal? You're in *my* house. I have a right to know if you're mixed up with something that's going to backfire on me."

"You've done nothing. You're pure, Bernadette."

"Do you think it'll matter if I've done nothing and you have? Do you think *anyone* will care? Appearances—"

"Appearances won't land you in prison." He gulped the Scotch and banged the glass on the counter, refilled it. "I'm going to bed. I'll be out of here this weekend. Then you can start pretending we were never married."

"I've already started," she said, regretting her acidic comment immediately, if only because it would put him more on the defensive. "Cal—please. I don't want to argue with you. If you're in trouble, you know what to do. You'ro a capable attorney."

He gave a bitter laugh. "Thanks for that, Judge."

"What aren't you telling me?" She stepped toward him. "What's happened to you, Cal?"

"Do you believe in the devil?"

Her heart jumped. "What?"

He abandoned whatever he'd started to say. "You'll be gone in the morning before I get up. Have a good trip to New Hampshire." He managed a small smile. "Say hi to the loons for me."

"Cal—"

"I don't want anything to happen to you, Bernadette. I never have."

He walked away from her, taking his drink with him. She debated following him, but what good would another fight do? He was stubborn and secretive by nature, qualities that had their advantages, as well as their liabilities. But she'd never been able to penetrate the hard shell that he'd developed to protect the most vulnerable parts of him, where his insecurities lived. She'd gotten tired of trying. If he gave in to his compulsions instead of rising above them, what could she do?

Get out of range when they backfire, she thought.

But she knew better. She adhered to the judicial code of ethics as strictly as any of her colleagues, but that wouldn't help her when it came to appearances. If Cal was in trouble, she had no idea if their divorce would protect her from public backlash, or if she'd end up like Harris Mayer, disgraced and ostracized.

No charges were ever brought against Harris, but that didn't make him innocent, she reminded herself. Regardless of his personal culpability, he'd had a hand in some shady dealings.

Most people she knew appreciated her unwillingness to completely cut off an old friend, even if they didn't understand it. But would they understand if she'd unwittingly paired Harris and Cal, and they'd cooked up some fraudulent deals?

"You're getting ahead of yourself," she said aloud, looking around at her empty kitchen. Cal would be gone when she returned from New Hampshire. She'd have her life back. She smiled suddenly, surprising herself. "Thank heaven."

She headed upstairs, replacing visions of unpleasant imagined headlines with real memories of the lake, the mountains, the feel of cold dew on her feet on a lute summer morning, memories, she thought, of home.

Twenty-Four

Mackenzie noticed a fat spider scurry in front of Cal Benton's shoe into the lush greenery of the "natural" courtyard of his condominium complex on the Potomac. Cal had called her on her cell phone, reaching her just after she'd had her stitches removed. He'd asked her to meet him privately as soon as possible. Since she'd allowed for more time than she'd ended up needing for her appointment, and had her own reasons for talking to him, she'd agreed and drove straight to his condo. He'd met her in the lobby and brought her out to the courtyard.

He was visibly tense, sweat already glistening on his upper lip as he stood on the cobblestone walk in the shade of a clump birch. The air was dead still. Nothing but the spider moved. A perpendicular walk led to an air-conditioned glass breezeway that connected the main building with the parking garage. Cal was undeterred, apparently, by the oppressive heat, dark clouds and rumble of thunder.

The spider disappeared, and Mackenzie tilted her head and gave Cal a long look. He was dressed casually, appropriate for a blistering Friday in August—not to mention his impending move. "Not going to give me the grand tour of your new condo?"

"Another time, perhaps."

Meaning never, she thought. "Bernadette's on her way to New Hampshire?"

"I assume so. She left before I got up this morning." He nodded to the sky. "I hope she can make it to the lake before this line of storms reaches her."

"She's been making that trip for a lot of years."

He lowered his eyes. "Yes, she has. Mackenzie—I'll be blunt." He raised his gaze to her, his expression serious, but she thought she detected a measure of embarrassment, too. "I have no intention of telling Bernadette about what you saw earlier this summer. If you weren't in Washington and seeing her regularly, you wouldn't consider telling her, either."

"That's not true—"

"It's not that you feel she needs to know as much as it is you don't like keeping something from her. You're worried what she'll think of you if she finds out you knew about this situation and said nothing."

Mackenzie didn't let him get to her. "The attack on me at the lake changes the equation. It happened on Beanie's land, and that puts her under scrutiny. The police, the FBI, the marshals—reporters, even—will look into her background for any evidence she has a history with this man. The longer they can't find him, the more likely her life at the lake will go under the microscope."

"That means my life, too," Cal said quietly. "I hadn't looked at it that way."

"Cal, she can't find out about your brunette from the police or reporters. She needs to find out from you."

"You saw me with a woman with dark hair?"

"Yes—shoulder-length dark hair. I was canoeing. You two were on the screen porch. There's no need to—" She broke off midsentence and grimaced. "Oh, hell, Cal. She wasn't tho only one. There have been other women."

He took in a sharp breath through his nose. "You have no right to judge me."

"Just stating the facts."

"I'm normally not that promiscuous," Cal said. "The divorce affected me more than I thought it would. I guess I was sowing my wild oats ahead of the official paperwork. I'm hardly the first man to give in to . . ." He trailed off, waving a hand as if Mackenzie was free to finish his sentence for him.

She wished the spider would poke back up out of the decorative grasses and crawl across Cal's foot. "I wish I'd gone canoeing someplace else that day. If you believe word of your affair—or affairs—is about to come out, will you at least tell Beanie before it does?"

He nodded. "I will. Right now, it's not my biggest concern—or yours, I would think." Clearing his throat, he reached into a side pocket of his pants and withdrew a folded sheet of paper. He opened it carefully, then showed it to her, revealing the police sketch of the man who'd attacked her a week ago. "Is this a decent likeness?"

"Except for the eyes," she said. "It's hard to capture just how soulless and eerie they were. Why? Do you recognize him?"

He flipped the paper over on the fold, as if he wanted that face staring up at him. "I don't know." Cal seemed to regain some of his natural arrogance. "When I first saw the sketch last week, nothing hit me. But I keep thinking about it."

"Keep thinking what, Cal?"

He shrugged. "I don't know. I can't put my finger on it." He thrust the sketch at her. "Do you suspect he's one of the people Bernadette's helped?"

Mackenzie took the paper but didn't unfold it. She didn't need to. "I have no idea."

"You still haven't been able to place where you've seen this man before?"

"Not yet, no."

"Strange, isn't it?" Cal he didn't wait for her to reply. "I'll call the detectives in New Hampshire and let them know he seems familiar to me, too. Maybe it'll help, maybe it won't."

"I'll follow up and let them know we've talked."

He gave her a cool look. "Of course. If Bernadette did help this man, it's more likely it was before I was in her life. She's become more circumspect. I keep telling her she doesn't need to engage in direct charity. She can give money to organizations and lend her credibility to her favorite causes." He took out a folded handkerchief from his back pocket and blotted the sweat above his lip. "As she did with the literacy fund-raiser last week."

Mackenzie tried not to show just how irritating and condescending she found him. "Beanie's a generous person."

"It's odd, don't you think, for someone who's as tight with a dollar as she is?"

"Makes perfect sense to me. Charity isn't always about money."

"That's because you're from Cold Ridge, too. You all think alike up there." He glanced at his watch. "I have to go."

"Cal—"

"Thank you for coming."

"You asked me here just to tell me you weren't going to level with Beanie?"

He didn't answer, simply shot up the walk toward the breezeway. Mackenzie, feeling the ninety-plus degree heat herself, stepped into the shade he'd vacated and debated whether to follow him and push him for more answers. Why he'd stopped at Rook's house last night. What he knew about Harris Mayer's whereabouts.

But she heard footsteps behind her, and when she turned, she saw Rook and T.J. making their way up the walk from the lobby door in their FBI suits. She dropped onto a stone bench.

"Special Agent Kowalski, Special Agent Rook," she said, stretching out her legs. "If you're looking for Cal Benton, he went that way." She pointed toward the breezeway. "He's got about a minute's head start. He must have seen you, because we were having this nice conversation about three-legged puppies and—"

"I'll go," T.J. said, heading off at a light run.

Rook sat next to Mackenzie on the bench. "You look hot, Deputy Stewart."

"I am hot. Cal hogged the shade."

"Get your stitches out?"

"I did. Before you know it, I'll be able to run, jump and shoot without pain." Feeling sweaty, she looked up at the sky, but it was unchanged, no sign of the front moving through. "Cal's trying to manipulate me. I can't figure out why."

"To save his own skin, probably."

"I think he enjoys it." She glanced at Rook, who didn't seem to be sweating at all. "Did the doorman tell you we were out here?"

"You should have seen T.J.'s face when he mentioned a redhead," Rook said.

"Cal called me. I didn't just turn up. Why are you two here?"

"To follow up on last night. Time to get some answers from Benton." Rook settled back on the bench. "I'd have told you T.J. and I were headed over here if you hadn't sneaked out this morning while I was in the shower."

She shrugged, pushing back a wave of heat that had nothing to do with the temperature in the courtyard. "You didn't have the kind of doughnuts I like."

"I didn't have any doughnuts."

"That's what I'm saying." She pointed toward the ornamental grasses. "There are spiders in there. Big ones. Of course, you're from this area, so you're probably used to them."

"Mac—"

"Cal wanted to talk to me about a private matter."

Rook leaned closer. "What private matter?"

She told him about Cal and his woman-of-the-moment at the lake, and her conclusion that there'd been other incidents. Rook listened without interrupting, and when she finished, she said, "It's sordid behavior, but not illegal."

"Did you recognize the woman he was with?" Rook asked.

"No."

"How long has Cal known you saw them together?"

"Since I moved to Washington—about two weeks after I saw them. I considered pretending I hadn't seen anything, but I couldn't do it. I didn't trust him not to raise the stakes. I figured at least if he knew he'd been caught, he'd knock it off."

Rook didn't respond right away.

"What?" she asked.

"Are you sure you didn't feel violated yourself? You grew up on that lake. Judge Peacham's been a strong figure in your life—"

"Sure. I felt violated, too. So?" But she pressed ahead, not wanting to delve into her childhood on the lake. She opened up the sketch. "Cal now thinks our guy looks familiar."

"Do you believe him?" Rook asked.

Mackenzie shrugged "I don't know. It could be more manipulation, but it doesn't make sense that he'd lie. It doesn't make sense he'd take a woman to Beanie's lake house, either."

"Why not? It's quiet, isolated. Your parents are in Ireland. Most of the other people out there would be tourists. And if you like the idea of secretly sticking it to your soon-to-be-ex-wife—"

"That's a sick way of thinking."

"Who else might know about Cal's flings?" Rook asked.

"Gus, maybe. He looks after the place when Beanie's not there. But I haven't said anything to him—to anyone except Cal, and now you."

T.J. returned, not even remotely winded. "He took off. We can try him at his office."

"He wasn't dressed for the office," Mackenzie said. "Of course, it's Friday. I suppose he could stop in. He didn't tell me where he was going."

"I'll wait in the lobby, where it's air-conditioned and there's cover if there's a tornado," T.J. said.

The bench was starting to feel very hard, but Mackenzie figured she'd let Rook and T.J. be on their way, then be on hers. But Rook didn't move. She glanced at him. "Thinking?"

"Yeah. About last weekend at the lake. Did you put me in the room Cal and his brunette used?"

"I don't know which room they used. I assume they used the downstairs bedroom." In other words, Bernadette's room. Mackenzie grinned at Rook and said, "I put you in the room that gets the bats."

After T.J. and Rook left, Mackenzie returned to the lobby of Cal's building, where the doorman, who had to be at least seventy, gave a low whistle. "You better take a few minutes and cool off."

"I'm red?"

"Tomato-red."

She made a face, although she wasn't surprised. During training, she was known for getting red and splotchy during physical exertion. No matter how fit she was, heat had a way of turning her red. "It's about a million degrees out there."

"Yes, ma'am." He seemed untroubled. "Need some water?"

"I've got some in the car." She opened up the sketch and smoothed it out on the desk in front of him. "Any chance you've seen this man?"

He studied the drawing. "I don't think so. Maybe."

"Take your time," Mac said.

"Does he live here?"

"You tell me."

But the doorman frowned, straightening. "Are you a cop?"

"I'm a federal agent." She showed him her credentials and gave him her name. "You're . . ."

"Charlie. Charlie West, ma'am." He glanced back at the sketch, rubbing his chin with one hand. "What'd he do?"

"He knifed two women in New Hampshire."

His hand dropped from his chin. "We don't have anyone like that around here, Agent Stewart."

"Deputy Stewart, sir. Just focus on the face. Is it familiar?"

"I don't know." He held up the paper. "Mind if I keep this?"

"Not at all. But if you see this man, don't approach him. Call the police. You should consider him armed and dangerous." She handed him her card. "If you have any questions or think of anything, call me, okay?"

"Yes, ma'am, I will."

"Do you know why Cal Benton insisted on meeting me in the sweltering courtyard instead of up in his condo?"

The doorman grinned, but quickly turned serious. "He had painters coming this morning, but he canceled them. I was supposed to let them into his place. They were on my list."

"When did he cancel them?"

"I found out this morning—early. Right after I got in at seven."

"He called you?"

"He came down here."

"Was he alone?" Mackenzie asked.

"Yes, ma'am, he was alone."

She thanked Charlie West for his time and headed out into the heat, just as thunder cracked and lightning flashed over the river. She ducked into her car, leaving the door

open to the breeze, and dialed Joe Delvecchio's number. When he answered, she told
him everything that had transpired since her
arrival at the condominium complex, leaving
out only her exchange with Rook about the
room with the bats.

"I figured I'd call you first," she said.

"You didn't call me first, Stewart. You
called me last. You've already talked to Benton, Rook, Kowalski and the damn doorman."

"I haven't talked to Detective Mooney in
New Hampshire yet."

"Don't let me hold you up," he said.

She ignored his sarcasm. "Someone
should show the sketch to other people in
Cal's building, just in case the doorman did
recognize him but isn't sure. Another worker
or resident might be more certain, one way
or another. I'd do it, but I'm personally involved."

"You think?" He sighed. "I'm on it."

"For the record, Cal Benton's flings might
not have anything at all to do with the attack
on me."

"Deputy, don't second-guess yourself. The
more pieces we have, the better. They won't
all have a place in the puzzle. That's nothing
new. Are you on your way back here?"

"Give me an hour," she said, fastening her seat belt.

"It's a ten-minute drive."

"Traffic."

One beat, two beats.

Mackenzie pulled her car door shut. "I need to make a stop. It's personal."

"It was personal when you went to see Benton, too." But Delvechhio relented. "All right. An hour."

She didn't know if his modest acquiescence was a sign of trust or if he was just giving her enough rope to hang herself. Either way, she was committed now. She started her car, cranked up the air-conditioning and headed toward Massachusetts Avenue just as a fat raindrop hit her windshield.

Twenty-Five

Mackenzie had her own key to Bernadette's house off Embassy Row. She'd had it since college, when Bernadette had given it to her before setting off on a six-week trip to Asia. *"Come when you want. Just no wild parties."* As if bookish Mackenzie were known for wild parties.

When no one answered the door, she let herself in, announcing her presence. "Hello—anyone home? It's Mackenzie."

Thunder rumbled, and with the darkened sky, the light in the house was more like dusk than late morning. Before she'd left for the lake, Bernadette had obviously turned down the air-conditioning. Never mind Cal, Mackenzie thought. Of course, he could always turn it up, but he'd notice the gesture—the reminder that it wasn't his house and he was no longer welcome there.

As generous as Bernadette was, she was not a pushover.

Mackenzie made her way to the guest suite on the first floor. The door was unlocked and the drapes were still shut. "Cal?" she called, just in case.

The covers were pulled back and half on the floor, as if he'd passed a bad night. She checked the bathroom. Towels on the floor, shaving materials scattered around the sink. The mirror was splattered with dried soap. Would he clean up before he moved out? Or just leave the place a mess as a final thumb-in-the-eye for Bernadette?

The two of them, Mackenzie thought. Bernadette was a role model in so many ways, but not so much when it came to relationships. She volleyed between being too forgiving and too unforgiving, confusing herself and the men in her life. She'd never found anyone who really understood her—

her keen intelligence, her drive, her generosity, her contradictory nature. But she never expected to, either.

Mackenzie saw nothing in Cal's room that suggested he was the victim or perpetrator of blackmail, or knew where Harris Mayer or her attacker were. Nothing that suggested he was in any trouble at all. From his living quarters, Mackenzie could see a man in a hurry, perhaps. And agitated. He was a busy attorney in the midst of moving, and he had her on his case about his brunette at the lake.

She ventured into Bernadette's study. Forbidden territory. Bernadette hated anyone trespassing in her space, but not so much that she kept the door locked. Files, yes. Her computer was password protected, but Mackenzie checked just to be sure. No sensitive files related to Bernadette's work as a U.S. district court judge were out in the open.

Was *she* a victim of blackmail?

Not a perpetrator, Mackenzie thought. That was beyond the realm of possibility. Bernadette was in the position to know other people's secrets, but she didn't have the temperament—or the skill—to act on them for her own profit.

And what would she have to hide?

Her friendship with Harris was out in the open. She'd had little to do with him in the five years since his public disgrace, but she hadn't abandoned him entirely. Since he'd gone to the FBI, the blackmail, extortion, fraud and whatever else he'd been whispering about to Rook had a federal interest. Harris was a former judge. He would know. He wouldn't need Bernadette's advice. But he would want it anyway.

"Breaking and entering, Mac?"

She spun around at Rook's voice. He was leaning in the study door, as if he'd been there awhile, his dark eyes leveled on her. She shrugged. "I'm here to feed the cat."

"There is no cat."

"I could have sworn Bernadette said she'd gotten a cat. I have a key." She held it up for him to see. "We seem to be on the same wavelength this morning."

"I stopped to see if Cal was here."

"He's not. Did you check his office?"

"He didn't go in. He told his assistant he had a client emergency. He doesn't answer his cell phone."

"Is T.J. with you?"

"No."

Rook's mood was difficult to read.

Mackenzie glanced around the study, which was dominated by Bernadette's surprisingly simple desk. She had an ergonomically correct chair and glass-front bookcases that ran along an entire wall. Law texts and art history picture books were shoved in among paperback Regency romances she read for relaxation, and bird books, hiking books.

Several photo albums were scattered on the floor in front of one of the bookcases. Mackenzie squatted down and opened one to pictures of Bernadette and Harris at the lake.

"Those were taken awhile ago," Rook said, standing over Mackenzie.

She looked up at him. "You FBI types must get more training in being stealthy."

"It's not that difficult when someone's preoccupied."

"I remember this visit," she said, pointing to the pictures. "It was the summer between my junior and senior years in college. I had a part-time internship at a local museum and a job cleaning rooms at one of the inns in town. Bernadette had my parents and me over for dinner, and I remember how fascinated I was listening to her and Harris talk. He's a smart man."

"Judge Peacham must have been devastated when he let it all get away from him."

"She was." Mackenzie shut the album and rose, feeling the stiffness of the healing cut in her side. So many questions would be answered by now if she'd been able to hang on to her attacker. "She worried he'd commit suicide in the beginning. I was here once when he called her. It was right after the scandal broke. I was in graduate school—I was down here for research, Harris was drunk, angry at himself at having been exposed. He couldn't see that he'd done anything wrong, legally or ethically. Beanie convinced him to tell her where he was."

"Where?"

"A rooming house. It was some kind of secret hideout for him. He'd go there and indulge his dark side, I guess. I went with Beanie to collect him. She dropped him off at his house in Georgetown and gave him an ultimatum—never again."

Rook glanced down at the shut album. "Did she keep that promise?"

"As far as I know." Mackenzie stepped past him, but turned as she reached the door. "Would you like to check out the rooming house? I hadn't thought of it until now. I don't know if Harris still uses it."

"Can you find it?"

"I think so, If I can't, I can call Beanie. She'll remember where It is."

Rook considered a moment. Outside, Bernadette's tall shade trees swayed in the wind, and rain lashed the windows. Finally, he said, "We'll take my car."

Mackenzie nodded. "All right." As she started out of the study, she smiled back at him. "Try not to let the cat out when we leave."

She thought he might have cracked a smile, but she wasn't sure, which, she realized, was part of the fun of being around him. But she couldn't think in those terms right now. She had to focus on the job at hand.

"He took the place for a month." The superintendent, a wiry, middle-aged man with sparse tufts of close-cropped hair, had led Rook and Mackenzie to an ell off the rundown building. "That's the most he ever takes it for. He comes and goes. He don't call himself Harris Mayer, though. Harry Morrison. Pays in cash."

Rook stood on the sidewalk behind the

super. The rain had stopped, but thunder still rumbled in the distance. "When did you see him last?"

"A week ago. Maybe more." He stuck the key in the door, shook his head. "Hear that? Air-conditioning. He keeps it going full blast. His choice—he pays the bills." He unlocked the door, pushed it open, then jumped back. "Oh. My goodness, my goodness."

Rook drew his weapon and saw that Mackenzie had done the same. He instructed the superintendent to move back onto the sidewalk and gave the door a kick to open it wider.

The worn wood floor of a small entry was splattered with dried blood. It was plainly blood. Careful of where he stepped, Rook entered the studio, immediately recognizing a smell that air-conditioning couldn't suppress.

He glanced at Mackenzie, right behind him. "Mac, this isn't going to be good. You've never—"

"I'm okay, Rook."

"You know Harris."

A tightness around her eyes betrayed her emotion, but she gave a curt nod. "So do you. Let's just do this."

They moved into the adjoining room, the

furnishings threadbare and cheap but serviceable. Ancient air conditioners in a front window and a window in the kitchenette clunked and groaned.

"There," Mackenzie said, nodding to the floor in front of a shut door. "More blood."

She stood to the side, and Rook pushed open the door.

The smell was worse. There was blood everywhere.

Harris Mayer was sprawled in the old bathtub, his body partially covered with a flowered shower curtain that had been ripped from the rod.

"Knife wounds," Mackenzie said from the doorway.

Rook looked back at her. "They're not self-inflicted. He's been here awhile. Days, not hours." He shook his head and grimaced. "Hell."

She didn't respond, just spun around without a word and bolted. Rook didn't follow her and he couldn't do anything for Harris. Whatever his flaws he hadn't deserved this. Rook returned to the main room and checked the rear exit next to the kitchenette, but it was secure. He got out his cell phone and made the calls he needed to. The D.C. police. His superiors. T. J. Kowalski.

T.J. was to the point. "Mackenzie led you to him?"

"Just get here."

"On my way."

When Rook returned to the street, Mackenzie was talking to the superintendent. Her skin was grayish, but she was rallying after the shock of finding Harris. Already, he could hear a siren. Cruisers would arrive first, with D.C. detectives not far behind. Harris's murder fell under their jurisdiction.

Rook stood close to Mackenzie. "Anyone you need to call?"

She nodded. He still had his phone out and handed it to her. Her hands shook slightly. "I got sick to my stomach," she said as she dialed. "Bet I wouldn't have if I hadn't been on antibiotics." She cleared her throat. "Chief? Yeah, it's me. It's not a good scene here." She'd called him on the way to the rooming house and now gave him the facts of what she and Rook had found. She spoke crisply, without emotion. But when she disconnected, she tilted her head back and exhaled at the sky. "I should have thought of this place sooner."

A fresh breeze stirred, the storm quickly blowing out the heat and humidity—the stink of exhaust fumes, garbage and dog excrement. That no one had smelled the body in the studio wasn't a huge surprise. And if someone had and not reported it? Again, no big surprise.

"I didn't know," the superintendent said, repeating his mantra about minding his own business.

"Did you see anyone with Mr. Mayer?" Rook asked.

"No, sir. I mind my own business."

The first cruiser stopped in front of the building, with T.J. right behind it, his grim expression underlining the stark reality of the scene in the seedy studio. Rook had quickly adjusted his thinking. J. Harris Mayer, his would-be informant, wasn't hiding at the beach. He was dead.

Twenty-Six

Bernadette wasn't surprised to find Gus's truck in her driveway when she arrived at the lake. The weather had delayed her, and it would be like him to make sure she got home alive. As she got out of her car, she could feel the stiffness from the long drive in her lower back, her right hip.

Getting old, she thought, welcoming the feel of the cool early evening air, freshened by the passing front. A stiff breeze blew through the trees. She could smell the sharpness of wet pine needles and hear birds all around the lake, twittering and fluttering now that the storm was over.

She found Gus down on the dock, the wood soft and wet under her driving shoes. The lake was choppy, churned up by the wind. "My cell phone died or I'd have called," she said. "I pulled over during the worst of the storm and had coffee and pie." She smiled and added, "Peach pie."

Gus eyed her in that frank, uncompromising way he had. "I almost called the marshals on you."

Bernadette's heart jumped at his seriousness. She knew him so well. She remembered the tears and anger and hope she and her friends had felt when he'd left for Vietnam. They'd thought they understood the world, but they'd understood nothing. He didn't write during the months he was gone. But she didn't write, either, and only years later did she recognize her fault in that omission. She'd simply tried not to think about Gus Winter and what he was doing, where he was. And when he came back and kept to himself, hiking, working, she'd pushed ahead with her own life and left him to his. Then came his brother and sister-in-law's deaths, a tragedy so impossible to imagine that it paralyzed everyone—everyone except Gus.

"Gus," she whispered. "What's happened?"

"Harris Mayer is dead. Mackenzie and Andrew Rook found him earlier today."

"Harris? How?" Bernadette tried to grasp what Gus had just said, and pictured Harris, with his bow ties and wingtips, his patrician manner, his compulsions. "I can't believe it. Did he have a heart attack? It wasn't—" She paused to catch her breath. "Gus, was Harris murdered?"

Gus wasn't one to dance around a point. "He was knifed to death."

Bernadette heard herself gasp, but she couldn't speak. She stared out at the water, spotting two loons near the opposite shore. They were territorial birds, the only pair on the relatively small lake. They'd had babies in June, and she'd taken delight, as always, watching them ride along on their parents' backs.

I just want to watch the loons.

"Beanie?"

Years in the courtroom had accustomed her to suppressing her emotions, but she could feel her throat tighten. "Harris got such a kick out of the loons. He and his wife would sit out here for the longest time. I never had the patience." She blinked back tears and turned to Gus, who didn't seem to have moved at all since she'd arrived. She tried to pull herself together. "Things change. Harris was flawed, troubled, brilliant, selfish . . ."

"I'm sorry, Beanie."

Gus's simple statement ripped right through the shield she was trying to put up around her emotions. Tears spilled down her cheeks. She wiped them away quickly, turning from him. "Who told you?"

"Nate called. Mackenzie and Rook found Harris at a rooming house in a rough section of Washington."

Bernadette nodded. "I know which one. Mackenzie and I—she was with me when I went to rescue him one day. She must have remembered. Is that what Nate told you?"

"Yes."

"Harris was a friend, and he called me for help. I picked him up and took him home, and I never did it again. He never asked, so it was easy to just . . . to just walk away." She turned to Gus. "Do the police have a suspect?"

He shook his head. "Nate asked if I'd seen Cal."

"Cal? What? Is he a suspect?"

"I just said—"

"I know what you just said." She immediately regretted her sharp tone. A strong breeze brought out goose bumps on her bare arms, and she shivered. "You've never liked Cal."

Gus shrugged. "I don't have to like him. I'm not the one who married him."

"You didn't approve—"

"Was I supposed to?" He didn't raise his voice. "He's out of your life now. Maybe it's time you stopped looking after him."

Bernadette grabbed Gus's arm just above the elbow and squeezed hard. "Gus, what aren't you telling me?"

"Beanie . . ."

"We've known each other since we were kids," she said. "I was here when you went off to Vietnam. I was here when Harry and Jill were killed. I'm not a stranger. I know you." She dropped her hand from his arm. "If there's something you need to tell me, just do it."

He squinted out at the lake, the loons gone now, as if they'd sensed the tension across the water on the dock and had taken cover. Without preamble, Gus said, "Cal brought women to the house."

"Here?"

"Yeah, Beanie." He shifted his gaze back to her. "Here."

More to grasp. Harris was dead, and Cal—her husband, she thought, had betrayed her. She couldn't bring herself to look at Gus. "When? For how long?"

"I don't know. I first noticed about eight months ago. It was obvious you two weren't going to make it."

She felt heat rise into her face, embarrassment and anger boiling up in her. "Why didn't you tell me?"

"I didn't want to stick myself between the two of you."

"Why tell me now?"

"Because I don't like what's going on around here, and I figured it's time to get everything out on the table. Doesn't matter if it has anything to do with Harris's death or the attack on Mackenzie and that other hiker last week."

"They were both knifed," Bernadette said, almost to herself. "Like Harris."

"I'm not saying Cal had anything to do with the attacks."

She nodded, more in control of herself now. Of course Cal had women, especially in the past year. And of *course* he would have them here, at the lake.

She faced Gus. "Did Mackenzie know about Cal's women?"

Gus scratched the side of his mouth, as close as he would get to displaying any discomfort. "She caught him just before she headed to Washington. It's eaten at her. She was in the same pickle I was. She didn't know what to do."

Bernadette stiffened. "I've been played for a fool."

Gus sighed. "No one wanted to see you hurt."

"How was your silence supposed to change the facts? Cal took women here, to the one place he knows it would hurt me most for him—" She didn't finish, just crossed her arms tightly across her chest and faced the water. "Well. You can see why we didn't make it. And don't stand there and tell me you told me so."

"I didn't say a thing."

"You didn't have to. I know you, Gus." The wind blew her hair into her eyes, and she pushed it back. "I've arrived safe and sound, and you've delivered your news. You can leave now."

He started off the dock. "I'll get my gear and sleep on the couch tonight."

"You will not."

He ignored her. "I'll be back here in an hour."

Bernadette couldn't focus her thoughts enough to come up with an argument against his plan, and by the time she started to say something, he'd walked back up to his truck. She ran to the yard and looked for something to hurl into the lake. An Adirondack chair was too big. She picked up a rock the size of a golf ball and threw it as far as she could, watched it plop into the water, then found another and heaved it.

She hadn't loved Cal in a long time, but she couldn't believe he'd want his affairs to get out into the open. Even if he wouldn't mind humiliating her, he'd resist because of the likely backlash against him. He'd been extra difficult, tense and preoccupied for weeks. She'd blamed their divorce, the stress over his move.

"Wasn't *that* stupid," she said aloud, flopping into one of her Adirondack chairs. She could smell old ashes in the stone fireplace.

Had Cal and his women sat out here, toasting marshmallows?

How the hell could she have been so naive? So damn blind?

Harris's death—his *murder*—would put both her and Cal under greater scrutiny by the police, the media, their colleagues, the public. There'd be an investigation; with any luck, an arrest; then a trial, a conviction. The whole sordid, horrible ordeal would go on and on.

The wind was uncomfortably strong, and she needed a sweater, but Bernadette stayed where she was, running through the litany of choices she'd made in her fifty-seven years that had led her to this point.

A car sounded in her driveway, and when she looked up and recognized the two men walking toward her as local FBI agents, she knew they were there to talk to her about Harris. About the rooming house.

About Cal?

But she had done nothing to wrong and she had nothing to hide, never mind that a similar attitude had landed more than one defendant in her courtroom.

Bernadette rose, smiling as she walked

up to greet the two men. "I assume you're here because of Judge Mayer's murder. I just heard. Please, come inside."

She led them onto her screened porch and began to answer all their questions.

Twenty-Seven

Mackenzie walked across the sprawling lawn of the historic house that she'd called home for almost two months, the smell of hydrangeas and wet grass mingling on the breeze, the sunset glowing through the trees. After hours of answering questions and writing up her report on the events of the day, she'd ventured back there for a shower and a change of clothes.

But when she'd arrived, Nate's car was in the driveway. They took a walk on the grounds, and she'd told him everything.

"I finally called my parents in Ireland and told them what's been going on," she said as she and Nate approached the back end of the property. "I hated to do it—they're having such a good time."

"Your mother's getting into her Irish roots?"

"She says there's nothing like Irish butter." And if anyone deserved simple pleasures, it was Molly Stewart. Her hard work, frugality and dedication to her husband, regardless of his disability, hadn't dampened her good nature. "I don't know if I have any business worrying her this way. If I'd stayed in academia—"

"You'd have been killed last week, and Harris would still be dead."

At Nate's blunt words, Mackenzie shoved her fists into the pockets of her lightweight jacket. "I asked my folks to find an Internet café and take a look at the sketch. Maybe they saw this guy at the lake or around town before they left for Ireland."

"The couple who swapped houses with them didn't recognize him."

"Maybe he was there before they arrived."

She and Nate had walked to the house's century-old dump, where Nate's wife, a historical archaeologist, had conducted a dig, unearthing artifacts—mostly ordinary household items that would go on display when the house finally opened to the public.

"Harris Mayer might have been killed before you were attacked," Nate said. "If his killer is the same man—"

"Then I'm not responsible because I let him go?" Mackenzie could hear the self-recrimination in her tone. "That's not I how I look at it."

"You didn't let him go." A note of mild exasperation had crept into Nate's voice. "If you're going to do this job, you have to get some perspective on what's a real mistake and what isn't."

Mackenzie looked away from him. "I don't know if I can do this work. I look at you—"

"I've been at it longer."

"I look at Juliet Longstreet, T.J., Rook."

"All more experienced than you. Just about every federal agent in Washington is. You're new. We all know that. So does Joe Delvecchio."

"He told me today I'm so smart, I'm stupid."

Nate grinned. "He didn't get to be chief by mincing words. It was your sneaking into Beanie's house that got him."

"I didn't 'sneak' in. I have a key. And it's not like I took anything."

"She's a federal judge in his district. What if you had found something relevant to Rook's investigation? It'd be subject to suppression."

"Delvecchio doesn't understand my relationship with her."

"Nobody does. After your father's accident . . ." Nate hesitated, then continued, "Beanie blamed herself as much as you blamed yourself. She was an adult, and you were just a kid, but that day was tough on both of you."

"I hardly remember any of it. I just remember this overwhelming feeling that I'd done something wrong."

"Like today."

Yeah, she thought. *Like today.* She took his hand and squeezed it. "Thanks for your friendship, Nate."

He slung an arm over her shoulder as they started back toward the house. "Harris should have been straight with Rook. He wasn't."

"Maybe because he was more afraid of whoever killed him."

"Possibly."

"Or," she said, "knowing Harris, he tried to have it both ways. Cut a deal with the FBI *and* with his killer."

"The rooming house isn't in the best neighborhood. For all we know, Harris walked into the middle of a drug deal, or someone tried to rob him. We have to let the facts lead us."

"There was no forced entry. The doors were locked. Either Harris let his killer in or gave him a key, or the killer talked the building's superintendent into opening up the door. There are a lot of possibilities." Mackenzie forced herself to smile. "Or it was a ghost."

"No wonder you and Sarah get along so well."

But his amusement came across as forced, and hers faded almost immediately. "The FBI wants to talk to Cal," she said. "He was supposed to meet Rook and T.J. this morning, and now they can't find him."

"He could be a lot of places," Nate said.

"I know. It doesn't mean he's dead on a bathroom floor."

"Or that he killed Harris or had anything to do with his death, except perhaps a premonition. Who knows. Where are you staying tonight?"

"Rook's, I guess." Mackenzie kept her voice matter of fact. "I stayed there last night after the little incident with the hydrangea and the knife. He has a decent guest room. One wall's full of pictures of Rooks."

Nate dropped his arm from her shoulders but said nothing.

"His nineteen-year-old nephew is there," Mackenzie added.

"Think so?" Nate opened up his car door and grinned at her, showing a spark of real amusement for the first time since she'd found him in her driveway. "Bet the nephew's not there tonight."

Rook found his nephew out on the bent and rusted swing set in the backyard, another area that needed work. Shrubs his grandparents had planted when they'd moved into the house were in need of serious pruning or outright replacement, and, stuck in a tangle of weeds and ground cover in the far corner of the yard, was a faded, chubby gnome that just had to go.

So did the swing set. "I need to take this thing to the dump," Rook said. "Your great-grandmother got it when you were on the way. She was so excited to have a baby around again. Knew you'd be a boy."

Brian hooked his elbows on the chains of

the swing, barely fitting onto the seat. "Her sons and grandsons all turned out great." He squinted up at his uncle. "I guess odds were there'd be a screwup in the next generation, huh?"

"That kind of negative talk doesn't help, but I understand it." Rook ran a palm up the dented metal support. It'd been an old set when his grandmother had taken it off the hands of a friend whose grandchildren had outgrown it. Just a teenager himself, Rook had helped his father, a retired Secret Service agent, set it up. "I lost an informant today. A man I should have protected. I didn't know he was in danger."

"That sucks. What happened to him?"

"He was stabbed to death."

"Ouch." Brian grimaced. "I don't like real violence."

"Me, either."

"But you're an FBI agent."

"I didn't go into law enforcement because I like violence, Brian. I went in because it interested me and I thought I could do some good."

"And because all Rooks are cops."

He shrugged. "Maybe so, but at the time I thought that was more of a negative than a positive. When I started out in college, I didn't have a clue what I'd be doing in six months, never mind ten years."

"You didn't know you'd go into law enforcement?"

"It was an option, but there were a lot of options."

Brian shifted, the old swing set creaking under his weight. "I don't even know what you majored in."

"Political science." Rook smiled. "Don't tell Mackenzie. She's a dissertation short of a Ph.D. in political science."

His nephew grinned. "Imagine if you'd been her student."

Probably not a good idea, Rook thought.

Brian pushed back in the swing, straightening his legs as his dark eyes focused on the wet grass. "Do you feel like a screwup because of what happened to your informant?"

"It doesn't really matter, does it? I still have a job to do."

"A job you're good at." Brian swung forward, the swing set sagging dangerously. "I'm good at video games."

"When your father was nineteen, he was good at anything having to do with a motorcycle."

"He never flunked out of college." Brian pried himself out of the swing. "I'll help you get rid of this when you're ready. I'm heading home. You don't need to worry about me, Uncle Andrew. My mom and dad don't, either. I'll figure things out."

"Fair enough."

"Hey, I got a job today—washing dishes at a restaurant near the International Spy Museum." He grinned suddenly. "Maybe that's what I'll be."

Rook raised an eyebrow. "A dishwasher?"

"Uh-uh. A spy."

Plans afoot, Brian trotted off across the yard. Knowing his nephew, Rook wouldn't be surprised if he did end up as a spy. The kid would be all right. His battles with his parents were normal fare. He'd never had to find his father bloodied by a malfunctioning table saw, out in the middle of nowhere.

As he headed into the house, two cars pulled into the driveway. They belonged to his brother Jim, a Secret Service agent like their father, and his brother Steven, an Arlington detective. Behind them came his brother Scott, Brian's father and a prosecutor.

"Has something happened?" Rook asked when they got out of their cars *en masse.*

"Yeah," Steven, the youngest, said. "To you."

"I'm not bleeding."

Finally, their father pulled in behind Scott's car, and as he got out, Rook realized that Sean Rook was the spitting image of his eldest grandson, Brian, in another fifty years.

Scott clapped his younger brother on the shoulder. "You might not be bleeding, Andrew, but you've had a hell of a day. A murdered informant. No leads. That's a tough one. We're here for moral support."

"Plus," Jim said, "we want to know about the redheaded marshal with the freckles."

He was outnumbered, one of the hazards of being back in Washington—and, he acknowledged, one of its benefits. His brothers and father would want to know everything he could legitimately tell them. They'd offer their opinions and advice, and they'd ask questions, take him through how J. Harris Mayer had started out with vague tales of blackmail and conspiracy and ended up knifed to death in a seedy rooming house studio.

But as he welcomed his family into his house, Rook decided his father and brothers would have an easier time understanding the circumstances surrounding his dead informant than his redheaded marshal with the freckles.

Twenty-Eight

Mackenzie drove around the block twice before the last of the unfamiliar cars in Rook's driveway had departed. He stood at the screen door in the front of the house. He was dressed in jeans and looked more relaxed than she'd expected. Certainly more than she felt herself.

"I had to talk my brothers out of running your plates," he said. "Suspicious vehicle circling the block."

"Unknown, not suspicious. There's a difference."

"Not to them." He pushed open the door. "They'll be sorry they missed you."

"Just what I need. More Rooks."

But as she entered the foyer, her humor deserted her, and her injured side ached. He swept a look over her that, in spite of her fatigue, or perhaps because of it, set her senses on fire.

"Lousy day today," he said.

"That sums it up." She headed down the short hall to the kitchen. "I called Beanie before I left to come here. She's talked to the FBI. She never thought of the rooming house, either."

"You did think of it."

"Not soon enough. And Cal—she hasn't heard from him. He still hasn't shown up, has he?"

"Not yet," Rook said. "It's an August weekend in Washington. No one's here who doesn't have to be."

"He's supposed to move—"

"He can afford to pay someone while he heads to the beach." But when she didn't respond, Rook added, "Cal Benton's not a stupid man."

She stared out the window above the sink, distracting herself by wondering what Rook would say if she asked him if he needed a roommate to help with expenses.

She felt rootless, in a way she never had in New Hampshire or even during her weeks in Georgia. During the weeks of intense training, she'd been too busy, too focused on not failing to notice. Now, failure was a more deadly proposition. It wasn't just about herself anymore. When she screwed up, people could get hurt.

She glanced back at Rook, leaning against the hall doorjamb. "I saw two of your brothers. They look a lot like you. How many siblings do you have?"

"Three brothers. Scott, Jim and Steven. A prosecutor, an Arlington detective and a Secret Service agent. My father is retired from the Secret Service."

"I guess I should be glad they only wanted to run my plates instead of shoot out my tires. Your nephew's father is the prosecutor?"

"Scott. He's the eldest. I'm number three."

"They all live around here?"

"They do. They're all married with kids."

"Ah. That makes you the black sheep, doesn't it? Do you get along with their wives?"

"For the most part."

"They're not cops," Mackenzie said, making an educated guess.

"One's an E.R. nurse, one works at the Smithsonian and one's a homemaker."

"What about your mother?"

"She and a friend opened up a gift shop a couple of years ago. Drives my father nuts. They finally put him to work to shut him up—he's in charge of the homemade soaps."

"You have quite a clan. It's always been just my folks and me. We get along with the rest of the family, but my relatives are a small group and we don't see that much of them. Of my grandparents, I only knew my mother's mother, but she died when I was in high school. But I always had the Winters." Mackenzie sank back against the sink. "And Beanie."

Rook said nothing.

She angled a look at him. "I didn't see Brian's car."

"He's gone home for the weekend. Lives right around the corner."

So Nate was right, she thought with a smile. "Oh. Well. Then it's just you and me? Your brothers aren't going to turn up in the middle of the night, are they? They're not keeping an eye on you, checking for strange cars in the driveway—"

"No."

"Good, because they look like humorless hard-asses." She smiled. "I can't wait to meet them."

Rook moved toward her and slipped his arms around her, just above her healing knife wound. She sank against his chest, and he kissed the top of her head. "If you don't mind, I'd rather not talk about my family right now."

"No, huh?" She lifted her head and draped her arms over his shoulders, locking her fingers behind his neck. "Imagine that."

"Forget the guest room. Stay with me tonight."

She felt a ripple of awareness and remembered their lovemaking two nights ago in her kitchen. "And if *you* don't mind, I'd rather not make love to you here in the kitchen. This floor looks hard."

His mouth was tantalizingly close to hers. "We didn't make it to the floor last time, as I recall."

"My stitches are out."

"Yes, I know."

"The wound's healing nicely."

He kissed her ever so briefly, and she took it as just a taste of what was to come. "I'll be careful."

"Not that careful, I hope."

He lifted her up onto his hips. "Rook—"

"Give up a little control, Mac," he said, grinning.

She sank into his arms, letting him take her weight. "Fine by me."

He carried her back to his bedroom, its rich colors and dark woods as thoroughly masculine as he was. With one hand, he drew back the covers of his bed, then set her down. She lay against two soft pillows and watched him crack open a window, the air almost cool, the less humid breeze another tease on her already overheated skin.

She started to undress, but he sat next to her and took her hands. "Allow me."

She smiled. "Who am I to argue?"

He raised her arms above her head and skimmed his palms down them, until he reached her breasts. At a maddening, deliberate pace, he found buttons, hooks, a zipper, tugged at fabric, every touch of his fingers drawing a response from her. Her skin heated, her pulse quickened.

She started to bring her hands down to speed up the process, but he gently shoved them back. "Uh-uh. My job."

He continued until he had removed every

last stitch of clothing from her. And still he kept her hands in place as his explored her. He kissed her so deeply, so erotically, it was as if their mouths had fused together.

Mackenzie wriggled under him, fought for air. "Andrew . . . I don't think I can stand it anymore...."

"Do you want me to stop?"

She shook her head. "Not ever. I just . . ."

But he'd already lowered his mouth to her neck, trailed kisses down to her breasts, lingered there, stealing all thought of what she'd intended to say, all thought of anything except the exquisite wet heat of his tongue. The fact that he was still fully clothed only made her ache more.

He moved lower still, circling, flicking, nipping, and she gave herself up to the sensations roaring through her, opened herself up to the movement of his tongue and the scrape of his teeth, the probing of his fingers. She spun closer and closer to the edge, to abandoning all control.

Then he pulled back suddenly, and raised up, a flash of amusement in his dark eyes. "My turn to get undressed."

She tried to sit up and at least help, but her body wouldn't cooperate. She was quivering, aching. He had no trouble managing on his own, tossing his clothes onto the floor with hers, then coming to her, letting her cup his firm bottom and smooth her hands up his hips and along his back, every inch of him warm and hard. She reached between them, but he lifted himself up, then filled her with such suddenness and ferocity she cried out.

But he didn't stop, and she didn't want him to. He plunged impossibly deep into her, stretching her, filling her with a kind of sweet agony she'd never known, and when he thrust again, he went deeper yet. All his confidence and drive made her want him even more. She grabbed his hips, felt her fingers dig in, and held him still, just for a moment. Their eyes locked, and he gazed down at their joined bodies, then looked back at her again, mouthed her name as he drove into her, faster and faster, taking her breath away.

She came in waves, feeling her release down to her toes, but he wasn't finished. She threw her arms over her head and let herself feel nothing but each quick, hard thrust, until he moaned, grunting as he exploded into her.

Finally spent, he rolled onto his back next to her. A stiff breeze blew over them, and she could feel her pulse racing, although her body was relaxed and loose from their lovemaking.

"I hope we didn't disturb the neighbors," she said, still a little breathless.

He eased onto his side and smiled at her. "We?"

"I don't know, Rook. You break all my rules. You're in law enforcement, you're a total hard-ass, you're a city guy—"

"My brothers and I hike all the time." He traced a finger along her upper arm. "What kind of man do you want?"

She grinned at him. "One who's handy."

"After the past hour I'd say I'm pretty damn handy."

"Touché."

"Not as humorless as you thought, am I?"

"You're full of surprises, I'll say that." Mackenzie felt a rush of heat, remembering the feel of him inside her. "I meant, do you know how to use a hammer? Can you build things?"

"I've done most of the work so far on this place."

"It's nice," she said, her energy suddenly starting to fade. "You've done a good job. I like the skylights."

"There's more work to do."

"I've never owned my own house. I've always rented." She caught his hand in hers, looked him in the eye. "We were doing fine. A couple of nice dates, enjoying each other's company. Then you dump me."

"And you flew to New Hampshire to lick your wounds and got into a knife fight." He locked his fingers with hers and drew closer to her. "I don't claim to know what the hell's going on, but if you'd stayed here last weekend things would have been different."

She rose up slightly, feeling a tug of pain in her side, a reminder that she wasn't fully healed. "If I'd stayed, we wouldn't have a description of Harris's killer."

"His likely killer."

"I know. 'Be led by facts, not speculation.'" She dropped back onto the pillow. "My brain's not working anymore. It's fried."

He kissed her on the mouth, the nose, the forehead. "Sleep," he whispered. But she touched his side, ran her fingertips along the muscles of his abdomen, and, impossibly, felt a renewed spark.

"Mac . . ."

She climbed onto him, felt the heat and hardness of him. It was dark now, and the breeze felt cool on her skin. "I don't need to think," she said as he reached for her breasts, cupping them as she rose up, then lowered herself onto him.

They made love slowly, thoroughly, pushing off any doubts and questions for another time.

Twenty-Nine

Jesse shivered in the cold, early morning mountain air and crept across the bare rock to Cal, who hadn't moved much in the past three hours. They'd made camp amid a cluster of granite boulders well off the main trails in the hills above Bernadette Peacham's lake house. No tent or sleeping bags, just a couple of emergency blankets that packed up to the size of a deck of cards.

"Morning, Cal."

Jesse pulled the gag from Cal's mouth, not that Cal showed any gratitude. He coughed and spat. "You sadistic bastard. I could have *died.*"

"Died of what?"

"Thirst, choking on my own spit—I could hardly breathe." He hacked some more, turning red. "Bastard."

"If you were in danger of dying, I'd have woken up." Jesse calmly cut the ropes on his captive's hands and feet. "Give yourself a couple minutes for the circulation to return."

He'd had three hours sleep himself, max. He'd picked up Cal yesterday after his little *tête-à-tête* with Mackenzie Stewart and took him out to the airport, stuffing him in his plane and debating whether just to shove him out over the Atlantic. For years to come, people could wonder whatever happened to Calvin Benton, Judge Peacham's ex-husband.

Instead, Jesse fed and watered the turncoat and flew him up to New Hampshire, then dragged him into the hills. Clearly, nothing about the White Mountains calmed or rejuvenated Cal. He'd gone silent, tight and tense, obviously plotting his way out of the mess he was in.

The mountains had focused Jesse's mind. Dragging Cal up there overnight maybe hadn't been the greatest idea, but leaving him in Washington to cut his own deal with the FBI, or whatever, wasn't an option. Now that Deputy Mackenzie and her FBI guy had found Harris, the police and the media were all over his death. She and Rook weren't identified in media reports, but Jesse knew it had been them. They'd found the rooming house. Was it because of Bernadette Peacham? Her friendship with Harris?

Doesn't matter.

Of course, the reporters were all saying Harris was murdered. Jesse considered what he'd done that night was self-defense at its most elemental and pure.

Cal slowly rubbed his wrists and ankles where the rope had cut deep into his fair skin. "I will die, anyway, won't I?" His tone was surprisingly matter-of-fact. "Sooner or later, I'll pay for my sins."

"We all pay for our sins."

With the passage of the cold front yesterday, the air was downright chilly. Jesse could have slept for hours, if not for Cal gagged and bound a few feet from him. Awake, Jesse had his assault knife to keep his prisoner in line. Asleep, he needed Cal quiet and immobile.

"Oh, God." Cal abruptly rolled onto the knees and vomited into the dirt, moaning as he finished up and sat back on his heels, his face ashen. "Damn you to hell, Jesse. Harris was right about you. You are the devil."

"We had a good arrangement, Cal. You profited, Harris profited, I profited."

"But for how long? You'd never take your million and go way. You'd be back for more. You wouldn't be satisfied, and I'd get in deeper and deeper, until one day I found myself in the middle of a scandal, just like Harris." Cal's voice croaked, and he spat again. He looked haggard, his lips cracked dry from the gag. "I didn't want to end up like him."

Jesse thought of the way he'd left Harris at the rooming house. "That I can understand, but you should have come to me, talked to me. Treated me like an equal, a partner, instead of something you wanted to scrape off the bottom of your shoe."

"I don't have any intention of keeping one cent of your money. The rest is just to make sure you go away and never come back."

Jesse opened up a plastic water bottle and handed it to Cal. "Don't drink too fast. You'll throw up again."

"Do you think I care?" But he drank, water spilling down his chin like drool, and he didn't stop until he'd drained the bottle. He tossed it aside, not bothering to wipe his mouth. "I wish I'd run you over on the street when I first met you."

"Yes, well, you didn't," Jesse said. "Stop thinking about jumping me now. You're in no condition, and I'll kill you."

"If you kill me, you won't get your damn money or anything else."

"Your ex-wife—"

"Bernadette doesn't know anything. Just leave her out of this mess."

"You're trying to make sure I don't throw you over a cliff and rely on the sainted Judge Peacham instead. You don't care what happens to her. Don't pretend you do."

Cal's eyes darkened. "Did you kill that poor girl in Washington?"

"Your little blonde? Why would I kill her?"

"For leverage. If there's one thing you understand, Jesse, it's leverage."

"True."

Jesse reached into his pack and produced a protein bar—peanut butter and chocolate chip. Not his favorite, but he tore it open and took a bite. He had his knife tucked in his belt. One wrong move by Cal, and Jesse would cut him and enjoy doing it. The guy was scum.

The protein bar was dry and purely utilitarian. He loved the stripped-down life the mountains required. No distractions, no excesses. The ability to survive was all that mattered up here. He took another bite of the bar and drank some water.

"Don't think I don't know you, Cal," he said. "I'm a great observer of people. That's how I make my money. You're bored."

"I'm fighting for my life and you think I'm bored?"

"You brought your women to New Hampshire because you were bored with the status quo. Bored with yourself. You let your boredom turn into anger and recklessness. Why do you think you hooked up with me in the first place?" Jesse took another drink, then gestured at Cal with the water bottle. "Boredom."

"No, Jesse. I hooked up with you because you and Harris threatened to expose me. I wish the hell I'd let you. You didn't want money from me—you wanted access and information. You've been squeezing Harris for years, but the very weaknesses you exploited finally got the better of him. So you pressured him into getting you someone new." Cal touched a fingertip to a cracked spot on the corner of his mouth that had turned bloody. "Me."

Jesse shook his head. "You didn't walk away, did you? And you know why?"

"Boredom?" Cal snorted. "I'm not bored, you son of a bitch. I'm scared. If you don't kill me, the damn FBI will toss my ass in prison."

"Have a little faith." Jesse felt his smile become distant, nasty. "Lucky you didn't try to make your own deal with the FBI."

"Harris . . ." Cal turned pale, and the cockiness went out of his voice. "Jesse—what have you done to him?"

Jesse didn't respond. Harris and Cal's betrayal had set off something in him. But that wasn't all. Being in Cold Ridge had tripped a switch deep inside him, reminding him of the first time he'd come to the White Mountains as an isolated, angry, frightened young man. He'd had to get control of the violence that raged inside him. He'd had to find a way to make it work for him.

And here he was again, taking risks, telling himself he had to be bold—that boldness had always worked for him.

He thought about Mackenzie Stewart and felt an urge to see her, talk to her, hear her voice. He pictured her blue eyes, her creamy skin, the spray of freckles across her nose. How could she have become a marshal?

"Never mind," Cal said quietly. "I don't need to know about Harris."

Eventually, Harris had recognized Jesse's capacity for violence, but not Cal. The dossier he and Harris had put together on their partner in crime didn't include that aspect of Jesse's life.

Even after spending a night tied up and gagged, Jesse thought, Cal Benton would find a way to believe he had the upper hand and was dealing with a man who, ultimately, would make a deal with him.

"You need to pull out," Cal said. "Go back to Mexico and let me wire you your money. It's too risky now to force me to do anything. You've got the FBI, the marshals and local and state police on your ass. Trust me to keep up my end of our bargain."

"*Your* bargain. I never agreed to anything."

"Come on, Jesse. It's an easy million for you—"

"Not easy. I worked for that money. It's *mine.*"

Cal gulped in a breath. "Things have changed. For both of us. We need to reassess our situation."

"You're arrogant, but you're not as smart as you think you are. You like the action, Cal." Jesse finished the last of his protein bar. "You're like me in a lot of ways."

"What you're doing now will destroy both of us. Jesse, you're a smart man. You're good at what you do. Why risk everything?"

"My million's here in New Hampshire, isn't it, Cal?"

He didn't respond. Squinting, he gazed out across the mountains, a cold breeze lifting the ends of his thin air.

"I was right to come up here last week."

Cal looked at him, even paler now. "What?"

Jesse got up, wishing he'd had more sleep last night. Three hours would have to do. "On your feet, Cal. We've got some rough hiking to do before we get to the lake."

"Jesse—was Harris right?"

"Am I the devil, you mean?"

"It *was* you who attacked Mackenzie."

"Don't be so taken aback, Cal. She fought hard. I underestimated her. In fact, if she hadn't just come from the lake, she'd have had me."

Cal didn't seem to be breathing. "Then you are violent."

Jesse smirked and said, "We're all violent."

Thirty

Rook listened to the water run in the shower as he put on coffee. What could be more normal on a summer Saturday morning? But nothing was normal. Not today. Mackenzie had slipped out of bed early and logged on to Brian's computer to buy an e-ticket for a shuttle up to New Hampshire. T.J. was on the way. They had work to do. As of yesterday afternoon, J. Harris Mayer had become a priority.

Last night, Rook's brothers and father had all described incidents where they'd faced similar intransigence, arrogance and manipulation on the part of a conflicted source, with a bad outcome of one kind or another. In his own case, the outcome was as bad as it could get. Harris was dead.

T.J. turned up with a bag of doughnuts. "I figured you could use a shot of sugar this morning." As always, he looked as if he'd stepped out of an FBI recruiting ad. But he raised an eyebrow. "Mackenzie?"

"In the shower," Rook said.

"Sure you know what you're doing?"

"She's heading to New Hampshire today to see Judge Peacham."

T.J. pulled a glazed doughnut out of the bag. "She should leave the investigating to the rest of us and go read a book." He sat at the table. "Maybe you should, too."

"If you'd been attacked on the lake where you grew up, would you be reading a book?"

"I wouldn't have been in a pink swimsuit when I was attacked, that's for sure. I'm not criticizing. I'm just saying what I think."

"Understood."

T.J. bit into his doughnut. Rook picked out a plain one. Too much sugar and he'd be bouncing off the walls. Mackenzie hadn't invited him to fly to New Hampshire with her. He'd awakened before dawn and watched her sleep, realizing that a part of this woman he'd made love to was still up north. She'd lived in New Hampshire all her life. No matter how committed she thought she was to her new work, he could tell she wasn't convinced yet it was where she belonged. It wasn't just other people's doubts. It was her own.

She entered the room, dressed in jeans, a summer jacket and a shoulder holster. Her wound had stood up to their gymnastics last night. Rook had tried to be careful, at least when his mind wasn't totally elsewhere.

"Don't you two look ready to climb tall mountains and slay dragons this morning," Mackenzie said cheerfully, the ends of her hair still wet from her shower. "You don't have much of a blow-dryer, Rook." Her eyes lit up when she spotted the doughnut bag. "Ah. Doughnuts. You didn't bring just two doughnuts, did you, T.J.?"

He grinned at her. "I'm a trained, experienced FBI agent. I knew you'd be here."

She smiled, the freckles standing out against her cheeks. "Good thinking." She plucked out another glazed doughnut. "My cab's about to pull up. I'll wait outside. Thanks for letting me leave my car here, Rook."

"Not a problem."

"See you tomorrow night. Let me know if there are any developments here."

"We'll tell you what we can," T.J. said.

She obviously didn't like that, but didn't argue. "I'll do the same."

She picked up her backpack, which she'd dragged into the kitchen first thing, as if she'd wanted to avoid going back to the bedroom with T.J. there. But Rook wasn't convinced he knew everything about how Mackenzie thought, what drove her. For answers, he suspected he needed to spend more time in New Hampshire, where she'd lived her entire life before packing up for the training academy.

He heard the cab arrive, then pull back into the street.

"You could you have stopped her," T.J. said.

"Uh-huh. I have more guns. And you'd back me up."

"No way. I'm staying out of whatever you two have going on. When I see sparks, I get out of the line of fire." T.J. finished the last of his doughnut and rinsed off his fingers. "So when are you going up to New Hampshire?"

T.J. could read people better than anyone Rook had ever worked with. He sighed. "My flight leaves two hours after hers."

"Then let's get rolling."

They headed straight to Cal Benton's condominium complex. If he hadn't returned overnight, someone there might know whoro he was.

A different doorman greeted them in the lobby, young, rail-thin, with a calculus textbook open on his desk. "You the ones who left that sketch?" he asked.

"A colleague did," Rook said.

"I think I know the guy."

Rook suppressed any reaction. "From your work here?"

"Yeah. I'm on part-time, mostly nights and weekends." He pushed back his chair and yanked open a drawer, pulling out the crumpled copy of the sketch of Mackenzie's attacker. He thumped a finger on it. "Yeah, he's the guy. I saw him getting on the elevator just the other night. Two, three days ago."

"Was he visiting someone here? Do you have a log—"

"What?" The kid seemed to be confused. "No, he wasn't visiting anyone that I know of. He's got a place here."

T.J. straightened, and Rook couldn't hide his surprise. "Where?" he asked.

"Sixth floor. It's a corporate condo. He's

leased it for six months. I don't remember the name of his company. It's Virginia-based, but he's not from here—works for them, or he owns it. I don't know. I didn't ask."

"What's his name?" T.J. asked.

The kid shrugged. "No idea."

Rook nodded to the sketch. "Are you sure it's him?"

"Yeah. Pretty sure. It looks like him. I don't know if I'd have recognized him if I'd just seen the sketch on TV, but I figured there's a reason you guys brought it by."

"Why didn't the doorman who was here yesterday morning recognize him?"

"This guy's not around a lot."

"Call up to his condo," Rook said. "Let's see if he's home."

There was no answer, nor was there any answer at Benton's condo. Rook and T.J. thanked the young doorman and stepped back outside. T.J. gave a low whistle. "We're going to be busy this morning."

Rook agreed. Time to get a couple of search warrants. Fast.

Thirty-One

Mackenzie walked into Gus Winter's store, as she had on countless other bright, clear summer mornings. If she'd simply stayed in Cold Ridge and hadn't decided to become a federal agent, would Harris Mayer now be alive? Had her decision to put in her application to become a deputy marshal somehow set events into motion that had culminated in his murder?

She didn't blame herself, but she wondered about her role in the events of the past couple of weeks. She was a passive, unwitting participant, which she hated. She and

Rook had met because of Harris and his manipulations, because of her friendship with Bernadette. In all likelihood, the attack on her and the hiker and the hydrangea and the assault knife—the anonymous calls—all tracked back to Harris and to his friendship with Bernadette.

A teenager Mackenzie knew from town— an avid mountain climber—was folding hiking shirts on the worn counter. "Is Gus here?" she asked.

"He'll be in soon. Five, ten minutes, maybe." The teen, blond and tanned, grinned suddenly, as if just recognizing her. "Hey, Ms. Stewart. I mean, Agent Stewart."

"Just Mackenzie is fine."

"I heard about that fight up at the lake. Man. That was close. Hope the police catch the guy."

"Me, too."

"Mackenzie!" Carine Winter North waved from near the back wall of the store. "I didn't know you were in town."

Mackenzie smiled at the sight of her friend. "I just got here." She threaded her way through the racks of clothing and gear to Gus's display of maps and hiking guides.

"I only decided this morning at the last minute to come up."

A week after her own close call, Carine seemed back to normal, little Harry snuggled onto one hip. "I'm looking for a map of Mount Desert Island. Tyler's on his way home, and we're thinking about getting out of here for a few days." She smiled, color rising in her fair cheeks. "I think Maine might be nice. I haven't been to the ocean yet this summer."

"Did you tell him about last weekend?"

"No, but I should have. He read about it on the Internet. Can you believe it? Never occurred to me. My name wasn't mentioned, but yours was. So he knew damn well I was in the middle of it all." She abandoned the maps and shifted Harry to her other hip. "He says we can work on our communications skills while he's here." She grinned. "Sounds kind of good, doesn't it?"

Mackenzie had known Tyler North as long as she had the Winters. He'd left Cold Ridge early for the air force, but kept coming back, hanging on to the house where his eccentric mother, a well-regarded artist, had raised him on her own. He'd seemed to know, on some level, that he and Carine were destined for each other and a life together in their hometown.

"Mackenzie?" Carine touched her friend's shoulder. "You okay?"

"Just drifting."

"Did you come here alone?"

Mackenzie nodded, not sure how much detail she wanted to go into now. But eventually Carine would drag it all out of her—the creepy events of the past week, Harris's murder. Rook.

"Your FBI guy—Andrew—"

"He's still in Washington."

Carine raised an eyebrow. "But you two are getting along?"

"Better." Mackenzie smiled, thinking of Rook and his fixer-upper house within blocks of his father and brothers. A complicated man and yet totally straightforward. "I don't know. I think Rook might want a woman more like his grandmother. Someone to bake cookies."

"Have you told him you make a mean chocolate chip cookie?"

Mackenzie laughed, but her laugh sounded forced even to her. "No, because it's the only thing I *can* make."

Carine's expression darkened. "We heard about Harris Mayer. I called Nate, but he wouldn't tell me a thing. Told me not to bug you. You found the body?"

"Yesterday afternoon," Mackenzie said.

"That must have been awful." Carine winced; she'd come upon a murder scene once herself, before she and Tyler were married. "I remember Harris visiting Beanie. He always struck me as one of those people who had it all but still wasn't satisfied."

"I guess it wasn't in his nature."

Carine hoisted Harry higher onto her hip and smiled, kissing the top of his little bald head. "Little mister here is getting to be a lug. What are your plans?"

"I'm meeting with the state police this afternoon for an update."

"Beanie?"

"I'm on my way out to see her right now."

"Harry and I have had either Gus or friends staying with us this week, but Tyler gets back tonight. We'll be at the house if you need anything."

"I'm sorry about what happened, Carine. This guy should never have gotten away from me."

"It wasn't your fault. You're not superhuman. This man had his chance with me, and he didn't take it. He let me go. For what it's worth, I wasn't his target, whether or not he was thinking rationally."

"If Tyler doesn't make it back here tonight, will you call me?"

"Don't worry about me, okay? You've got enough on your plate." Harry gave a huge yawn, and Carine kissed him again. "Nap time." She smiled, winking at Mackenzie. "For me, too."

Two minutes after Carine left, Gus entered the store from the back room, grunting when he spotted Mackenzie. "When did you get here?"

"And a bright and cheery good morning to you, too, Gus."

He sighed. "I'm in a lousy mood."

"I can see. I arrived about fifteen minutes ago. You just missed Carine and Harry."

"I'm running late. I was up at Beanie's last night. She wasn't nervous about staying at the lake by herself after her friend in Washington turned up cut to pieces, but I was." He pushed a palm over his gray hair and glanced around the store, as if someone might have moved everything while he'd been gone. "She kicked me out an hour ago. I've always gotten under her skin."

"And vice versa."

"I guess." He waved a hand irritably. "She's upset, but she won't admit it. I heard you and your FBI agent found Mayer yesterday?"

"We did."

Gus sighed, bending down suddenly to scoop up a shirt that had fallen off a hanger. "That can't have been good. Finding bodies— that's worse than teaching college freshmen, don't you think?" Gus laid the shirt on the counter, not waiting for an answer. "I assume you're on your way out to Beanie's."

Mackenzie nodded. "She's not expecting me, though."

"Just as well. She keeps saying she's missed something. She's driving herself crazy."

"I know the feeling."

"Yeah." Gus softened, some of the energy going out of his irritation. "If you need to borrow my truck—"

"I rented a car at the airport."

He grinned at her. "The world must be coming to an end."

Having a car gave her freedom of movement, but she'd also used the drive from the airport to think. She hesitated, then said, "Gus, have you talked to Beanie about Cal?"

He blew out a breath. "Yeah. She's not thrilled with you or me right now."

"What would she have done if she'd been in our position?"

"I tried that one on her. Didn't work. She went on about honesty, keeping secrets from friends. She's just embarrassed. That rat-bastard brought those women out to the lake knowing it'd humiliate her if she found out."

"Then there *was* more than one. I figured as much, but I only saw him with a dark-haired woman."

Gus seemed uncomfortable with the entire subject. "There were at least two that I know of, probably more. I drove by one day and saw him out on the dock with a blonde—young, pretty. I was tempted to stop, but I didn't." He added awkwardly, "Figured it wasn't my business."

Mackenzie picked up a notepad from his counter and handed it to him. "Write down a description. Everything you can think of—hair, eyes, height, weight, dates. Don't censor yourself. I'll take it with me when I meet with Detective Mooney this afternoon."

"All right, Deputy," he said with a sudden

flash of amusement, taking the pad. "I'll do that."

"Thank you."

He gave her a grudging smile "It's good to see you, kid. How's the cut?"

"Healing well."

She said goodbye and headed out, yesterday's storms leaving the air feeling washed and clean, the mountains in sharp relief against a cloudless sky. Cold Ridge was home in a way Washington never would be, but, she thought, climbing into her rented car, why not have both?

Before she was out of range of any cell service, she checked her phone for messages. T.J. had called, asking her to get in touch with him. She dialed his number, and he picked up on the first ring. "Hey, T.J. What's going on? Is Rook with you?"

"He's on his way up there. Mackenzie, I'm in your guy's condo."

"You mean Cal?"

"No. I'm talking about your stalker-attacker. A part-time night doorman recognized him from the sketch you left. He leased a corporate condo on the floor above Cal Benton's place."

"Do you have a name?"

T.J. didn't hesitate. "Jesse Lambert."

Mackenzie shook her head, as if T.J. was in the car with her. "The name doesn't sound familiar. Not at all. Any hard evidence it's the right guy?"

"Just kitchen knives so far. The place is pretty sterile."

"What about Cal? Any sign of him?"

"Not yet." T.J. paused a moment, then went on. "Rook's on his way to New Hampshire. He'll be at your meeting this afternoon with the investigators up there. His flight's just a couple hours behind yours."

"He planned this all along, didn't he?"

"He had his ticket before I arrived with the doughnuts this morning."

Mackenzie sighed. "The man's relentless."

"I'm not going there," T.J. said with a small chuckle. "Stay safe, Mackenzie. This guy—"

"I know. It's that hydrangea. Creepy."

This time, T.J. didn't laugh.

When she hung up, Mackenzie debated waiting in the local diner and watching for black sedans, but she didn't. She wanted to see Bernadette, and, she thought, the lake, the shed, the brush where her attacker had hidden, the route he'd taken into the woods. The entire scene, with fresh eyes.

Jesse Lambert.

The name didn't do anything for her. It was still the eyes that seemed familiar.

Thirty-Two

Bernadette unlocked the padlock on the shed door. She'd walked down here, realized she didn't have the key, then had dragged herself back to the house to hunt it down. She knew she was more annoyed than the situation warranted, but the padlock was another reminder of what had gone on here last week, when she was in Washington, oblivious. Just as she'd been when Cal had slipped up here with his women.

She felt violated. The lake was her refuge, but she could no longer pretend she could simply dismiss what had gone on here over the past few months.

With a burst of frustrated energy, Bernadette pulled open the shed door. She couldn't remember the last time she'd locked it. She'd never worried about burglars— there was nothing of real value inside. Occasionally, she worried about kids sneaking in and making off with the canoe or the kayaks and ending up drowned. But it wasn't enough to make her change her habits. Kids had never been a problem on the lake.

Even Mackenzie, Bernadette thought as she wrestled the lock from the latch. She'd been spirited—a hellion, according to Gus— but *normal,* wandering off on her own, not so much fearless as unaware of any dangers lurking out in the woods.

Bernadette let her gaze drop to the old bloodstains on the concrete floor. If only she could go back in time and warn Kevin Stewart about his saw, tell him to inspect it for problems.

If only she could go back in time and find him herself, and keep his eleven-year-old daughter away.

But how many times had she looked at a defendant in the courtroom and known he was running a litany of if-only scenarios through his head? Not all defendants had regrets, or regrets for the right reasons, but some did.

She propped the door open with a rock she kept nearby just for that purpose. She wanted to stay focused and keep moving, hoping activity would renew her spirits. She'd slept poorly, and as much as she'd appreciated Gus's concern for her, she couldn't stand having anyone around her right now. It wasn't him. It was her—her fatigue, her mounting sense of doom and depression.

Maybe she should just grab her garden tools and dig weeds for the rest of the day.

But she pictured Mackenzie fighting for her life in front of the shed. And Harris, five years ago, coming to the lake to tell Bernadette in person that he was in trouble. He'd found her in the shed, looking for her favorite kayak paddle.

This place is bad luck.

As she stood on the threshold, she realized she'd forgotten why she'd even decided to open up the shed. Not nostalgia, that was for damn sure.

I'm losing my mind.

She stepped back out into the sunlight. Ordinarily, the cool, bright morning would have had her out on the lake by now, kayaking, swimming, watching the loons, but not today.

"Hello, Judge Peacham."

A man emerged from the tangle of brush and small trees between the shed and the lake front. Startled, Bernadette almost fell backward, but she maintained her balance and stared at the man, recognizing him—the dark hair flecked with gray, the pale gray eyes. He wore expensive hiking clothes and boots but seemed at ease in his surroundings.

He smiled at her. "Beanie—that's what they call you up here, isn't it?"

It took a moment for her to place where she'd seen him before and remember his name. He wasn't from Cold Ridge. "Jesse," she said. "Jesse Lambert, right?"

"That's right, Judge."

His tone was calm, controlled, but something about his manner unnerved her. She took a step back from him, but remained polite and nonconfrontational. "We met a few months ago . . ."

"That's right. At a boring Washington party. It's much nicer up here." He breathed in the pleasant air, but his eyes—such strange eyes—never left her. "I love it, don't you?"

Bernadette felt a pang of real fear. She remembered now. Cal had introduced them at a cocktail party they'd both attended, separately. As she recalled, he'd indicated that Jesse Lambert was some kind of consultant with a small company based in Virginia. She'd run into him on at least two more occasions, but she hadn't really paid any attention. She had many casual acquaintances and hadn't thought twice about Jesse Lambert.

"Did you come up here with Cal?" She struggled to keep her tone light. "If you two want to borrow a canoe or a couple of kayaks, by all means—" But she broke off abruptly. The way he stared at her was as frightening as anything she'd witnessed in her years as a prosecutor and a judge.

"That's not why I'm here. You know that, Judge."

"I only know you're a business consultant of some kind."

"Cal and I did a few deals together. And Harris," Jesse added with a cold smile. "Oh, wait. Let's be accurate. J. Harris Mayer. Always a stickler for accuracy, your friend Harris."

Bernadette gasped, her knees weakening. "I haven't seen Harris in ages." She didn't dare say she knew he was dead. "I didn't realize you two knew each other."

"He's the one who introduced me to Cal."

She was too shocked to respond. What else didn't she know? Yesterday, she'd learned about Cal taking women here to the lake—and Harris's murder, she thought. She'd tried not to envision him lying dead in the run-down rooming house, but rather how he'd looked during his many visits to the lake with his wife and children, in happier days, before he'd let his compulsions dominate him. Or maybe they always had, but he just hadn't been caught and exposed.

"Aren't you going to ask me how I know Harris?"

"It doesn't matter. I don't care. Just tell me what you want."

Jesse pointed at her, almost with glee. "I know Harris because of you."

"I don't understand. I didn't meet you until Cal introduced us—"

"I know. Complicated. But Cal and Harris are irrelevant right now."

His stark words jolted Bernadette. "Jesse," she said, her voice cracking, "where is Cal?"

Ignoring her question, he glanced at the shed, the brush, as if he hadn't noticed them before. "I heard about the marshal attacked out here."

It was you, you bastard.

Bernadette could see that he was enjoying manipulating her. As surreptitously as she could, she took another step back. She knew the lake, the woods around her house. If she could get away from him, she'd have at least a chance to run, elude him until she could get help.

But if she was right and he was the man who'd attacked Mackenzie last week, he could know the area as well as she did.

Get to your car. It's your best hope. And keep him talking until you can make your move.

She tried to steady herself. "Jesse, why are you here?"

"I'm like you. I don't want to get bit by what Cal's into."

She faked a laugh that sounded even more hollow and weak than she'd expected. "You're a wealthy, respected businessman. How could anything in which Cal might be involved hurt you? And he and I are divorced. I'm not worried—"

"If you cooperate, he'll live," Jesse said abruptly. "If you don't, it's simple. He'll die."

Bernadette went still. She felt the blood draining out of her head, but tried to force herself to assess her situation objectively. She needed a weapon. There were tools in the shed. The sticks she used for toasting marshmallows near the fireplace. Rocks.

But before she could figure out what to do, Jesse produced an assault knife, pointing it at her in an obviously well-practiced move. "No one's protecting you, Judge." His tone was mild, even matter-of-fact. "No one can save you. You have to deal with me and only me."

"All right." She was surprised at how calm she suddenly sounded. "Tell me what you want."

He ran his thumb along the smooth edge of the blade. "You've alienated a lot of people, haven't you, Judge? Your pretty marshal friend, for one."

His eyes flashed, and with a deep sense of revulsion, Bernadette realized he was attracted to Mackenzie. "Mackenzie knows I care about her."

"You don't give her enough credit," Jesse continued, as if they were teachers discussing a student progress report. "She's good at what she does. She's still new, but she has sharp instincts. I've seen them at work. Hell, I almost got my ass kicked because of them."

"What do you want? I can't help you if you don't tell me."

The matter-of-fact tone vanished. "I want what your ex-husband stole from me."

What? Bernadette pushed back her confusion and shock. And her fear. This man thrived on his sense of power and control over others. Over *her.* She had to use that to keep him talking.

"I don't know anything about that," she said. "Cal and I live separate lives."

"Think, Judge. Focus your mind. Your ex-husband's in a tough situation." Jesse paused, watching her reaction, relishing it. "If I'm not able to get back to him soon, he'll die before anyone can find him. It's a nice day, but he's cold, wet, hungry and thirsty. He's also scared. You don't like that, do you? The idea that he's scared?"

"I don't know anything about your dealings with Cal. If you give me more to go on, perhaps I can help you."

He nodded toward the open shed. "Let's take a look in there. Okay, Judge?"

As if she had a choice in the matter. But

she knew she had to do what she could to delay him. "Why?"

"Because I've been trying to think like Cal, and I figure he'd hide what I'm looking for in a place where he could secretly stick it to you."

"But—"

Jesse shook his head. "No more stalling, *Beanie*." He waved his knife at her in a threatening manner. "Into the shed."

If he killed her, she thought, she hoped he'd make a quick job of it. If he was as skilled a fighter as he wanted her to believe, he could kill her instantly with a quick, targeted stab to the heart.

Don't go quietly. Fight him to the end.

Surprised at her steadiness, she went ahead of him into the shed. Her knees were shaking, but not, she hoped, visibly. She didn't want to give him the satisfaction of seeing her tremble in fear.

She noticed the tools hung neatly on hooks and nails, each a potential weapon. She'd never attacked anyone before in her life, but she knew she could do it if she had to.

"I searched Cal's condo," Jesse said, remaining between her and the shed's only door. "I went through your house in Washington. You didn't even know, did you? You should have a better alarm system. It's not 1950 anymore."

Her heart thumped wildly in her chest, but she manufactured a smile. "You're probably right. Look, if Cal stole something from you, I don't blame you for being upset."

Jesse didn't seem to hear her. With his free hand, he pulled something out of his shirt pocket—thick paper, folded in half.

A photograph.

He flipped it onto the floor in front of Bernadette. "Pick it up."

She hesitated. Jesse wasn't allowing himself to be distracted from his search for whatever it was he thought he'd find there. She knelt down slowly, the image on the paper at her feet taking shape.

It was a picture of Cal, the man with whom she'd once planned to spend the rest of her life, in bed with a pretty, fair-haired woman.

In my bed here at the lake.

The bastard hadn't even had the courtesy to use one of the guest rooms.

"You took this picture?" she asked, angling a look up at Jesse.

"It was easy enough. If they'd been upstairs . . ." He shrugged, obviously pleased with himself. "That would have been more difficult."

"Have you ever spied on me?"

"I wasn't spying. I was collecting information—intelligence, if you will, that I could use when I saw fit. I don't believe for one second that Cal feels inferior to you. You worried about that, didn't you?"

Bernadette stared at Jesse as he spoke so calmly and rationally, as if they were best friends discussing personal matters over a beer. "I—" She couldn't focus on what to say. "Jesse, please. Tell me why you're here. What do you want?"

"He's shallow," Jesse said. "Your ex-husband. He doesn't believe in anything but his own bank account and his pleasures. That kind of cynicism is tough." He gave her a long look, as if he expected her to see something she hadn't noticed before. "Why aren't you cynical, Beanie Peacham?"

The voice . . . the eyes . . .

Bernadette clutched her chest and sank onto her knees. "Oh, my God."

Jesse smiled and lowered his face to hers. "You remember me now, don't you?"

Thirty-Three

The cool breeze off the water made Mackenzie shiver, but it felt good. A year ago on a
beautiful Saturday in August, she'd have
been kayaking by now, contemplating what
life would be like if the Marshals Service accepted her for training.

Now, she knew.

She started onto the bottom step of
Bernadette's screen porch, but saw the shed
door propped open and headed down the
slowing lawn. If Bernadette was preoccupied
with Harris's death and in a prickly mood after Gus's revelation about Cal, she would

turn to activity—to doing something useful. She'd mow, dig weeds, finally paint her flea-market table.

"Hey, Beanie," Mackenzie called, in case Bernadette hadn't heard her car in the driveway. "Gorgeous day, isn't it?"

As she approached the shed, she resisted an outright shudder and pushed back the overpowering sense of dread she'd felt so often as a child when she'd get near it. She'd envision monsters in there in the dark, as if somehow the prospect of monsters would mitigate the blur of real memories she had—of her father's blood and moans, of her own terror and guilt. Ever since that awful day when she'd found her father, her memories of what had happened were jumbled up with nightmares, trauma, fear and confusion over which of the images stuck in her head were real and which weren't.

She heard a sound—a groan—and immediately drew her gun.

"Beanie—what's going on?"

But there was no answer. Careful not to expose herself more than was necessary, Mackenzie moved toward the shed, the door swung open. She squinted against the bright sun and angled a look inside.

"Beanie?"

"I'm okay." Bernadette's voice was high-pitched, laced with fear. "He's gone . . ."

She staggered into the doorway, her face ashen as she gripped her left shoulder with her right hand. Blood oozed through her fingers and down her wrist.

With her free arm, Mackenzie caught Bernadette around the waist and held on, taking her friend's weight. "I've got you. It's okay. Is anyone—"

"No one's in the shed. He heard your car and ran."

They edged out of the shed. Bernadette looked on the verge of passing out, but she rallied as she sat on the grass, her hand still clutching her shoulder.

"Who ran, Beanie?" Mackenzie asked.

"Jesse—Jesse Lambert." Bernadette grimaced, sinking slightly. "Damn, this thing hurts. At least it's not deep."

"Let me see."

Bernadette shook her head, with the authority of a woman accustomed to commanding a courtroom. But her eyes, normally a light green, were dark and glassy with pain and fear. "He says Cal will die if I—" She broke off, wincing in pain, then continued.

"He wants something Cal stole from him. I don't know. I couldn't make sense of half of what he said."

Mackenzie noticed something—a paper ot some kind—stuck in Bernadette's blood stained hand. "Beanie, what's that?"

She seemed confused. "What?" But she drew her hand from the wound in her shoulder. A photograph, smeared with blood, stuck to her palm. "Oh." She stared at it, then pried it loose. "Here, see for yourself."

Mackenzie made out the bloodstained image.

Cal's blonde. She felt a pang of sympathy for her friend. "This Jesse showed the picture to you?"

"As if it were a trophy."

"I'm sorry you had to see such a thing." But Mackenzie shifted her attention to Bernadette's wound, a slash across the meat of the shoulder and down to the collarbone. "Here." She pulled off her jacket. "Use this for compression. Hold it as tight as you can against the cut. Okay?"

"He didn't want to kill me. He could have, but he—" Bernadette stopped herself, taking the jacket, pressing it against her bleeding shoulder. "I can call the police." She gave

Mackenzie a weak smile. "As backup for you.
I know—you *are* the police."

"I can't leave you. If he doubles back—"

"You won't let him." Bernadette staggered
to her feet, pushing away Mackenzie's hand
and looking back at the shed. "This man . . .
Jesse . . . I should have recognized him...."

Mackenzie stiffened. "Why, Beanie?"

But when Bernadette turned back to her,
Mackenzie could hear her father arguing
with a man twenty years ago.

**"Find another place to camp, Jesse.
You're trespassing. Time to move on."**

She'd been hiding in the trees, playing
spy. Her father and the younger man didn't
know she was there.

"You remember him now, don't you?"
Bernadette asked quietly, but she didn't wait
for an answer. "Your father kicked him off the
property."

"I know. I remember." Mackenzie's voice
was just above a whisper. "He was worried
about my safety—and yours."

"It wasn't your fault," Bernadette said.

Mackenzie forced herself out of the past.
"It doesn't matter right now. Andrew Rook is
on the way. He shouldn't be too far behind
me." She saw that Bernadette's color had

improved, and she seemed focused, able to handle a call to 911. "If he gets here before I'm back, tell him to meet me at the clearing we went to last Saturday."

"Mackenzie—"

"I can't take the time to explain now. Beanie, are you sure you can do this?"

"Yes." She gave a faltering smile. "I know you marshals don't like federal judges to get slashed, but please don't worry about me. Just go, Mackenzie. Do what you have to do. Be safe."

Mackenzie waited just long enough to make sure Bernadette wasn't going to pass out on the porch steps before, gun in hand, she ducked through the brush, a barberry scratching her arm as she fought her way out to the trail along the lake.

A red squirrel scurried in front of her.

"Be out of here by noon or I call the police."

Not a nightmare, she thought. A memory. But she felt the pull of her own healing knife wound and focused on the present. On finding Jesse Lambert, the man who'd attacked her, the hiker and Bernadette—and who'd tried to kill her father all those years ago, and just last week had succeeded in killing Harris Mayer.

Mackenzie knew she had to find Cal, because if he'd stolen from this man—this Jesse Lambert—then Bernadette was right.

Jesse would kill him.

Thirty-Four

Rook pulled in behind what he assumed was Mackenzie's car in Bernadette Peacham's lake house driveway. The judge, he noticed, drove a basic sedan that wasn't fancy, expensive or new. But she had this place, he thought as he got out of his car. He stood in the shade of a tall maple, its leaves rustling in a steady breeze, the air cooler than it had been last week. T.J. was en route. He'd made a joke about all roads leading to New Hampshire, but it fell flat, neither he nor Rook in any mood for humor. The search of Jesse Lambert's condominium had yielded information on a small plane that was now parked at an airstrip about an hour's drive from Cold Ridge.

Rook appreciated the clear air and the view of the sparkling lake, but he felt a ripple of uneasiness. Why wasn't Mackenzie out here already, pressing him for details on what he and T.J. had found in Washington?

He walked around to the front of the house, hearing the door to the screen porch bang shut.

Clinging to the rail with one hand, Bernadette Peacham staggered down the steps. "Agent—" She clutched a bloody hand to her shoulder. "Agent Rook . . . we have a situation here."

He leaped to her side, grabbing her around the waist. Her hands and the front of her shirt were smeared with blood, but Rook saw it was from a cut in her shoulder. "Here, sit down." He lowered her onto a step. "Where's Mackenzie?"

"You have to go after her. I've called 911. The cavalry's on the way."

He heard a vehicle in the driveway behind the house.

"Gus," Bernadette Peacham said, then tried to smile. "I recognize the rattle."

"Tell me what happened," Rook said.

"Mackenzie's gone after Jesse Lambert. He's—"

"I know who he is. He stabbed you?"

She nodded. "To give himself a head start. He—he has Cal slashed somewhere. I think Mackenzie knows where."

Gus Winter rounded the house. "Beanie—" His gaze took in the bloodstains, her pale face. "Ah, hell."

"Don't get hysterical, Gus, for heaven's sake," she said sharply. "I'm fine. You and Agent Rook need to go after Mackenzie."

Gus sat next to her on the steps. "Rook'll go. He's armed to the teeth. I'll sit here with you."

Bernadette gripped his hand, her eyes shining with tears, but she rallied, looking up a Rook. "She said to find her at a clearing—"

"I know the spot."

"The local police must be right behind you," she said, but Rook was already on his way across the lawn and into the woods.

Mackenzie crossed the rock-strewn stream in a single leap and cleared the mud on the opposite side with inches to spare. A small victory after last Saturday's miss. With her weapon in hand, she headed up the trail, listening for anything out of the ordinary—the crack of a fallen branch, excited birds, chattering squirrels. Anything that suggested that Jesse Lambert had taken cover nearby.

She wasn't worried about him shooting her sniper-style. He liked knives.

And he liked getting under her skin. No fun in just shooting her.

She moved steadily, familiar with every exposed root and rock on the trail, focused on what she needed to do now—not on what had happened twenty years ago.

That could wait.

She heard a distinct rustling sound in the undergrowth to her left. It stopped abruptly.

Not a squirrel or a bird, Mackenzie thought, ducking behind an old sugar maple on the right side of the trail. "Come out, Jesse," she said. "Put your hands in the air and show yourself."

The man from last week—Jesse Lambert—jumped lightly from the cover of trees and brush, landing in the middle of the trail a few feet from her. He opened his hands for her. "See? Not armed." He grinned, cocky, unconcerned. "I knew you'd come."

Staying close to the tree, Mackenzie pointed her gun at him. "Get your hands up, Jesse. Now. Hands up!"

"Mackenzie, Mackenzie." Still grinning, he kept his hands open and took a half step closer to her. "Here we are again after all these years. It's fate, don't you see?"

She ignored him. "I'm a federal agent, and I'm ordering you to get your hands up. Now!"

"You know who I am, don't you, Deputy?" The soulless, colorless eyes gleamed, and he lowered his voice. "I'm the man in your little-girl nightmares." He waved his fingers at her, as if to taunt her, tell her that, even without a gun in hand, he was in control. "If you shoot me, you won't find Cal in time. He'll die. You're just a rookie agent, Mackenzie. You're small. You've never shot anyone for real. You know you can't handle me by yourself."

"Last time, Jesse—"

"You're just as helpless as you were at eleven, when your daddy was trying to protect you."

She knew he was trying to get to her, but she wasn't going to let him. "I'm not saying it again. Hands up."

"You can't shoot an unarmed man."

"How do I know you're unarmed? I

wouldn't know until I've cuffed you and searched you." She could feel the weight of the gun, the pull of pain in her knife wound, but she kept her voice steady, her focus on him. "So, are you going to cooperate or not?"

"Mackenzie, you're the reason your father kicked me out of here all those years ago. You know that now, don't you? He didn't trust me near you."

Her father had always been a good judge of character, but Mackenzie refused to indulge Jesse by commenting. She'd practiced this scenario dozens of times—the uncooperative, unarmed suspect. The appropriate use of deadly force. With her injured side, she wasn't in the best shape to tackle him.

"I wasn't trying to kill your father. I just wanted him to suffer for not trusting me."

She spotted Rook moving into position in the trees behind Jesse and decided to play him for more time. Push him. Let him make his move.

"Yeah, well, Jesse," she said, "just give me an excuse to kill you, and I will. What about that poor woman you carved up last week in the mountains? That was to throw us off, wasn't it? Make us think you were a deranged hiker picking his victims at random."

He shrugged, obviously pleased with him-self. "It worked."

Bastard. "And Harris—you left him to rot like a dead rat in that rooming house." Her arms were tired from holding up her Brown-ing and keeping Jesse in her sight, but she didn't waver. "Since you aren't putting your hands up, as I've instructed you several times—"

"I want to go to Mexico and live out my life." His voice took on a pleading note that she assumed was entirely phony, intended to manipulate her. "Why don't you come with me? I have money, more than you'll ever make as a marshal. I haven't done anything someone similarly provoked wouldn't have done. It was self-defense with Harris. What-ever happens to Cal is his own doing."

"Shut up already. This conversation is over. I've had enough."

That was her cue to Rook.

He leaped, tackling Jesse, both of them crashing to the ground. Mackenzie jumped forward, keeping her gun on Jesse.

A knife appeared in his hand. She reacted instantly, stepping on his wrist. He yelped in pain and released the knife. She quickly kicked it away from his reach and helped Rook cuff him and search him.

"Butcher," she said, standing back from the man who'd maimed her father twenty years ago, who'd slashed her and another woman a week ago and had murdered Harris Mayer. "How many people have you carved up?"

Jesse leered at her. "More than you'll ever know."

Rook glanced at her. "Mac—you okay?"

She noticed the blood on her left side. "Just watching you two fight opened up my knife wound." Actually, more likely jumping over the stream had, but she figured he knew that. "You were stealthy for a city guy, Rook. I'm impressed. I expected an elephant tramping through the woods."

Jesse spat into the grass. "Cal's dead because of *you.*"

"If he dies," Rook said, "it'll be because of you."

Mackenzie stared into Jesse's eyes, remembering herself crouched in the woods and her father—so handsome, so strong— arguing with this intransigent, arrogant man. She'd sensed his violence. But she was only eleven, and if her father hadn't known what Jesse would do, how could she?

She looked at Rook. "I know where Cal is."

"The clearing?"

She nodded. "I'll go. It's just up the hill "

"We'll go together." He grabbed Jesse by the shoulder. "On your feet, pal."

Mackenzie scooped up Jesse's knife and led the way to the clearing. It had been one of her favorite escapes when she'd first started wandering off on her own as a child, never imagining that anything out here could hurt her—or her family. Jesse had camped there, without permission, all those years ago. And her father had discovered him and worried that the young trespasser posed a danger to his daughter.

When they arrived at the clearing, no one was there. Sunlight shone on the field grass and ferns, and the shade shifted with the wind.

"You had your chance," Jesse said. "You lose."

Mackenzie didn't even glance back at him. "You wouldn't leave Cal out in the open," she said, inspecting the trees along the edge of the clearing.

Behind her, Jesse kept talking. "The

crooked bastard double-crossed me. Harris helped him." Anger and entitlement crept into his voice. "I only want what's mine."

"There he is."

Mackenzie crouched under the low, dead branches of a hemlock. Cal was shoved up against the trunk, bound and gagged and in clear physical distress. "Don't try to move," she said gently, strands of her hair catching in branches, the acidic smell of pitch and brown needles filling her nostrils. "Hang on, Cal, okay? Help is here." His gag was yanked so tight, it cut into the sides of his mouth, and she had to use Jesse's knife to cut it from him. Gingerly, she pulled the bandana from his mouth. "More help's on the way. We'll get you to a hospital."

He blinked at her, tried to speak, then tried again. "Beanie?"

"She's fine." Mackenzie couldn't remember him ever referring to the woman he'd married by her nickname. "Gus is with her."

"Gus . . . those two . . ." Cal's shoulders sagged, his head lolling to one side, but his eyes focused on Mackenzie. "Jesse—I wanted to get him out of my life. All our lives."

"Save your strength, okay? We can talk later."

She cut his hands free. He was dehydrated, his arms and face bruised and beaten. He licked his parched lips, his tongue swollen. "He killed Lynn. She wasn't . . . I helped Jesse extort money from her boss. But Lynn and I . . ." He caught Mackenzie's fingers in his. "I loved her."

Mackenzie thought of the photograph in Bernadette's bloody hand. Lynn must have been the name of the blond woman with Cal.

"Jesse was right about the shed," Cal whispered.

"What about the shed?"

But he drifted into unconsciousness. She felt for a pulse, but it was thready. She broke off dried branches above them, trying to give him more room, more air, and get a better look at him.

And she saw the blood on his lower left side.

She and Rook had gotten to Cal in time to save him from dehydration, exposure and a beating, but not from a stab wound—not, she realized now, from Jesse Lambert. Jesse had lied. There was no hope for Cal, no chance to save him regardless of what she or Bernadette or anyone did.

Cal was another of Jesse's victims.

Thirty-Five

The loons circled in the water in front of the dock, closer to Bernadette's house than usual, and Mackenzie wondered if they knew, on some instinctive level, that their presence was a comfort. As a child, she'd hide among the rocks and trees along the shore and watch them, always careful not to disturb them.

She stood on the threshold of the shed, smelling the lawn mower grease and the dust and the half-opened bag of composted cow manure. Bernadette was at the hospital, getting stitched up. Gus had accompanied her.

Cal had died before paramedics could get to him under the hemlock.

As she stepped into the shed, Mackenzie was aware of Rook behind her. "Before my father was hurt, it never occurred to me I could be in any danger out here at the lake. In town, maybe. But not here."

"Sounds like a normal kid to me."

"I suppose."

She glanced back at Rook, any effects of his encounter with Jesse Lambert impossible to detect. She and Rook had turned Jesse over to the state police. Jurisdictional issues would get sorted out. In the meantime, the locals had their slasher in custody.

"You FBI types won't object if I take a look around in here, will you?" she asked.

Rook shrugged. "Would it matter?"

Mackenzie didn't answer. She was focused on what Cal had told her before he'd died. She found a sawhorse on the back wall and dragged it to the middle of the floor, near her father's old bloodstains. He hadn't been distracted or careless that day—and his maiming wasn't an accident. Jesse had sabotaged the saw, setting off a chain reaction her father had been helpless to stop.

It had been one of Jesse Lambert's early acts of deliberate, malicious violence.

Mackenzie was convinced there had been

others over the years. They hadn't started up again just with the attacks on her and the hiker last week, on Harris—on Bernadette and Cal. They'd been ongoing.

Instead of telling authorities that Harris had sicced Jesse on him, Cal had joined forces with them and profited. When he realized he was in too deep and couldn't get out, he hadn't come to authorities and confessed, tried to work out a deal, but decided to pressure Harris to help him get Jesse out of their lives once and for all.

And if their plan backfired, he wanted to lead Bernadette to answers.

Mackenzie started to climb onto the sawhorse, but Rook touched her arm and shook his head. "No way, Mac."

"Relax. I used to climb trees all the time as a kid."

"Not with a knife wound in your side."

"It's healing—"

"You don't want to end up with a fresh set of stitches. Besides, I'm taller. And," he added with a smile, "I used to climb trees as a kid, too."

He had a point. She stepped back out of the way. "Have at it."

With an agility that surprised her but probably shouldn't have, he climbed onto the sawhorse and reached up into the rafters. "What am I looking for?"

"Money? Anything that seems out of the ordinary for a lake house shed."

He hooked one arm on an exposed beam and reached up higher. "Ah. What about an overstuffed dry pack tucked up in the rafters?" He glanced down at her. "I think this might be what Jesse was after, Mac."

Rook lowered the dry pack down to her. She set it on the concrete floor and pulled open the drawstrings, peering inside. "It doesn't look as if there are any kayak supplies in here, that's for sure."

She noticed a yellow-lined sheet of paper folded into thirds and clipped to some kind of folder on top of the rest of the contents. She lifted out the folder and removed the paper.

"Mac," Rook said as he dropped lightly next to her.

"I know. I'm not wearing gloves. We can separate my prints out from any others, if prints are going to matter." She unfolded the paper. "I'm guessing they won't." She recognized the handwriting, large letters in black marker. "It's from Cal. 'Dear Bernadette: If something happens to me, bring the contents of this bag to the FBI. I'm sorry. Cal.'"

Rook set another overstuffed dry pack onto the floor. "He made his deal with the devil, all right. He and Harris never should have gotten mixed up with blackmail."

"When you're in a hole, stop digging." Mackenzie opened up the file folder and flipped through the papers inside. "Spreadsheets. Addresses. A document map to the rest of the contents of the bag. Looks as if Cal turned the tables on Jesse and found out just about all there is to know about him. That should help prosecutors." She shoved the folder and the note back where she'd found them. "What's in this other bag?"

Rook opened it up and gave a low whistle when he peeked inside. "Cash," he said. "A hell of a lot of cash."

Mackenzie let out a breath. "If Cal had just taken this stuff to us—to Beanie—" She didn't finish. "He always thought he knew better. Information and access were his strengths. Now, they'll help us unravel what this Jesse Lambert has been up to. Other victims and associates. Who knows." Her gaze landed on her father's old bloodstains.

"Want to bet there are more violent crimes in his past?"

"Cal and Harris might not have realized they were dealing with a violent man until it was too late."

"Maybe so."

Suddenly restless, Mackenzie pushed out into the air and down to the lake, splashing into the shallow water. The loons were gone. She stood on a rock, the wind gusting in her face.

Aware of Rook on the shore behind her, she said, "When Jesse attacked me last week, I remembered his eyes. They were like something I'd conjured up in a nightmare."

"Repressed memory."

"I've always known I was in the woods the day of my father's accident, but I never could remember the details." She glanced back at Rook, but he wasn't a man who was easy to read. "I must have conflated what I did that day—the actual events—with my nightmares. After a while, I couldn't distinguish one from the other."

Making it look easy, Rook jumped to the exposed rock next to hers without getting his feet wet or losing his balance. "You were a little kid," he said. "This bastard manipulated you. He becomes other people's nightmare." Rook was silent a moment. "That's what Harris tried to tell me."

"He should have been straight with you."

She heard a car in the driveway. *More cops,* she thought. But when she looked back at Bernadette's yard, she saw Carine wave and break into a run. "Mackenzie!"

Nate was behind his sister, his wife at his side. He wasn't here as a senior federal agent, Mackenzie realized, but as a friend.

Rook winked at her. "You do the talking."

"Scared of Nate, are you?"

He grinned. "Not even a little."

Thirty-Six

After all the various investigators—local, state and federal—had left, T. J. Kowalski joined Rook and Mackenzie at the lake. "Quite a place," he said, settling into one of the Adirondack chairs in front of the stone fireplace. "I've never seen a loon, you know."

Mackenzie smiled. "You might hear one tonight."

"If I can stand the bugs and the cold."

Rook had built a fire and pulled his chair close to the flames. The night *was* chilly, but Bernadette had old wool blankets just for that purpose. Mackenzie had one opened up on her lap. But T.J. didn't look that cold to her.

"Long day," she said.

He shrugged. "Not for me. I took a nice plane ride north and talked to a few people. You and Rook are the ones who did the heavy lifting." He didn't smile, and in the light of the fire, his eyes were without humor. "Sorry I wasn't here to back you two up."

"If Jesse had managed to get away from here, you'd have kept his plane on the ground."

"We had him," T.J. acknowledged without pride. "Just not in time to save Harris Mayer or Cal Benton."

Rook tossed another log on the fire. "They made their deal with the devil."

T.J. nodded. "What about Judge Peacham?"

"Doctors are keeping her at the hospital overnight as a precaution," Mackenzie said. "They're watching for infection—the knife wound nicked muscle. She says we're all welcome to stay here and toast marshmallows and listen to the loons."

But another car arrived, Nate and Joe Delvecchio walking down to the fire.

T.J. gave a low whistle. "Guess the marsh-mallows and loons will have to wait."

"Welcome to life as a federal agent, Mac," Rook said with a hint of amusement.

She smiled at them both. "Fine with me."

On Sunday, after she was released from the hospital, Bernadette insisted on sitting out on her screened porch. It was a warm afternoon, with almost no wind. Mackenzie joined her, trying not to hover because, even after two years of marriage, Bernadette Peacham was a woman accustomed to her own company.

"New Hampshire isn't going to give up Jesse anytime soon," she said, sounding more like a judge than an injured victim. "They'll want to try him here—for Cal's mur-der." But the words seemed to hit her like a fresh wound, and she faltered, although only for a moment. "Chances are you'll have to testify."

"I don't mind," Mackenzie said.

"It won't be easy to see him again, but at least you'll know he can't hurt anyone else." Bernadette flopped back against her wicker chair, her face ashen just twenty-four hours after her encounter with Jesse—after learning that Cal was dead. "All these years, Mackenzie, and I had no idea that your father's mishap wasn't an accident. I feel like such a sap."

"You and Dad tried to get rid of Jesse."

"Your *father* tried to get rid of him. I can't say I did much of anything."

"But you never helped Jesse," Mackenzie said. "Don't beat yourself up, Beanie."

She stared out at the lake. "I let people take advantage of me."

"Don't we all, at some point in our lives?"

She snorted. "I did *repeatedly.*"

Mackenzie almost smiled at her friend's sudden drama. "There's nothing wrong with giving someone a helping hand, Beanie. Most people you've helped—including me—appreciate it."

"I've never . . ." She fought back obvious tears. "I've just never felt so damn alone."

"You're a brilliant and generous woman, Beanie, and you have good friends, people who care about you—people who don't want anything from you." Mackenzie smiled. "For example, Gus Winter."

"He's always been there, hasn't he? For

all of us. He and his brother would come out here to the lake as teenagers—Jill and I were friends."

Bernadette drifted into silence, and out on the lake, Mackenzie could hear the familiar, eerie cry of a loon. She wondered if T.J. heard it. He and Rook had taken two of the kayaks out onto the lake, leaving her alone with Bernadette.

"The worst day of my life was when Harry and Jill died up on Cold Ridge," she said. "It was such a freak thing. They'd never have gone up there if they'd known the weather would turn like that. How do you get over such a tragedy?" But she didn't wait for Mackenzie to respond and stood up, moving to the screen and gazing out at the water and woods that had been home to Peachams for decades. "Well, I can tell you—you don't."

Mackenzie remained in her wicker chair, remembering Carine explaining to her what it was like to have become an orphan at three years old. "That was the worst," she said. "And to leave behind three children."

Bernadette looked away from the lake, her incisive gaze now on her neighbor from across the lake. "But the scope of that tragedy made it all too easy for us all to minimize other things that happened here in the valley. It gave us a perspective we wouldn't have had otherwise, and we tried—I think we all tried to let it make us stronger, better people. Wiser, even. Because what other choice was there?"

"Beanie." Mackenzie thought she could see where this was going. "Please. Don't judge yourself."

"We were all too slow to recognize the effects of what happened to your father on you. Kevin hadn't died up on the ridge. You weren't orphaned." She sighed, turning away from the screen and sitting back down. "Well. The past is what it is. I can't take any of what I did back."

"None of us can," Mackenzie said.

Bernadette frowned at her. "You're so young. You can't have many regrets. What would you do differently?"

"For starters, I'd have recognized Jesse when he slashed me."

"That was only a week ago!"

"It's in the past. It counts."

At first, Bernadette look dumbstruck, a rarity for her. Then, all at once, she burst into laughter. "Oh, Mackenzie. I swear, if changing anything about the past made you any different . . ." But she didn't finish, just motioned toward the lake with the arm on her uninjured side. "I want you to have your own spot on this lake."

"I do—"

She shook her head. "You don't. Your parents do, and I do, but we're all going to live to a hundred. You should have a spot now, while you're young. Let your children grow up here, even if it's only for summers and holidays."

Mackenzie stared at her, not quite grasping what Bernadette was saying. "I can't afford a place in Washington, never mind *two* places."

"I'm *giving* you the land," Bernadette said, exasperated. "I had a waterfront lot surveyed when I drew up my prenuptial agreement with Cal. I just haven't gotten around to doing anything about it. I'm not trying to steal you away from your family, Mackenzie. But I've no one else, and you love it here as much as I do."

"I do." Knowing Bernadette as well as she did, Mackenzie didn't let her emotions get the better of her. "Thank you."

Bernadette smiled, obviously relieved. "You're welcome." She nodded out toward the lake. "I think your FBI agent likes it here, too."

"Beanie—I don't know if Rook and I will work out."

Gus grunted, coming onto the porch from the kitchen. "You two? You're lifers."

"It's true," Bernadette said. "Everyone can see it."

But Mackenzie had no intention of discussing Rook or her love life with either of them, and she excused herself and ran outside, out to the end of the dock. She was barefoot and wearing shorts, and she was tempted to dive into the lake with the same abandon as she had a little over a week ago, before Jesse Lambert had come at her with a knife.

What was it Delvechhio had told her last night?

"Give yourself a day to put this behind you. Be back at work on Monday."

That meant she wasn't fired for having too much baggage.

It meant catching a plane back to Washington tonight.

And *that* meant she had the afternoon. She glanced back at the porch, where Gus and Bernadette were arguing about something, and then squinted out across the lake, trying to spot the two FBI agents in their kayaks. But there was no sign of them, or of the loon she could hear warbling out by the opposite shore.

Bernadette was right, Mackenzie thought. She loved it here.

With a running start, ignoring the healing knife wound on her side, she leaped into the cold, deep water.

Bernadette struck a match and touched the tiny flame to the edge of rolled-up newspaper. "It's the obituaries," she said, feeling Gus's eyes on her. "Somehow, I think Harris would approve." But not Cal, she thought. Irony had never suited him.

Gus said nothing.

She sat cross-legged in the grass as the fire burned through the newspaper and caught the kindling. By Gus's standards—by her own, really—it was early yet for a fire, not yet dusk. And warm. But she'd wanted one.

She winced, feeling a tug of pain in her hip. "It used to be easier to sit cross-legged. I'm creaking these days."

Gus grunted without sympathy. "Getting out of Washington more often would help. You sit too much." He settled back in the old

Adirondack chair. "You should go mountain climbing while you're up here." Then he added simply, "I'll go with you."

There were no deep corners, no layers and odd places, with Gus Winter. He'd seen war, he'd endured the tragic loss of his brother and sister-in-law and he'd stepped up to raise his orphaned nephew and nieces—and yet the complications of his life had never become excuses for him, rationalizations for bad behavior.

"That'd be good." Bernadette kept her eyes on the fire. "I have regrets, Gus."

"Tell me about it."

She straightened her legs, relieving the strain on her hip. Her injured shoulder ached, too, but she didn't want to take more pain medication. Without looking at Gus, she said, "I won't survive the scandal of what Cal and Harris did. Who Jesse is. That so much of it went on for years under my nose."

"You didn't do anything wrong."

"It doesn't matter. I won't survive it, and perhaps I shouldn't. I should have pressed Harris for the truth about what was going on with him five years ago. I knew for months something was wrong with Cal." She noticed the newspaper turning black, crumpling into the ashes. "I'm too trusting. People won't see that as a good thing in a judge."

"Cal didn't get mixed up with Jesse Lambert because of you. Neither did Larric. They had their own reasons." Gus pulled himself out of the Adirondack chair and sat in the grass next to her. He was fit, but not as limber as he'd once been. He grinned at her. "Remember sitting next to each other in first grade when they sent in that clown?"

"It was a juggler."

"Same difference."

"You misbehaved, as I recall."

He shrugged. "I always misbehaved. When I started climbing mountains, I did better. When I came back from Vietnam, I had a lot on my mind. I'd spend days at a time on the ridge. Then Harry and Jill died up there."

"You're a hero to a lot of people, Gus."

"Just did what I had to do. That's what you're doing now, isn't it?" He looked at her with those penetrating blue Winter eyes of his. "Beanie, what do you want?"

"Want?" She heard her voice crack and looked away from him. "I don't even know. Right now, sitting here with you in front of the fire is good enough."

"You're thinking about quitting, aren't you?"

Her eyes filled with tears. "Retiring, not quitting. I never expected to go out of the courtroom on a board. I always knew one day I'd come back here. Gus, I want to be here listening to the loons and growing tomatoes."

"You'd miss locking people up."

"That's a simplistic reduction of what I do."

He grinned. "You'd miss your gavel."

She rolled her eyes. He was baiting her, enjoying himself. Trying, she thought, to get her going, distract her. "I will *not* miss my gavel. One day, Gus, I swear—"

"One day when you're up here for a court break, you can explain to me what you do."

"You know what I do."

"I know who you are. There's a difference."

He leaned back on his elbows. "We're going to grow old together, Beanie Peacham."

She smiled at him. "I hate to tell you, Gus, but we've already started."

Thirty-Seven

The glasslike lake reflected the dark ever-greens along its shore and the grays of dusk. Mackenzie, changed into dry jeans and packed for her trip back to Washington, jumped from an exposed rock to a bigger one at least ten yards into the water. She was just below the clearing where Jesse had taken Cal—and where, it turned out, Bernadette had carved out a lot for her.

If she didn't make her peace with this place now, Mackenzie thought, she never would.

She heard a movement on shore behind her, but this time it wasn't a knife-wielding lunatic. Rook emerged from the cover of the pines and hemlocks, dressed casually and as striking as ever.

Mackenzie grinned at him. "I can't go anywhere without the FBI following me."

"You marshals." He jumped lightly onto her rock without teetering even a little. "Enough room here for the two of us."

"Always so confident."

"Did you break open more of your wound jumping into the water earlier?"

She angled a look at him. "You saw me?"

"T.J. brought binoculars. He wanted to check out the loons. Says you count as a loon all by yourself—"

"Where is he now?"

Rook gestured back toward Bernadette's house. "He's saying goodbye to Gus and Judge Peacham. He's catching an earlier flight to Washington. He can pave the way with our superiors."

"Meeting with the big guns of the FBI?"

He nodded.

"You're still one of their rising stars. T.J., too." She dipped a toe in the water, which felt colder than it had out by the dock. "Jesse could have killed Beanie yesterday."

"Mac—"

"The only reason he didn't is because he wanted her to delay me, so he'd have more of a head start. It didn't do him any good." She pulled her toe out of the water, remembering Jesse Lambert's eyes yesterday when she'd confronted him. But she pushed the image out of her mind and continued. "Beanie says she had no intention of making it easy for him to kill her. She was going to fight back with whatever she could reach."

"She might have succeeded," Rook said.

"I wouldn't put it past her." Mackenzie put her hand on his arm, feeling his warmth and strength. "I love it up here, Rook."

He nodded. "I know you do."

"But Chief Delvecchio likes me. He says it's a bad sign and he probably should have his head examined."

"He knows you're good. And smart."

"I became a marshal for a lot of reasons, Rook. My father's accident, Nate's influence, the action, a chance to prove myself— maybe all of them weren't good reasons, I don't know. Maybe I'll end up back on a college campus one of these days. But right now, the service is where I want to be."

"Mac." He touched his fingertips to her lips. "You don't have to explain to me."

"I fell hard for you, Rook. You know that, don't you? That night in the rain, when I thought you worked for the IRS or something."

He smiled. "You have to work on your FBI radar."

"I should have known. You were so damn good-looking and sexy out there in the rain, and such a hard-ass—"

"I shouldn't have dumped you the way I did."

"It was the right thing to do. That's why you did it—not because of ambition or anything else."

He lowered his mouth to hers.

"If T.J.'s out on the dock with his binoculars—"

"Do you care?" Rook kissed her softly, obviously not caring if anyone was watching. "I love you, Mac."

"Rook . . . Andrew . . ." Mackenzie almost lost her balance on the rock. "If we fall into the lake, we're not going to make our flight. Then we'll have even more explaining to do in Washington." She grinned at him. "My ghosts await my return. Sarah says she can give me another two months before I have to find my own place. I don't know about Nate, though. He's not convinced I won't attract some other creep to the place."

"Then you still need a place to live."

"I do."

"Brian's moving out. I'm renovating. Suppose we see what happens?"

"Just one thing." Mackenzie slipped her arms around Rook and kissed him again. "The Cupid wallpaper stays."